CONVERGENCE

Shirley J. Naas

Saguaro Books, LLC
SB
Arizona

Saguaro Books, LLC
16845 E. Avenue of the Fountains, Ste. 325
Fountain Hills, AZ 85268
www.saguarobooks.com

ISBN: 978-1-0881-3159-6
Library of Congress Cataloging Number
LCCN: 2019954945
Printed in the United States of America
First Edition

Dedication

In memory of my loving mother, Phyllis Jane Etherton Davis, my greatest supporter of my work. May my work honor her faith in me.

Prologue
"The Banished"

The mists dispersed and provided images around me. Finally, I had a signal of the return of my sensors and detectors. Unspecified sounds came from my left but they were faint, minuscule sounds. Something moved slowly and deliberately toward me, intermittently stopping then cautiously continuing forward. For some reason, I wasn't overly concerned because it didn't register strongly on my preceptors, an exclusive celestial attribute. I detected nothing threatening from the movement then the sound was simply gone. Much later I would learn exactly what generated that movement and noise but for now it was gone and inconsequential.

Simultaneously, I became aware of my physical appearance. I observed some normalcy except for the smaller size and bearing a markedly different coloring. More "pinkness" tinged the outer surface with a vague outline of something in my appendages. Had I become something else? Was I now a part of this lower realm? Were my celestial attributes intact, or did I even still possess them? Soon after this revelation, I lost all conscious thought.

Ignorant of how long I functioned in this state of "non-awareness, this abyss," I finally noticed my surroundings. A great deal of time had passed because the environment had indeed changed. Only a dull, brittle "brownness" existed where before a lush green growth covered the area. Now, the surface where I lay provided no cushioning with only a dry and bristly covering, much rock stretched before me and I sensed I had landed on a high elevation.

It must have been a mountain, however, it puzzled me there was no snow anywhere. Evidently, I landed on a lower part of that mountain and sheltered in a remote, valley-like area. My entire body was sprinkled with layers of dust and debris. A strong force had blown across me and partially covered me. After slowly lifting myself into a sitting position, I surveyed the area around me. Next, I scanned myself and my complete nakedness startled me for a moment. The apparel worn on the "Day of Destruction" had completely disintegrated leaving not one thread of the garment. Yet, I experienced no coldness. Although I looked somewhat different, I later learned it was "human-like" but not human. Indeed, I wasn't mortal, had never been mortal and felt no discomfort from the elements. Instinctively I knew that like a human I would need some type of covering in order to venture out.

With doubts of whether I could still manipulate physical elements, I hesitated to alter my present state. Was I now to be forever visible in this form? In time I would know those answers along with many other perplexing emotions. When I finally came face-to-face with a particular human, it would change me forever. I soon learned to blend in without drawing unnecessary attention to myself. I harbored no desire to be of interest to humans or one to be despised and hunted by them. Time; I needed time to learn and find out if any other "renegade" celestials survived that fateful day. I knew only I was Grinstead, a former level-three guardian angel but I remembered nothing more. When I attempted to recall the final events of that cataclysmic day, I found only "empty" spaces with no recollection of those events. I wondered if it were lost to me forever.

I ran a hand across the back of my head. Crustiness covered a deep indentation at the base of my skull. Consequently, my head received the brunt of the impact justifying my confusion and lack of memory. Definitely my processing center was damaged but, thankfully, not destroyed. An audible sigh of relief verified the durability of that center. Fortunately, an angel's "brain" is more complex than a human brain. For one thing, it's larger and filled with additional sections and folds and, of course, an angel's brain doesn't deteriorate. It remains strong and functions at full capacity forever. Our entire cognitive processes are enriched with heavy levels of iron and magnesium. If man had even a fraction of those levels in his brain, that brain would surely implode. Long before that, he would've been driven completely insane. Incidentally, many humans with elevated levels of magnesium in the brain are a constant threat to other humans.

The science of man has yet to comprehend the magnitude of this characteristic, although research scientists are closer to making that connection. Primarily, doctors acknowledge that too high a level of magnesium in the blood stream can cause major cardiac and kidney problems but they haven't seriously focused on those traces found in the human brain. Today's science begins to adequately study the human brain and its functions but I'm getting ahead of myself and need to go back to the beginning.

I rose, stood, waited until the spinning in my head receded and I cautiously headed down the mountainside. It came to me I should descend using my usual mode of travel but I quickly dismissed it. I wasn't ready to "test the waters," so I walked. While traveling, I saw not one living being and I concluded it was cold. If anything dwelt here, it would have sought shelter. After traveling several miles, I came upon a more pleasant region. The land laid level and barren with a beauty in its starkness. I continued and traveled for days and never found another celestial. In truth, I never found any living creature. I found absolutely nothing.

I slowed my progress, moved aimlessly without purpose and eventually developed a strong urge to hide myself away, to stop all functions and become as senseless as stone. The reality of my circumstances hit me full force with a vengeance. I was completely alone. This was, indeed, an unknown phenomenon for me. In Heaven, the highest realm, no angel or any celestial is independent. We are classified by our ranks or our roles. Those roles connected us, gave us purpose and directed our existence.

Our responsibilities are based on our capabilities at the time of our creation. I couldn't remember a solitary time I wasn't in the company of other celestials. This recollection generated feelings of complete loneliness and separation from all I knew and all I had ever known. A feeling of great sadness surrounded me and caused great sorrow. This was a new emotion for me yet one so typical of a human reaction. Miserably, I yearned for the total lack of conscious thought or awareness. The enormity of what had happened and the effect of the combined actions of so few began to take a toll on me. *What had I unknowingly been drawn into?* A deep depression settled over me, an attribute inconceivable before. In a miasma of confusion, I wandered on, aimlessly meandering for days, or it might have been weeks. I noticed nothing around me until one day, when I came upon a wall of rock with an opening that required bending down to gain entrance. I did so without a second thought and entered a small cave.

Immediately the light faded as I moved farther into the recesses, yet, this presented no problem for me. I could sense and feel my surroundings through my mind. I found a level shelf carved into stone, lay down upon it and became part of that stone. I closed my eyes and slept. Such a deep, penetrating sleep that carried me for eons of time, receding into a dormant state where nothing touched me and my body plunged into "hibernation", shutting down all processes and requiring nothing to sustain it. I slept on. I was unaware, totally, of the events surrounding me because I had no need for food, water, air, or anything else. I lived in an empty shell, void of cognitive and internal functions. I simply required nothing.

Time moved forward and things changed. God had been busy. Men and women now walked upon the earth in huge numbers. In time I would meet a woman and know the true meaning of desire that humans felt, which they were created to feel but that would come much later. I was dormant now. Healing, forgetting, evolving, turning within myself and merging with the stone of the shelf where I lay. Time passed and life began in earnest as I slept and humans multiplied and ruled this lower realm, this Earth.

Ultimately, after a great deal of time, something deep within roused me to full consciousness. I awoke alert and driven to move out of my haven and spring from my comatose-like state. I emerged from the rock, stretched, experiencing earnestness somewhere in the core of all that I was and all that I would soon become. An overwhelming urgency prompted me to seek answers, companionship and become useful again. In the end, I felt the need to gain redemption. A true hunger engulfed me but not for food. That wasn't necessary to me but I yearned desperately for light, the essence or the pulse of my being. I needed the nectar of energy pumping vitality and sustaining me. In the same way, most created things need light and, therefore, the black confines of the cave became oppressive and suffocating. My shell satisfied, I no longer needed to sleep or idle listlessly. I had to get out.

Before my exit, I studied the cave and noticed the remnants of life forms. They must have been animals though there wasn't enough substance left of the remains to determine what they'd actually been. I noticed many skeletal remains scattered around the interior of the cave. I was unsure exactly how much time had passed but I did remember there was nothing near me when I had entered the cave. Life around me had existed for quite some time. Actually, as I later learned, even the end of life occurred and began afresh.

Indeed, I encountered things I never dreamed possible here on this realm. Evil had come and gone many times throughout the centuries of time. Choices made so long ago fixed the events and would continue to do so until the Omnipotent One decided to collect all that was his due from the beginning. Somehow, I survived and would bear witness to it all. I became a vessel of time and I would record all that had come before and all that would follow. This I would learn after centuries and millennia of time.

I walked out of the cave and embraced the light for the first time in over sixteen hundred years.

Chapter 1

Cassamie James

The wind whipped violently against my lightweight jacket. Immediately I realized my folly in not preparing more carefully. Though it was the end of April, at this elevation, my baby blue North Face windbreaker was warmer than most but no match for these Arctic winds that arrived about thirty minutes ago. Typical that Malitar would have to choose the highest point in the region for our rendezvous. There was something about a high altitude and bracing winds that appealed a great deal to him. Perhaps he would sense my discomfort and bring something more suitable for these winds. After all, he knew my tendency to get distracted and forget the bare necessities.

Why were these meetings at the most inconvenient time? Literally, why meet in the dead of night or during the first promise of daylight? Angels. They had no need for sleep or rest in general because angels are not human and have no basic survival needs. I've been dealing with one angel in particular since childhood. Born with a unique trait that allows me to see them and I've had an association with Malitar, my angel, since birth. My uniqueness is based on bonus attributes that most people don't have. *Who would have thought that I, introverted Cassamie James, would be dealing with such celestial beings?*

I've lived in Scobey, Montana, for almost four years. After graduating from Harvard's journalism department, I accepted a job with the Scobey Sentinel, a small, family-owned newspaper that provides daily news for the surrounding area in a sixty-mile radius. The newspaper maintains a wide readership partially because some rural families do not have Internet and many are stubbornly loyal to the editor of the paper. Anyway, my family was shocked when I chose such a remote and isolated community. Always attracted to beautiful scenery and miles of open, unpopulated land; I accepted the job. After being raised in large metropolitan areas, the smaller communities held a strong appeal for me. I liked walking down the street and recognizing people. Not only that but I knew all the local gossip and could tell what tidbits of information were worthy of notice. Most of my investigative skills had to do with what specials were on the weekly menu at the local restaurant, The Shady Spot.

Mount Antelope is the highest elevation near the small town of Scobey. When the glaciers moved through thousands of years ago, this small mountain range formed. For some reason, the glacier stopped at this point and with its final thrust of energy, forged this mount that I now stand upon and raised 3,464 feet into the air.

Of course, Malitar would say nothing just happens randomly and this spot, this mount under my feet, was created years ago to prepare for this meeting. Meeting? I wouldn't really call it a meeting. Nope, this definitely would not be a meeting. In meetings, people tend to have some say in what is happening. Opinions are given and gathered but not in this "meeting." I would have no influence, power or effect whatsoever on what would be determined today. I would be given some role to play then I would be on my way back to little 'Po-dunk" USA, or my next location and whatever nondescript job was assigned to me. Come to think of it, I had been here for an extended period of time.

The wind moved and shifted differently. It wasn't getting colder but a bit warmer. A small tingle touched me, so I knew Malitar was close by. Angels are surrounded by an aura of energy. He called it a "cycloplasmic" energy source that surrounds angels and prevents them from being detected unless desired so by that angel. You see, angels tend to travel in a sort of mist interacting or counter-acting against any environment and they can alter or control all the elements of that environment.

Most humans are unable to visually see angels. That ability is based on an individual's brain functions and, of course, the willingness of the angel to be seen. The occipital parts of the human brain are so layered and complex that ninety-seven percent of humans have no ability to fully process what the eye is actually seeing. It's as a limited computer with all the attachments necessary but not having the right connection to get online; however, many people can actually sense the presence of an angel or celestial and, yes, there can be a difference. For instance, when a feeling of inner peace or intense happiness settles upon a person for no obvious reason, it's because a celestial has touched that person or been nearby.

I have that brain capacity and connection and I was born with it twenty-six years ago in a back room off a deserted train depot. Shortly after my birth, my mother died from complications. Malitar was present and took charge of what happened later. Of course, I don't remember any of this but Malitar had everything recorded so that one day I would be able to access it. That is, if I ever want to access it. Some things are better left alone or to put it more colorfully, some stones are better left unturned. I believe another expression is, "Ignorance is bliss". That's good because I live in a blissful state most of the time. I hold a great deal of ignorance when it comes to supernatural beings.

I waited for the rumble and loud clap of thunder. This time Malitar chose to arrive in a bolt of lightning. I could feel the hair on the back of my neck rise. To my left, approximately forty yards away, the lightning struck a huge boulder. I saw the reverberations of energy reflect then bounce off the limestone rock where I stood. When the noise died away, before me stood Malitar. No matter how many times I witness this event, it never ceases to impress me. Where nothing but a boulder stood moments ago, there now appeared the tall, angelic body of Malitar. He was over ten and a half feet tall. Although when necessary, he could adjust that height and assured me many angels were much taller. In fact, he had many more years to grow before reaching his full potential of fifteen feet. Malitar was young by angel standards. He had only existed for around 2300 hundred years. To me, he didn't look a day over forty.

Then came the smooth, lyrical voice, "Good morning, Cassamie. How are you?" I was continually amazed with how well he dressed for any setting. Today he was in knee high leather boots over form fitting riding breeches. The brown, leather bomber jacket and wool scarf gave him a rather rakish appearance although most definitely there was no rogue here. He was the most caring and compassionate being I had ever met, hence, the rank of angel.

Looking directly into my eyes, his usual custom, used to unnerve me. I've become accustomed to it now. He has the deepest, lavender-shaded eyes with the outer edges circled with crystalline shavings of ice blue. These eyes mesmerize and tend to pull one in and make concentration difficult. Perhaps it was intentional, although I doubt angels are cunning, at least not this kind of angel. So it must be characteristic. Surprisingly, angels were a lot like humans in many ways but with highly enhanced attributes. For instance, when Malitar moved; it was as a folding of energy. Immensely graceful with a musical symmetry, his speed could go entirely undetected. One moment he was a few feet away and by the next breath he was within inches. Normally he tried to approach more slowly. It took years for me to accept these behaviors. Fortunately, I had my entire childhood to help with this acceptance.

"Good morning, Malitar. I see you've chosen your typical meeting place. Is it easier for you to meet at high elevations, or do you just prefer challenging me?"

"Now, you know I'm not that type of angel, Cassamie. Surely by now you've learned to trust me and know I will protect you at all costs."

I felt a little guilty when recalling how many times Malitar had saved me from imminent danger. Tasting a little salty chagrin, I replied, "Sorry. I'm just not an early morning person. If I had my second cup of coffee, I would be much more amicable. Can we get down from this mountain and go get some?"

"Of course. Do you want to walk down, or shall I carry you?" He flashed a lop-sided grin.

I almost let him take me down but, remembering back a long time ago, I decided to walk down. Though I would get the coffee sooner if I left it up to Malitar, I was not quite prepared for such a dramatic trip. I told him I would meet him down at my car and we would drive into town.

While descending the mountain, I thought of the first time Malitar had carried me. It was an experience I immediately feared, though some would have found exhilarating. Because of being a reserved and cautious child, I possessed too many uncertainties and worries. Grams said I was born that way, too wary and cautious of new experiences; always sitting back, observing and letting others take the risks. She said it was as if I had an internal thermostat that kept me from being reckless or foolhardy. I thought of it as having levels of restraint. Maybe I was a bit too careful but it had come in handy for most of my life.

My mother, on the other hand, Shelby Annette Kensington, never had any restraints. She lived her life and enjoyed all the amenities it offered. A direct result of her lack of caution took her life. I had a great deal of blame in that along with the one who sired me but I wouldn't think of that right now.

The first time Malitar carried me was when I was six years old. I attended a family reunion at a park in a small, rural area. Grandpa and Grams always felt strong family connections and we would travel a great deal to meet with our relatives. Grandpa's huge family, the Kensington clan, came from Scotland in the late 1800s and had primarily dealt in textiles and manufacturing. Some were even merchant marines and sailors adding to the shipping company that later followed. My grandfather's expertise was managing the legal aspects of the companies and he was quite good at his job.

On the other hand, Grams' family was much smaller. I really never knew much about her family. She rarely mentioned them; however, on this particular occasion, we were visiting with Grams' side of the family. The day had started out cloudy with some periodic sunshine filtering through but I recall the thickness of the air, an almost oppressive humidity.

I went with a group of cousins to explore rock formations near a cave. We were only a few hundred feet from the group of adults cleaning up after the noon meal. Grams had made her famous blackberry dumplings and I'd probably eaten too many. The sugar high had worn off. Anyway, I was beginning to tire of the group. Reynolds, a slightly older cousin, had dared me to climb up to the highest formation extending over the face of the cave. A dangerous outcropping of jagged rock protruded over the face dropping steeply to the river below. From that moment, I learned to dislike him. His hair shone with an eerie blackness, so black it was almost purplish-blue. He had disturbing eyes, unfriendly eyes that never warmed when he smiled. It was as if he had a cruel smirk on his face trying to tempt me. Even his name irritated me. Interestingly enough, none of my other cousins were paying any attention to us. They ignored Reynolds completely as if he weren't there. Later I would learn the reason why they "overlooked" him. Anyway, I remember him walking over to me and whispering in my ear.

"You're a chicken, Cassamie Anne, you can't do anything."

"I am not a chicken. I could go up there if I wanted to." I defiantly hissed back.

"Then show me. You won't because you're a momma's baby."

"I'm not a momma's baby. You'll see."

I never liked to talk about my momma because Grams always got sad when her name was mentioned. Even at that young age, I sensed I had something to do with her death. Yet, no one had ever told me that. Any time her name came up, adults would always give me a sympathetic look. I wanted to scream, "Don't look at me that way." Then they would transition to another topic and completely ignore me for a few minutes. On this particular day, as usual, I was the only child in the family without parents present. So, already fueled by misgivings and resentment, those feelings quickly turned to anger.

The anger filled me with enough daring to head toward the rocks jutting out over the face of the cave. Climbing higher, I could hear Reynolds taunting me saying I wouldn't go all the way, that I would turn around any second. With the wind building, I continued to climb until I no longer heard him. When I got farther away from the group, the wind strengthened and I noticed the clouds darkening. One great gust pummeled me mercilessly and I began to lose my bravado. Instantaneously, my anger left me and my natural sense of caution rushed in. I was terrified. Unable to move another inch and rooted to the spot, I began to cry. Stubbornly not calling for help because I didn't want Reynolds to hear the fear in my voice and taunt me even more, so I clung to the rocks while the rain pelted me. Unbeknownst to me, the other children had returned to the picnic area. They'd been called back when the weather began to look threatening. A summer thunderstorm was coming.

The thunder boomed and the wind grew in intensity and I hunkered down on the rock face. What seemed to be hours but actually only a matter of minutes passed before I looked up and saw Malitar. Though this was the first time I remembered seeing him, I wasn't afraid. He gently knelt down, picked me up and wrapped me in his arms. Before I could open my mouth to speak, he folded into himself and carried me away. Complete terror seized me. My body seemed to turn inward with a great penetration of pounding pressure. My lungs clamped shut and I began gasping for air. I couldn't expand them. There was no air and I felt similar to the time when I had the breath socked out of me by a large black dog knocking me to the ground. I wanted to scream but there wasn't enough oxygen in my lungs to fuel it. Within seconds I was placed safely inside the cave to wait out the storm. Malitar whispered to me everything would be OK. He stayed with me until Grandpa came to rescue me. Of course, Grandpa couldn't see the angel and, for some reason, I never said anything about him to either of my grandparents.

Today I made another descent; only this time I was a grown woman, an experienced climber. I proceeded slowly down the mountain. I saw Malitar sitting in the front passenger seat of my classic 1989 Volkswagen Beetle. A comical sight to see him scrunched into the compact car. Many times, he'd tried to persuade me to buy something more "conducive" to his great height but I got my small amusements wherever I could. It amazed me even with the passenger seat pushed all the way back; he could barely stay contained within the space. He would need to shrink before we could head back to town. The moment the thought left my mind, I saw him make the size adjustment.

When I opened the door and climbed in, Malitar gave me that indulgent smile that parents must give their children when they mean, "Why didn't you do what I suggested?" Although I really wouldn't know about parents since my mother died at my birth and my father, well, that was another story I wasn't prepared to deal with yet. My maternal grandparents had raised me. Sadly, my grandfather died last April but my grandmother, "Grams" as I called her, was still as active and alert as ever.

There was nothing she couldn't do when she decided on a course of action. Usually her energy was concentrated on helping others and caring for their needs. Financially comfortable because of my grandfather's businesses and investments, one could not tell of her wealth by her lifestyle. She lived modestly and spent much of her wealth on charities and church needs. Her special gift of "second sight" kept her busy trying to avert danger or misgivings for others. She sensed things. Throughout my childhood, I'd been a witness to her many premonitions that had indeed come true; however, she cautiously guarded her "gift" and only a privileged few knew of it. My mother had also had the "sight," yet it had not saved her. The gene hadn't transferred to me in the same venue. My special gift dealt with sight as well but mine was that my brain could rearrange energy and penetrate the barriers that kept most people from seeing what was actually behind that energy, thus, my ability to see angels.

Malitar leaned over and asked, "Where exactly are we going for your desired coffee, your nectar, your life-sustaining drink?"

I knew he was teasing me or trying to anyway. He had no earthly or heavenly knowledge of the effects coffee can have on a person. What a waste to never need any caffeine or have a hunger for any particular food. As my mind wandered to all of my favorite foods, a plethora of food items crossed my mind.

"Chocolate. Have you ever tasted it?"

"Yes, I have tasted chocolate and many other foods. I find some to be pleasing but have no need for that type of sustenance. Our hunger is caused and quenched in ways other than food."

The road became more winding, so I concentrated on my driving and we rode silently for the remaining two miles to the local café. Luckily, there was a parking space in front of the building and I whipped easily into the spot. There most definitely were advantages to driving a compact car. I hopped out and bounded around the front of my car as Malitar came crawling out of his seat. Amusing.

The café wasn't crowded, so we took a booth toward the back wall to give us some privacy and to present a clear view of the street and anyone entering the café. I learned a long time ago to always be strategic about these details. Also, I positioned close to the back exit in case we needed to make a quick departure. Malitar had taught me well.

Today I didn't recognize any of the customers. That was good. Brooke, our waitress, came to take our order. I ordered my coffee black with sugar only, added a plate of fresh fruit to go with it then leaned forward and waited for Malitar's response.

"I would like one of those deliciously smelling rolls I see on the counter. Please, may I also have a tall glass of iced water?" He gave his most engaging smile to Brooke. I felt a little sorry for her as she tried to stammer a response. No one was immune from his charms. I knew he had no desire for the pastry, wanted to appear as human as possible, so he improvised with duplicating a comment he thought normal. Of course, "normal" could never describe Malitar.

Malitar hadn't told me much about Heaven. Oh, he hinted at things, always making comments about the plan and how everything happened for a purpose. He never really told me anything about why he was here with me instead of being 'there'. I always wondered about the angels up 'there'. From the little I remember from my childhood Sunday school classes, angels were supposed to have wings. I had never seen Malitar with wings. I needed to check the scriptures and brush up on the information concerning them but I don't remember much written about them. Secrecy evidently shrouded the heavens. Looking at Malitar, I knew there was a higher order, a supreme God who had a hand in making this beautiful creature, this spirit and heavenly angel. I needed to try and find some answers to so many questions. Yet, the questions and answers would have to wait because Brooke brought out our order and I could definitely smell freshly brewed coffee. This was my heaven right here on earth.

After thanking Brooke, I drank most of my coffee and ate some fruit before leaning back against the booth and asking Malitar the reason for this visit. He smiled and asked, "Do I need a reason to visit my favorite human?" When I continued staring at him and gave no response, he smiled and began filling me in on the "situation" that would require my involvement.

Chapter 2

Looking out the window of the plane, I mentally went over the instructions Malitar had given me. I had contacted the person Malitar informed me about. I was to meet Ransfield Steward in the Holiday Inn Express at Marion, Illinois, in the lobby at 8 o'clock, sharp. He would help search for the child that had gone missing while on a school field trip. The outing had been in the Shawnee National Forest in southern Illinois. The child, Sarah Bennington, a fifth grader, was last seen at the picnic area on her way to the restroom.

According to what Malitar had told me, the child's abduction took place in a rural setting with lots of trees and underbrush. The students had finished a short hike on the lower trails of Rim Rock. It had been a hot day and most of the students were thirsty, hungry, tired and a bit grumpy. With plenty of adult supervision, some of the teachers had been helping the bus drivers unload the coolers filled with sandwiches, sodas, along with boxes of chips, fruit snacks and paper products. From what I had read on the Internet, other teachers supervised students playing Frisbee or using the facilities. One teacher stood within a few feet of the restroom and had seen Sarah enter. However, she had been distracted when another child called to her to ask where he could get a drink of water. Other teachers wiped off and cleaned the picnic tables for the students to use. Therefore, from my deduction, there were many people in the vicinity of where Sarah had been taken.

Sarah had stayed with her best friend for most of the trip but had separated in order to go to the restroom. The facility was located in the open except for one part of the building that was secluded by low, lying limbs from the nearby ash trees. Sarah, being a little bit over the top on cleanliness, had gone back to wash her hands even though the teachers provided hand sanitizer wipes. Sarah never came back. Her backpack and camera had been found about sixty feet from the restroom facility with the contents scattered about.

Initially the group wasn't too concerned. The science teacher, Mr. Orr, was in charge of Sarah's class. The report stated that he thought maybe she had wandered off on the path headed toward Pounds Hollow but when he came across her belongings strewn across the grass, he became concerned and went into the woods looking for her. Using his cell, he called a fellow teacher to ask for additional help looking. They spread out calling for Sarah. The rest of the students were left under the care of the other staff members and the bus drivers. After ten minutes of searching, Mr. Orr called their principal at the school. Within 20 minutes, the principal and a deputy sheriff came to the location. By then the teachers had gathered all the students together under the shelter and anxieties were high. The children were visibly worried and many were crying. I could certainly understand this.

I continued to scan the report and read the comments of the teacher, Mr. Orr, including his quote, "It wasn't like Sarah to wander off from the group or her teachers. She is an obedient and conscientious child." Shortly after the arrival of the principal, the teachers were instructed to load the students onto the buses and return to school. Additional search parties along with Sarah's parents were on location looking for her. Search and rescue dogs were brought in but no trace was found of the child. Her trail led down to the creek along the lower Rim Rock trail then up and through what was known as Fat Man's Squeeze, a naturally formed limestone passage carved by years of rain and wind. In some areas of the trail, the squeeze was quite close, therefore, rendering the name. The authorities found two sets of distinct tracks leading up to the higher ridge. One investigator added that a smaller set of tracks showed some type of resistance. Those tracks looked as if someone had struggled on the path. All traces ended at the top parking lot where Sarah had seemingly vanished.

When the plane descended toward the Williamson County Airport, a small, regional airport outside the Marion, Illinois, city limits, I noticed cornfields in the background. Southern Illinois was definitely an agronomy region. I read in the brochure that Marion was one of the fastest growing towns in Illinois. The present population was around 17,000 people. Only about fourteen miles to the west was a university town, Carbondale. Southern Illinois University was the closest university and many employees at this airport probably gained training from there. The plane taxied down the runway and I spotted a pizzeria close by. I planned to make a stop on my way out.

When walking across the tarmac, I noticed the tower, scattered hangars around the perimeter and the small airport terminal. However, for its size, there was a great deal of activity. Fed Ex and UPS trucks were backed up to planes, many small aircraft were positioned for takeoff and there appeared to be a media crew on location. Later I would check to see if their presence had anything to do with the missing child because this was the closest commercial airport to the area of Sarah's disappearance. During my flight, I had put my laptop to good use. Uncovering seemingly unimportant details was a part of my talent. With added insight, I was usually able to piece together a detailed web of connections. Soon I would begin to hone that skill.

Entering the terminal, I was greeted by a young woman from the Hertz rental cubicle. She asked if I needed a rental. As I looked around the building, I could plainly see there were no other car rental booths, so, I willingly followed her to a nearby desk to fill out the paperwork for a vehicle. I wanted one that would be able to go off-road if the need arose. As she filled out the paperwork, I casually asked about all the media that I had seen at the gate. She told me that some politician was flying into the area.

After noticing only a few rental cars lined up, I easily found mine and stowed my gear in the back. Leaving the terminal, I was behind the wheel of a recent model Ford Explorer, a navy blue one. Probably not going to look too good with a layer of country road dust but they surely had car washes somewhere. I headed toward the pizza joint I had noticed when landing. Take care of the basic needs and the brain functions much more productively.

Entering the building, I accidentally bumped into an older woman. For some strange reason, I detected a strong earthiness like a forest glade in early spring surrounded by an overwhelming smell of fresh air. I turned to apologize to her and noticed she was staring at me.

"Excuse me. I was so intent on getting inside that I was careless. I hope I didn't hurt you."

"No, dear, you didn't hurt me. I should have moved out of your way," she answered.

There was something about her, something vaguely familiar but I couldn't quite pinpoint it. My travels had mainly been in the northern part of this state near Chicago or at little towns along the Ohio River but I never remembered visiting Marion, Illinois. Interestingly enough, she asked if she could be of some help. Failing to suppress my look of surprise, she added, "Oh, allow me to introduce myself. I'm Myriad Dupree and I've been expecting you."

Instantly I became suspicious and observed her more closely. Although at first glance, she appeared to be an older lady, though her face was surprisingly void of any wrinkles. Her hair was definitely gray but it was thick and possessed a deep luster. Her eyes were ice-blue with tinges of gray around the edges and her smile was radiant showing a full set of bright, white teeth. At the corner of her mouth were deep dimples. She looked ethereal and seemingly ageless. Though she was short in stature, her bearing held a great deal of poise and grace. On second thought, there was nothing at all elderly about her. I must have been suffering from jet lag when I first surmised that she was older.

I blatantly asked, "Who are you really and why are you here?"

"Well, dear, let's go order some pizza and I'll answer all your questions. One should always address the basic needs before beginning a deep conversation. Don't you agree?"

She was reiterating almost word for word my thoughts while leaving the airport. Was this a mere coincidence, or could she read thoughts from a distance? I was open to believing that some people had extra sensory skills. I personally knew a few. Indeed this day was proving to be an interesting one.

"I'll agree that I'm hungry. I'm going to order a loaded, thick crust pizza. Does that appeal to you?"

"Oh, most definitely. I shall wait for you in that booth at the back of the building, away from the rest of the crowd. That way we can have our privacy. Oh, please do order me a Diet Coke and may I please pay?" When she reached into her purse, I insisted that I would pay and that I'd meet her at the booth in a few minutes. She patted my hand, gave me a warm smile and headed toward the rear booth.

In spite of all the strange things that had happened since I came into this place, for some unknown reason, I felt comfortable with her; oddly enough, I even sensed a faint kinship with her. Surely, I was suffering from jet lag, or definitely, unusual circumstances were at hand Regardless, I knew this was no chance meeting and I was interested in finding out what this woman had to say. Something told me that she was going to play a major role in the upcoming events and it was more than coincidence that put her in this restaurant at the exact time that I entered it. Why here? Why not the burgers place across the highway? How did she know I would choose pizza and come directly from the airport to this particular place? Soon, hopefully, I would have some answers.

I made my way back to the booth where Ms. Dupree waited and strangely I felt an overwhelming sense of peace that somehow everything would turn out OK. Explain that. I maneuvered around a small child running down the aisle after her father, while her mother trailed behind. I made it to the booth and slid in across from my newly found companion. She was still smiling and licked her lips when she smelled the fresh, hot pizza on the tray.

"There's really nothing as appetizing as a steaming hot pizza fresh from the oven. Wouldn't you agree?"

Before answering her, I noticed where earlier there had been several people seated at tables and booths nearby but now they were all empty. In fact, the whole restaurant had just about emptied out of customers. There were two teenagers at the counter and one middle-aged couple at the front table near the door. Coincidence or was this all orchestrated? Looking around, no one was paying any attention to us and no one seemed to be "lurking" in the parking lot. Myriad was on her own.

"Sure. Let's eat then we can discuss why you're here." I bit off a mouthful of delicious pizza and noticed that Ms. Dupree was enjoying her slice. After inhaling three more slices and drinking most of my soft drink, I wiped my mouth with a paper napkin, took a deep breath and asked good ole' Myriad what she was doing here.

"Well, my dear, how can I say this?" She cleared her throat and appeared to compose herself before speaking, "I knew you would be here and that you'd need a friend. So, I came. I've watched you from afar for so long. I've seen you grow from a lonely and confused child to a beautiful and self-confident young woman, although still a little sensitive when you think about your mother. So, I thought it was time we met. You see, I knew your mother and I knew your father even better. I enjoyed watching him go through his levels of growth and I felt heartsick when he got caught up in the wrong movement. Though still unsure exactly what position he really took, or if he ever held any blame and I'm convinced that he was at the wrong place at the wrong time but that's another story for another time." She paused for a moment before continuing.

"Oh my, I am rambling and I'm sure you must think me quite senile. For now, we need to talk about what's going to happen in the next few days. I need to prepare you for what you'll soon learn and what you must do to prevent further tragedy. First, eat up. You'll need all your strength for the coming days. Mmmm. This pizza really is tasty, isn't it?"

I looked at my companion more critically. She was dressed with impeccable taste. Her suit had to be a designer one and looked quite expensive. The satchel beside her made of the highest quality leather. It looked soft, gently worn and pliable, probably handmade in Italy and I had seen none like it. She wore an unusual necklace with some kind of insignia on it. I couldn't quite make it out and didn't want to openly stare. I didn't believe she was from here. She had no noticeable accent but her mannerisms were those more typical of a European. She possessed an old-world charm yet seemed comfortable in her surroundings. When she made her next statement, I choked on my food.

"What did you just say?" I asked as soon as I could clear my windpipe, control a choking fit and manage to speak again.

"Yes, dear, you heard me correctly. I am what many people have called me for thousands of years. I am the one known as, "Mother Nature." I'm always amused with the term. It has sounded so comical to me for years. Feminine influence has been around long before Eve. Feminine and masculine celestials reside in the highest realm. Eve was the first woman made by God for this realm. Yes, dear, he is the creator of all that covers this earth and all the realms. God knew the importance of helpmates and companionship.

Because of what happened in the Garden of Eden, distrust emerged between man and woman. When Eve listened to the one so powerful and cunning and persuaded Adam to also partake of the fruit from the Tree of Knowledge; their peace was broken. Knowing God had forbidden it, they forfeited their home and were forced to leave their sanctuary. From that day forward, some rivalry and disharmony have existed between the two sexes and damaged God's initial plan for mankind."

She briefly stopped before saying, "Oh my, here I go again, rambling. Let me get to the purpose of my visit."

I sat stunned and I know my mouth had to be wide open. In order to gain some control of this discussion, I took another drink of my soda. Wishing I had something stronger in my cup, I cleared my throat and asked, "Why are you here?"

Chapter 3

Ransfield Steward

Ransfield Steward climbed out of his sleek, classic 1972 black Corvette with some effort. Having a sports car was not all it was cracked up to be especially if you were thirty-two years old and carrying a height of six and a half feet; not always an easy feat and no pun intended. He thought his Ford F150 was much more practical and convenient but on such a beautiful spring day he had to drive his convertible on the trip from Midway, Kentucky. Besides, he could move and maneuver more quickly. This probably wasn't the wisest decision because he would be traveling in a rural area that might require some off-road driving. If so, he would lease a pickup or a sports utility vehicle.

Earlier, Rann left one of the major thoroughbred breeding operations near Midway. One of the mares was a few weeks away from birthing a long-awaited colt. Matthew Elder had a lot riding on the success of this new colt. Lord only knew how many tens of thousands of dollars he had spent on the stud fees. April's Dawn was a fine racehorse but she was nearing the end of her breeding season. Soon she would have to be put out to pasture or sold for a limited profit. Many groups had shown interest in taking the aging mare but, so far, Matthew had put off selling. He believed she still had it in her to birth a real winner. Maybe he was right and only time would tell. Matt was a remarkable person and Rann had known him for most of his life. In fact, he had first become interested in horses while working in Matt's stables while growing up. Because he had no great love of the racing industry, his interest had always been with the well-being of the animals.

A racehorse was a unique animal with such speed and strength dependent on the mighty, yet small-framed legs. Because of his love of the animal, he chose a career to see to their needs in the best way possible. He had gone to vet school and graduated near the top of his class. It hadn't been easy. He worked his way through college and still maintained his grades. He felt the experience gained while working on the numerous ranches and horse farms had given him an education no amount of classroom time could provide. There was a lot to be said for on-the-job training. True, life experiences were priceless and he had been able to build his skills while becoming educated with the best practices. The connections he made along the way further benefitted his training and career.

For now, Rann would concentrate on today's events. This was going to be an interesting meeting at best or a major ordeal at worst. The woman he had spoken to on the phone was named Cassamie James. What would she be like? Over the phone, she transmitted a professional demeanor but he couldn't help detect a bit of wispiness in her voice. Was she a busy woman or an attractive one? He'd find out soon enough. According to his watch, he was only a few minutes late. He tended to run just a bit under the wire. Rann had a lack of regard for strict guidelines. Schedules were not his strong point. He didn't want to be controlled by a clock. Time was important but the exact management of it, not so much.

Delivering pureblooded thoroughbreds taught him patience and that things didn't always run smoothly or according to a schedule. He'd already been on the road for over five hours. Sure, it would have been quicker to fly but he preferred driving. He had more control of the variables when he was behind the wheel. He pulled into the Holiday Inn Express parking lot and noticed it was almost full. Climbing out he reached into the small compartment behind his seat and grabbed his duffel bag and laptop. Walking across the parking lot, he took a few seconds to look around. Multiple restaurants and gas stations nearby and he even spied his favorite burger chain, Steak and Shake.

He opened the lobby door and remembered to recognize the woman by a red satchel that she would be carrying. That should be easy. Most satchels were brown, tan, or black. So she didn't conform to the norm and had a little individuality. He scanned the lobby and saw a woman bending over a laptop. Beside her on the floor was a red satchel. Bingo. She had long, auburn-brown hair cascading across her face and he also noticed she wore black glasses. He walked over to her.

"Hi. I'm Rann Steward. I noticed your red satchel. Easy mark. We talked on the phone."

Trying to avoid that he had startled her, she forced herself to finish typing the sentence on her laptop before casually glancing up. So, this was Ransfield Steward. Nothing like being a few minutes late. She had come early and sat here for over thirty minutes waiting. She'd about given up on him. He was here now and so no need to show temper at this point; however, if they were going to work together, she wanted him to know she appreciated and expected punctuality. She looked him straight in the eyes and said, "I was about to give up on you."

Rann's smile faded just a bit. So, she was one of those, a "clock watcher." Figures. "Sorry if I'm a little late. Do we have our meeting here or do you want to go on up to my room so we aren't disturbed? We have a lot to discuss and the sooner we get to it, the quicker we can get started. Let me check in. Have you already checked-in?"

Cassamie could not believe what she was hearing. What nerve. Here he sashayed in twenty minutes late and he insinuates that I'm holding things up. I'm already feeling some animosity toward him but that's neither important nor relevant. I'll remember why I'm here and ignore that comment. She turned to him, smiled sweetly and said, "We'll have to meet in your room. I'm camping in the Shawnee National Forest and close to the site of the abduction. Just go ahead and get your key. I'll wait for you beside the elevators."

Rann strolled up to the front desk, smiled at the young woman behind the counter and gave his name and confirmation number. The clerk looked up from the counter and faltered for just a second. Here was a knockdown gorgeous man standing in front of her.

"Good evening. Let me take care of getting your room." She was able to collect herself in time to avoid making a complete fool of herself. Ransfield had dark brown hair with deep-colored green eyes. At the lower right side of his mouth was a small scar. When she finally noticed that he had handed her his credit card, she processed it then handed it back to him. She told him that his room was on the third floor, room 306.

Rann thanked the clerk, picked up his bags and walked toward "Ms. Outdoor Life". Camping near the site, is she? Bad choice. He understood turkey mites were really bad in this area, spring, summer or fall. Also, he had learned, a long time ago, sometimes you needed to distance yourself from your work zone but that was his philosophy. Evidently, she had her own feelings about work. Good luck, Madame Punctuality. While she's in tune with nature, he planned to be comfortably reclined on a bed tuning in with a remote control. That was his idea of remote. He preferred the one you controlled with the touch of your fingers.

Cassamie had observed the whole exchange with the young woman at the front desk. She marveled that the girl was even able to process his card by the way she was openly gawking at him. OK, so he was good-looking but he wasn't a Greek God, by any means. He was OK. She had seen better-looking men. So what if he was tall, lean and muscular. He even had that walk so many women seemed to find irresistible. She would also concede he was a pretty good dresser, as well. He looked quite comfortable in his jeans and button-down shirt. His boots were nice leather. They were a little worn but they looked genuinely broken in and not just worn for fashion. By her observation, he had to be in his late twenties or early thirties. He had no visible signs of age. There was no gray hair. Of course, that could be remedied with good old Grecian Formula or hair dye, although he didn't really look the type to be concerned with gray hair or aging, in general. Gray hair on him would probably make him more appealing to many but not to her.

Rann approached her at the elevator, smiled broadly and said, "OK, let's go up and see where I'll be bunking tonight. It's room 306."

He pushed the up-arrow button, waited for Cassamie to step in then followed behind her. He punched the third-floor number and the elevator smoothly ascended upward. When the elevator stopped and the doors opened, he waited for Cassamie to step out. They walked down the hall, Rann following and he noticed that she was slim with all the right curves. If she took those glasses off, she probably had beautiful eyes. He thought they looked blue and framed with long, thick eyelashes; however, from the few minutes that he had been around her, he wasn't getting good vibes on her temperament. Definitely, she was not his type. Besides, he preferred blondes with a pleasant attitude. *From her baiting me about being late, she definitely isn't the congenial type to make a good impression. Nope, she's not my type, at all.*

Cassamie was holding her tongue as she stepped off the elevator into the hallway. The decor was adequate with the usual placement of furniture near the elevator. The lighting was dim but suitable. Carpet looked fairly new with a neutral design. The walls were free of any marks or blemishes. It was a nice, well-kept hotel. His room wasn't far from the elevators but far enough not to be disturbed by late arrivals. She stopped in front of the door. Rann reached around her and inserted the key. *Amazing, it worked. The front desk clerk was able to multi-task. Who'd have "thunk it"?* Cassamie mentally recharged. It was time to get on task. *We have an important job to do and I need to be at my best. There's no sense wasting energy sparing with someone Malitar thought useful.* Malitar had good judgment and she trusted his instincts. After the child was found, she wouldn't have to think of Ransfield Steward again.

Cassamie stepped into the hotel room and found the light switch. The room was a little stuffy because the air was off. It had one of those heating and cooling units over by the window. Rann walked over and adjusted the settings. Soon the air was circulating around the room. It was decorated in neutrals with prints of landscapes hung over the bed. The prints were wildlife scenes with a pond and birds flying over the water. There was one king-sized bed. A huge armoire with a television sat directly across from the bed. Closer to the window stood a desk with technology information. In front of the window, a small table with two chairs angled against the wall. She thought about checking out the bathroom but decided against it. That was a little too personal.

When Cassamie glanced back at Rann, he was pulling out a laptop from one of his cases. He linked up to the free Wi-Fi before placing his computer back on the desk. So, he was tech savvy. Good. Next he threw his bag onto one of the empty chairs and unbuttoned the top two buttons of his shirt. He went to his bag, unloaded his toiletry satchel and carried it into the bathroom. Coming back, he bent over and opened the stocked mini fridge extracting a soft drink. Turning he asked what I would like.

"A Diet Coke would be nice."

"Sure thing," he responded as he opened and handed me one.

He had already started drinking his. Cassamie realized he didn't worry about the extra calories. Unlike him, it had been years since she had an honest to goodness real Coca Cola. The last time must have been in college while burning the midnight oil with calories. Though always a little on the skinny side, nowadays she needed to be more aware of caloric intake. At twenty-six, some restraint was in order.

Cassamie's cell phone rang and she reached into her pocket, pulled it out to turn it off when noticing the caller ID displayed her Grams's number. She would take this call. It was the only one she took no matter how busy or where she might be.

"Hi, Grams. How are you?" I felt the smile spread across my face. Grams's voice always put me at ease and lifted my spirits. She was my strongest supporter and my rock of strength. She never called to complain or try to make me feel guilty about my long absences from home. She called because she was wondering about me, concerned with my well-being and because she loved me unconditionally.

"Honey, I couldn't be any better. It's a beautiful day and my prize irises are looking like champions. Carlos tells me I should start collecting their seeds for drying. He seems to think I need another job. Never mind that, how are you? Where are you?"

"Right now I'm in a hotel in a small town in Illinois. I'm doing some investigative reporting. Nothing I can share right now but it should prove to be interesting. I'll let you know in a few days. Anyway, the weather is beautiful here. You tell Carlos that you have enough jobs and hobbies to keep you occupied for the next twenty years. How is he anyway?"

"Oh, you know Carlos. Never one to share too much information but he tells me his youngest grandson, Ryan, is the star cross-country runner and hopes to earn a scholarship this May, when he graduates from high school."

"Oh, I remember that little urchin, Ryan. I'm not a bit surprised he can run well. I was always chasing after him when one of his antics caused me more aggravation than usual. It's hard to believe he's about to graduate from high school. Wasn't it just yesterday he stole my favorite riding crop and hid it in the hay? I don't think I ever did find it."

Rann found it interesting to listen in on her conversation. Her face had softened and she looked more approachable than the "time master" she projected downstairs in the lobby. It was easy to tell she was talking to her grandmother and she was fond of her. There was mention of a Carlos and a Ryan but they didn't sound important, no mention of a husband and no designated ring on her left hand either. She probably wasn't the type to wear a ring. With her reaction to him, she probably was one of those women "libbers" with a low regard for men, in general. That suited him just fine. The sooner they completed their work together, the sooner he would be headed back home to the bluegrass state. He tried to get involved in his unpacking but for some reason his eyes were drawn back to her. She had removed the clip from her hair and pushed it away from her face. She had a nice face. Her complexion was flawless and she had removed her eyeglasses. She did have nice eyes, gray ones in this light. She also had high cheekbones and a strong chin. This probably is an indicator of a strong, stubborn personality, or more bluntly, a spoiled one, always wanting her way.

Yet, that didn't sound quite right because she was here, at her own expense, to help find a young girl lost in the woods or abducted, as he was beginning to believe. His skills of tracking were becoming better known and widespread, although he was usually only contacted when all law enforcement procedures had been exhausted. He had received the phone call from Cassamie early this morning and made arrangements to meet with her. He wasn't sure who had given her his name but that really didn't matter. He planned to gather as much information from her and hoped that they would have a successful working relationship. He realized that Cassamie had hung up and was now looking at him.

"I take it you were talking to your grandmother?"

"Yes, we talk every couple of days. Grams is something else. She leads an interesting life. I lived with her most of my life. Actually, I lived with both of my grandparents. Grandfather died a little over a year ago. Grams copes well now but it was a rough couple of months. She's a strong woman and has found her causes to keep her busy. She says she likes to stay busy because it helps her deal with her grief."

Rann looked at her, smiled and said, "She sounds like a great lady. I really never knew mine. All of my grandparents were deceased by the time I was in junior high. I remember some things about my dad's father but nothing about Dad's mother or my mom's parents. Dad's mother died when he was just six years old and my mom's parents were gone before I was even born but I still have my parents and they're great. They live in a retirement community in Florida. I try to get down there at Christmas and at least once in the summer."

"Families are important. I feel blessed to still have my grandmother. I'm sure the Bennington family is thinking about Sarah and wondering where she is tonight. They'll be praying for her safety. So, let me bring you up to date with what has gone on with the search. The location is about fifty minutes from here through some two-lane highways and blacktop roads. I understand you're from the bluegrass region of Kentucky and probably familiar with winding, rural roadways."

"Yeah, I've driven my fair share of rambling roadways with narrow shoulders or no shoulders at all. It's a little tricky pulling a horse trailer over some of those narrow roads, especially trying to navigate them on a dark, rainy night but, I'm pretty comfortable in small, rural areas. I spent most of my life around country people and horse breeders. I know this area somewhat because I've bought some quarter horses from a local trader that lives not too far from here."

"I thought you worked with thoroughbreds or race horses, at least that was what I was told," Cassamie added.

Rann smiled. "Most people don't realize quarter horses are raced, as well. They're good runners for a quarter of a mile, hence the name. Most of them make excellent horses for use at the tracks and trainers use the breed to help lead the higher spirited horses around the racetracks. A quarter horse's calm disposition helps soothe a higher-strung thoroughbred. They are also stronger in the front and hindquarters and can muscle the racehorse into position. A good quarter horse is just as valuable to any trainer as the thoroughbred. Now, the owner probably would feel differently about that but the trainer and stable hands appreciate the quarter horse."

After their discussion and exchange of ideas, Cassamie felt they were a little more comfortable with one another and in their combined abilities. Of course, she wondered about his expertise and how upfront she could be with details about her "talents". This would require more time to build trust in one another and in only extreme circumstances would she come forth with her additional attributes. These attributes were the ones Malitar felt necessary to find the missing child.

Rann had quickly caught on to the urgency in finding as many clues as possible at the site of the abduction. He would need to camp with Cassamie near Rim Rock. She was right and they needed to be closer to the location to gather as many clues as possible. The law enforcement agencies had used dogs to follow the trail. Dogs were helpful up to a point but their main usefulness was dependent on one sense and that was the sense of smell. More than one sense was necessary for interpreting the clues that had to be somewhere out in those woods.

Hopefully, early tomorrow they would be able to find what had been missed or overlooked. A child's life was at stake and one way or another that child was being harmed physically, emotionally or mentally. He persuaded Cassamie to stay in the hotel tonight and they could head out early tomorrow morning. He didn't admit it to her but he didn't like the idea of her being out in those woods alone with only a tent flap as a barrier. Those responsible for the kidnapping could still be in the area. He would feel better knowing she wasn't alone out in the forest.

They went down to the front desk and secured a room for her on the same floor three doors down. He told her they could change rooms and get one with two beds but she had definitely vetoed that suggestion. He marveled at her determination at having her own room. He thought it was silly to worry about propriety or any awkward feelings of forced intimacy. Both were here to get to the bottom of the abduction and find the child. There was no place for personal modesty. The quicker they could find the child the less chance of long-term effects.

Chapter 4

Sarah Bennington

It was a dark place and I was cold. My tummy kept rumbling. I was hungry. He hadn't given me any food since last night when he'd stopped somewhere and bought me a cheeseburger and fries. I'd been given two water bottles but one of them was empty and the other one sounded almost empty. I was scared. I wanted my mom.

I remember being on the school field trip and going to the restroom to wash my hands. Why did I have to go wash my hands? If I'd only accepted the hand sanitizer sheet as had everybody else and not worried about the germs, I wouldn't have been grabbed by this man and dragged through the woods and up that steep climb through that tight place. What had Mr. Orr called it? Oh yeah, Fat Man's Squeeze. My phobia for cleanliness had definitely put me in this predicament.

When he grabbed me, I wanted to scream but he clamped his hand over my mouth and whispered for me to be quiet and things would be OK. Everything in my bag was scattered all across the grass. I started to cry and he carried me a long way before putting me down. I must have passed out because I can't remember when we started moving again. I do remember he told me I would be OK in a little while and he wasn't going to hurt me. He said he wouldn't keep me long then he would take me home. He had lied. It had been a long time and he still hadn't taken me home.

When I was fully awake, I thought about what all had happened. I remember passing through that squeeze and climbing to the top. We came to a parking lot. He opened a trunk and dropped something into it. I must have fallen asleep again because I noticed my hands were tied, a scarf was over my mouth and I was in the trunk. I could tell we were driving. I had a pillow and a blanket. The blanket smelled clean and it was soft but it wasn't really warm. I cried for a long time until I fell asleep.

When I woke up, we were still driving. Some light came through the edges of the trunk lid. It was crowded with a suitcase and some sort of dark container. There wasn't enough light to see what was in it. Near my feet, there was a metal box. I had scooted over to it and tried to open it with my feet. I couldn't because it had a lock on it just like what we have on our P.E. lockers in the gym. Sometimes I forget my combination when I've been away from school for long. Then I have to go to the office and find out what it is. My friend, Jana says I should write it down somewhere or put it in the note section of my cell phone. If I wrote it down somewhere or put it in my phone, someone could find it. This made me start thinking again.

I thought a lot about my parents. I wondered what they were doing. I also thought about my friends and teachers at school. I bet my teachers got into trouble because I wasn't there any longer but I hoped they didn't. They were good about taking us on field trips and I wouldn't want that to stop. Kids like to get out of the classroom and go see things. It's fun to get to eat out in the woods with your friends. It made me sad to think about my friends. I started to cry again. I just wanted to go home.

I fell asleep again and when I awoke the car had stopped. I could hear noise. It sounded as traffic going by then I heard gasoline being put into the car's gas tank. We must have driven a long way during the night. I listened to see if I heard anything else but I couldn't hear anyone talking. I wanted to scream. I wanted to kick on the trunk lid but something kept me from doing it. I didn't want to make that man mad because he might hurt me. I was hungry and hoped he would give me something to eat as he did yesterday. Then the car door opened and closed; we started moving again. It was daylight now and getting warmer. I stretched out so I wasn't so scrunched and felt better. It wasn't long until the car pulled over and I heard him talking. He was ordering food: biscuits and gravy, a sausage biscuit and some orange juice. Then we were moving again. We drove for a few minutes until he slowed the car and it bounced down a rough road. He must have driven out of town and was driving in the country. Finally, he pulled over and turned the car off. I heard him walking around to the back of it then he opened the trunk. What was he going to do now? I held my breath.

He didn't look mad or upset and helped me out of the trunk. I looked around and saw we were in the country somewhere. There was no sign of anyone nearby. He told me to get in the backseat of the car. I did as he said and saw he had placed some biscuits and gravy on the seat with an orange juice in the cup holder. As he took the scarf from my mouth, he told me it wouldn't do any good to scream because no one was around to hear it. He said he would untie my hands so I could eat but he was going to put shackles around my ankles and this would prevent me from running away. I nodded I understood. I was so glad to be out of that trunk and I started to eat. I was really hungry. This time, I didn't even worry about washing my hands but he handed me a container of sanitation wipes. I used them to clean my hands and my face, being careful to keep the wipe away from my eyes. That stuff would sting if I got it in my eyes.

The man climbed back into the car and started it. He hit some kind of button that kept me from being able to open the door from the back. I also tried to roll down the window but it wouldn't budge. My mom had a button like that in her car. It was a rear window lock button supposedly for child safety. Ha. How safe was I now? I hated that button. I continued eating. The food was good and it felt good being out of that trunk and sitting up.

I didn't recognize anything around me. When he pulled out onto a highway, I looked for a sign beside the road but there was nothing. I noticed he would glance my way every few minutes. He was probably making sure I wasn't trying to do anything stupid. I didn't know what to do and I was afraid. I remembered a story we read in our reading textbook at school. It was about a boy named Willie who had been captured by the Indians, once. His family moved to the frontier to start a new life and traveled across the prairies and mountains in a Conestoga wagon. Soon after they built their log cabin, Willie had gone down to the stream to get a bucket of water. An Indian had captured him. Willie was afraid the same as I was now but later his father found him and took him home. I hoped that happened to me. I needed my cell phone. I could call for help but he had taken that away from me when he took me. Strange that he had put it up in a tree. What good did that do?

We seemed to drive for a long time. I don't remember much more because I fell asleep again. Riding in cars always made me sleepy. My parents liked that about me because when I was asleep, I wasn't always asking them how much farther. At least when I slept I wasn't worrying. A ringing phone woke me. When I opened my eyes, I saw the man was talking on a cell phone but I couldn't hear all he was saying. He was talking real low into it but I did hear him say he would call back when he reached checkpoint three. Whatever that meant. So somebody else knew about me being taken. Why did they take me? There were all kinds of kids out in those woods. Why was I the one taken? This kind of made me feel bad because it wasn't nice to wish that one of the other kids had been taken. Right now, at this moment, that was exactly what I was thinking.

Chapter 5

Cassamie and Rann

The next morning brought a bright, dry day and good conditions for the investigation. Rann showered, shaved, dressed then went down to Cassamie's room. Surprisingly, when he knocked she answered the door fully dressed and ready to go. She told him her first priority was coffee and breakfast. They decided to let her lead and she could pull into whatever restaurant she wanted. He had no preferences for what he had for breakfast.

They checked out and walked into the parking lot. Rann helped Cassamie to her vehicle and was glad to see it was an SUV. No need for him to rent one. He told her he would bring his car around behind her and it was a black convertible. He saw a smirk on her face before she climbed into the Ford Explorer. He jogged over to his car, stashed his gear in the back and pulled his car over to follow her.

Cassamie rolled down her window and said, "Might have known it'd be a Corvette. Follow me, if you can keep up." She gunned the engine and surged forward.

"Enjoy your entertainment, later we'll see who has trouble keeping up," called Rann, as he accelerated after her.

They made several turns and went through a road construction site. They didn't travel too far before she put her signal light on and pulled into a McDonald's. That surprised him. He wouldn't have taken her for the fast food type. He figured she veered away from those places and especially this one. Cassamie whipped into a parking spot close to the front door and he had to circle around to the side to find an open spot. He got out and sprinted around the building. When he entered, she had already stepped up to the counter and given her order. He walked up beside her and ordered two sausage biscuits, a hash brown and a cup of coffee. He asked her if it was for dine in or for the road. She told him they would eat in. Their food was brought right up and he followed her to a nearby booth. He noticed she had ordered an English muffin and coffee. First she took a drink of her coffee then began spreading jelly on her muffin.

"McDonalds. You got me there."

"They have good coffee and their mix for Diet Coke is the best. I love McDonald's. I always eat at one when I'm on the road. Don't you like it?"

"Sure, it's fine. I was just surprised, that's all."

They ate in companionable silence. The place was filled with little kids running around the play area. Mostly young parents and grandparents were seated in there. Over to the side, in a more secluded area, the regulars were enjoying their coffee and conversation. Many of them looked like retired folks having a leisurely morning.

After Cassamie drank most of her coffee, she leaned back against the seat and asked Rann what caused him to go to veterinarian school. She was curious about him. She had been told he was a highly skilled tracker and professional in his methods and she was interested in how the two became intertwined.

Rann smiled and told her that growing up near Midway, Kentucky, had a great influence on determining his choice of a career. When he was a kid, he worked for a local horse operation by mucking out stalls and helping to exercise the animals. His parents lived on a small farm near Matthew Elder's racehorse farm. Because Rann's parents weren't comfortable financially, he had gotten a part time job from Matt when he was eleven. That job turned into a regular job as he got older and had his driver's license. He always loved the horses but cared more about the animals' health than their performance on the track. His love for the animal helped seal his decision to go to vet school.

An old-timer named Hank Parson had taught Rann how to track. His great-grandmother lived to the ripe old age of 104 years and according to Hank, no need for a nursing home or assisted living for her. She was remarkably spry until her last winter when she came down with pneumonia. Hank said she wouldn't go to the hospital and died in her bed early one morning. Hank was the one to find her. She had looked peaceful as if she had just drifted off to sleep. Hank was only ten at the time and had a hard time accepting his loss. She had been his lifetime teacher and companion. He had to grow up quickly that winter but he always remembered what she had taught him and through the years honed those skills. He shared that knowledge with Rann.

Rann continued explaining Hank knew a lot of natural remedies and methods he used with the horses. "Actually, Matt allowed Hank full control on making the decisions on what was best for the horses. It was Hank who first encouraged me to become a veterinarian. He said modern times were far outdistancing his home remedies and I would benefit from learning from both modern science and tried-and-true practices of the past.

When Matt first heard Hank encouraging me, he piped in and told me he would help me get accepted into a veterinary medicine program. As the years passed, it became more common for our conversations to drift around that topic. Down deep, I knew I would enjoy that profession because it involved all the things I had come to love and understand So I worked hard in high school and earned a scholarship to the University of Louisville. It was close enough so I could be home on the weekends and still keep my part-time job with Matt. After graduating with my degree, I began a route running between all the major racing farms."

"Are you talking about the farms near Midway?" Cassamie had listened attentively as Rann shared his story. It was interesting and kept her engaged but she wanted to know more about his tracking skills. So, she asked him.

Rann had been looking out the window and turned his head to look at Cassamie and nodded. *So, she wants to know the whole nine yards. He would tell her most of it.*

"About ten years ago, an older man with Alzheimer's who lived with his daughter on a farm not far from Matt's home, wandered off from the front porch after she had gone in the house to check on dinner. She thought her father had fallen asleep in the swing but when she came back out, he was gone. Hank was out of town at the time, so when Matt received the call, he asked me to go with him in search of the elderly man.

This was the first time I became known for my tracking skills. I utilized what I had learned from Hank; he didn't add he also used a little assist from his own deductions and an uncanny sixth sense. I was able to find the older gentleman in a ravine down by a dried up creek bed on a neighboring farm. The old guy had gone through a heavy growth of briars and tripped over a large tree limb twisting his ankle and falling down the bank. He was scratched up, a little rattled and dehydrated by the time we found him but he suffered no other injuries. The family had been grateful for the help and they were quick to talk to the local newspaper reporter about the rescue.

The story was published in that newspaper and was picked up by the United Press syndication that ran in many national newspapers. I was bombarded by all kinds of journalists but refused any media coverage from the television networks. Soon after that, many people became interested in my tracking skills, including the local law enforcement agency. Throughout the years, they asked for assistance with many cases. I still help whenever I can."

"Where exactly is Midway? I'm not familiar with it. Is it known for racehorse farms?" asked Cassamie.

Rann smiled and told her about the region where he had lived his entire life. Midway was a small town with around 1600 people now and most of them were connected to horse farms. The town was actually built by the Lexington and Ohio Railroad in 1835. Previously, in 1833, the railroad had purchased a right-of-way passing through the center of Col. John Francisco's land Col. Francisco became angry after construction had begun and claimed they damaged his land He won his case against the railroad and the courts ordered the railroad to buy the entire 216-acre farm. They did for a grand total of $6,491.20 and, consequently, decided to build a town. It became Kentucky's first railroad town and a model for many other towns because of their street patterns.

Today the town is mainly a tourist stop with many shops, restaurants and specialty boutiques along both sides of Main Street. The horse industry has helped to bring many visitors to the town and the local chamber of commerce and historical society, along with various clubs, are active in generating activities and festivals in Midway. Midway's proximity to Frankfort, Lexington and Louisville has been instrumental to the town.

"Its location has definitely had an impact on my practice. My route takes me to Lexington, Frankfort, Louisville, including Midway and other surrounding towns. Now enough about me, what about your story?" He leaned in toward her and asked, "Who are you, Cassamie James? What makes you tick?"

Cassamie's fleeting smile vanished as quickly as it formed. She looked at Rann and said, "It would take a lot longer than the time we have right now for me to answer those questions. We'll have to continue that discussion another time because we need to head to the Garden of the Gods."

"Garden of the Gods? Is that the name of the area?"

"Yes and we need to go." She stood up and began gathering the trash and taking it to the receptacle. "Just follow me," Cassamie instructed as her mind engaged with the challenge ahead. *"Where will our path lead us and what obstacles will we face?"* Cassamie pondered.

Walking to our vehicles, we exchanged cell phone numbers in case we needed to make contact before we reached our destination. Rann followed, as they headed toward their destination.

It was an interesting drive. Part of the trip was on a four-lane highway, allowing them to make good time; however, the last half of the journey was quite different. Somewhere off the two-lane stretch of Route 13, between Harrisburg and Equality, they turned off onto a gravel road and traveled for around fifteen minutes on winding, dusty roads until coming to an asphalt-surfaced road. Using a local map, it directed them to travel on several paved roads until reaching the campgrounds near Glenn O Jones Lake. Cassamie noticed it was fairly close to the region they would be searching. Rann pulled up beside Cassamie. This would be their central headquarters for several days.

Cassamie climbed out of the SUV and opened the back tailgate to unload the camping supplies she had picked up earlier at a local sporting goods store in Marion. Surprisingly, they had a wide selection and she was able to pick up food and additional supplies right before driving to meet Rann. After placing a box of groceries on the ground, she turned around and bumped into him. He was there to assist in unloading. Cassamie surmised one good thing about him was he certainly had learned courtesy and manners. Someone had taught him well on that count and she appreciated his help.

"Hey, you've got some top of the line camping gear here. I take it you've camped before," commented Rann.

"I've been camping since childhood. My grandparents were strong believers in good stewards of the land and utilizing what nature had supplied with an eye on taking responsible steps not to damage or change any of the ecosystems. I love camping out. I'm also a pretty good camp cook, although you'll see I enjoy my comfort as well, thus, the well-stocked equipment and supplies. If you would, you can give me a hand with the tent. It shouldn't take too long to set up with both of us working. It's big enough for four campers, so we should have plenty of room. There's a privacy divide so each of us will have our own space. I'm sure you understand what I mean by that statement. Otherwise, you'll find yourself out in the cold and I mean that literally. Understood?"

"Absolutely. I wouldn't have it any other way," quipped Rann, looking her straight in the eyes without blinking. He mused he was here to do a job and find a kid, not to start some long distance romance with no future.

It only took about forty-five minutes to assemble the tent, set up the equipment and store all the supplies inside. This left plenty of time to drive to the parking lot where the fifth-grader's trail had ended. We would backtrack to the exact spot where Sarah had initially been taken. When I went over that plan with Rann, he was in agreement. We decided to leave his car at the campsite and take the Ford Explorer. Rann grabbed his large backpack from the trunk of his car and we headed out.

As I drove, I noticed him rummaging around in his backpack. He seemed to find what he was looking for and pulled it out. It looked to be a large magnifying glass with some kind of apparatus on the end of it. I wanted to examine it more closely but needed to keep my eyes on the winding road. When we stopped, I would ask him about it. I didn't know much about forensics other than what I'd seen on the television cop shows. I know that investigations were high-tech now but that particular apparatus looked primitive or homemade. As I pulled into the parking lot, I got a horrific smell of something. I glanced at him and he was holding what looked like a small leather pouch tied with rawhide. Before I could say something about the terrible stench, Rann looked my way with a sideways grin.

"What's wrong? Not your favorite scent?"

"My lord, no. What is that?"

"Something I learned from a descendent of the Shawnee Nation. It's not scientific or found in any of my textbooks but it's potent and useful. You'll see soon enough." He had a huge grin on his face and was enjoying my discomfort.

I rolled down my window and stuck my head out as far as I could. The air conditioning couldn't shield the stench now permeating the entire vehicle. I craned my neck around and asked Rann, "Are you sure that stuff isn't lethal or illegal?"

"No, nothing like that. It's just an unusual assortment of herbs and ointments. No danger other than the unpleasant odor. It won't cause you any health risks."

I turned off the ignition, removed the key and gladly hopped out of the vehicle as far away from it as possible. I noticed he took his sweet time gathering his bag and exiting the

SUV. He stood and looked around the parking lot, cocking his head to one side and closing his eyes. He stood that way for a few seconds then turned and looked at me.

"From the sheriff's report, I believe the trail is over to our right. Sound right to you?" He really didn't wait for my answer before heading in that direction. I grabbed a couple of water bottles, stashed them in my over-the-shoulder bag and scrambled after him. By the time I reached his side, he had found the beginning of the trail.

"Hey, aren't you going to check anything around here, in the parking lot?"

"No need. By now any electrostatic charges that were left on this hard surface are long gone. I'm sure the sheriff and the investigative team already combed this area gathering any evidence that might have been left, although I doubt they found anything useful. I'm more interested in getting to the trail, the softer surfaces and what might be found off the trail in the underbrush. I'm looking for anything that might have been overlooked. Let me see the bottom of your shoes so I recognize your imprints."

I lifted my shoe so that he could see the rubber pattern in the sole. He bent close, rubbed his hand across the tread then straightened. He seemed satisfied with what he saw. He started to walk away.

"Hey, what about your shoes and your footprints?"

"I don't intend to leave any tracks." Then he walked away, leaving me standing with my mouth wide opened.

What I hadn't noticed because I was so preoccupied with getting out of that SUV to avoid smelling any more of that terrible stench, was that Rann had changed into what looked like Indian moccasins. He had also disappeared down the incline of the trail. I took off running to catch up.

The light wind swept through the woods causing the young, spring leaves to gently bend with the swaying branches. This wind seemed to be searching for something or someone as it swirled from tree to tree and eventually settled on the lower branches of the poplar tree growing near the bottom trail of Rim Rock. Within moments, all was calm again. Where nothing was a moment ago, now a faint glimmer appeared. It intensified in clarity and, if one looked carefully with the keenest of sight and an unwavering trust in what was observed, one would see an opaque outline of a woman, a powerful and beautiful woman.

Not too far from this spot, Rann was searching for any clues to help find the missing child, Sarah Bennington. He had removed several items from his bag and laid them on the ground. Cassamie caught up with him and quietly observed what he was doing without interrupting. She appreciated the great care he was giving in placing many of his instruments in an orderly fashion. He looked back at her and smiled but continued on with his organization of the contents from his bag. As Cassamie watched, Rann straightened and held what appeared to be a string-like piece of leather. He used it to stretch across the earth near his feet. He bent over and scooped some dirt across the leather string. Straightening, he quickly pulled the string through the dirt. After this, he gathered the string and placed it in a plastic bag. Next he brought out the instrument she had seen earlier and placed the magnifying glass close to the area where he had drawn the leather string through.

The little device on the end turned toward the east. So she had been right. It was like a compass. Rann placed that instrument back into his bag and left the trail to walk into the underbrush. He carefully moved and inspected the small briars and brush near the ground. Two times he walked back into his previous steps and repeated the process. The final time he reached over to the left and removed a tiny thread that was caught up in the briars. He inspected it, smelled it and placed it in a small box. She noticed him briefly close his eyes and seemed deep in concentration. At this point, he pulled on a pair of gloves, turned around and headed in the opposite direction walking carefully back across the path toward a large oak tree. Here, he actually bent down on his haunches studying the bark at the base of the tree. Then he stood, leaning against the tree and reached above his head. It was as if he were feeling for something in the crotch, where the lower limbs met just above the trunk of the tree. When he turned back around, he held what appeared to be a cell phone. He carefully examined it then put it into another plastic bag.

How had he found that phone? What clue led him to search there, in that particular tree? What signaled him? Cassamie knew she was observing more than skill but she couldn't tell what sense or intuition had led him. She tried to comprehend what might have beckoned him to that particular tree.

Rann moved back to his beginning point where he had laid his bag. He reached over and brought out some type of measuring stick. He kneeled down and was inspecting something on the ground. Was it a footprint? Yes, it must be. Now he was measuring the length and width of it. He reached across to his bag and took out some colored tape. It looked to be electrical tape but was a bright orange color. He wrapped the tape around a point on his stick. From my observation point, the stick actually looked similar to a telescoping, trekking pole. After this, he grabbed a notebook and began making a sketch. I couldn't contain myself any longer.

"What are you drawing?" I asked.

"I wondered how much longer you'd sit there quietly, without asking questions," Rann said, as he turned toward me with a grin on his face.

"I knew you were deep into your work, so I tried to watch and stay out of your way. I followed most of what you were doing but there were some steps where you totally lost me."

"Come on down here. I've flagged a print. I've protected the track so it's easily seen and won't get disturbed. I'm finishing up by writing on the tape with this Sharpie pen. It should hold for a few days while additional evidence is gathered. I just drew a sketch of the indentations and the foliage in this area. I'll also take a couple of pictures with my camera. Then I'm going to use what I have in the leather pouch to smear around the perimeter. The stench will be effective in deterring inquisitive animals from the area. I'm sure you won't mind my use of it out here."

I was going no closer to that ointment but I watched as he took a brush and covered an area around the site. It was interesting to watch him work but I kept my distance from the contents he was smearing on the ground. I marveled how he could touch that stuff and not even flinch or grimace.

Rann continued explaining. "What I've done is simple forensic science; however, most of my skill came from what I learned from Hank. Remember his great grandmother was a full Shawnee tribe member. The American Indians were the earliest trackers and are quite knowledgeable in the traditional methods of tracking. Although they have possession of high-tech equipment today, they use the "cutting for sign" methods, primarily. You witnessed me using some of those methods; however, I use today's technology as well but the most effective trackers in the world are not instruments but people.

"Actually, the Tohono O'odham Nation in southern Arizona has the record of being the best trackers. Their reservation is in southern Arizona and parts of Mexico. They live in the Sonoran Desert in south central Arizona, not too far from Tucson. The best trackers make up a unit known as the "Shadow Wolves". Their unit is part of the U.S. Immigration and Customs Enforcement (ICE). The Shadow Wolves' primary task is tracking smugglers through a seventy-six-mile stretch of their reservation. They track drug smugglers, known as 'mules' as they try to bring their illegal pack across the border. Their unit has quite a remarkable history in tracking skills passed down from generation to generation."

"Can anyone become a Shadow Wolf?'

"No, a member has to be at least one-quarter Native American ancestry to qualify. There are nine different tribes that make up the Shadow Wolves. The protected skills are passed down from generation to generation in each tribe.

"How'd they get the name Shadow Wolves?

"From what Hank told me and from what I've researched, the name comes from the way the unit hunts like a wolf pack."

"Do they only operate near their homeland or do they track for anyone else?

"Actually, in 2003, they became part of the Department of Homeland Security when ICE became part of that department but, in 2006, the unit was transferred back to ICE. I believe the unit is made up of around fifteen members from various tribes. I know their skills have been used for tracking terrorists along the border of Afghanistan and Pakistan and by training border guards in Native American ancestral sign-reading methods, around the world."

Cassamie noticed Rann had stopped and was gathering up his supplies and putting them back in the bag. He looked up and informed me he was finished here for now and ready to head back to camp. It had been a long day and we were both tired. He suggested we start at daybreak and follow the trail as far as it led. We would backpack through the forest carrying basic supplies. So, we needed to return to camp and get a good night's rest.

Turning to head back up the hillside, I noticed a form or reflection at the bottom of the hill near the base of the trail. My senses went on alert. I could feel the rise of the hair at the back of my neck. I knew we were not alone and whatever was nearby was not human. As I continued to stare at the spot, the wind picked up and scattered some nearby leaves and brush. For a moment, I thought I could make out the form of a woman but, at the next instant, it was gone.

Rann was calling my name. He had finished packing up his supplies and was ready to go. I turned and hurried after him. Whatever that was, I had the feeling I would be seeing it again. Somehow, I knew its presence would reappear. Interesting, I noticed it just when we were getting ready to leave. For whatever reason, it wanted me to be aware of it. I would be on guard, next time. Now, I wasn't sure if what I saw was friend or foe but one thing I knew intuitively was its presence there was not accidental and somehow involved in this case. Whether or not it was involved in the disappearance of the child, I didn't know but I had a definite premonition I would soon learn those answers. I wasn't sure if that would be a good thing or a bad thing. Time would tell and time was definitely running out quicker for some than for others.

When we reached our campsite, the sun was starting to set and the temperature had dropped several degrees. While I began preparing our evening meal, Rann was busy gathering small limbs and twigs to start a fire in the ground pit. I had removed my portable butane cook top and was taking food items from the cooler and plastic containers. I noticed a strong blaze burning and I moved to the picnic table, within a few feet of the fire. I could feel the soothing warmth.

"You're pretty good at building a fire. Were you a Boy Scout?"

Rann laughed and told me while growing up, he didn't have the chance of belonging to the Boy Scouts or any type of extra-curricular club. Hank had taught him survival skills. He was self-sufficient on the land and usually slept on the ground, when he was out on a tracking mission. Most of the time he had a sleeping bag but he had slept on the ground with whatever provisions Mother Nature provided. When he referred to Mother Nature, I couldn't help but smile and think, *if you only knew*. It also prompted me to look around to see if I could detect her presence but I didn't sense her anywhere nearby. I'm not so sure I could unless she wanted to be noticed, although I had a feeling at some point in this search, she would make another appearance. That, in turn, caused me to wonder about Malitar. He had never told me about Mother Nature. I would be sure to bring her up the next time I saw him.

Dinner was ready. I set out dishes and utensils and brought the food over to the picnic table. I had cooked a type of vegetable and meat dish made up of ground turkey, tomato sauce, pasta and several veggies—my personal favorite. Seasonings were added and its aroma was pleasing and enticing. It was a simple dish but filling and full of protein and carbs. It should help to promote a good night's rest. I had also cooked some apples and cinnamon on the fire, just the right dessert to clean the palate and satisfy the sweet tooth.

Rann came over to the table with an appreciative look on his face.

"That smells great. Is it ready?"

"Yes, go ahead and fill your plate."

"No ma'am, ladies first."

"Fine." I filled my plate, poured a cup of coffee from the pot that had been sitting on the campfire and began to eat, while Rann was serving himself. I noticed he reached in the cooler and grabbed a bottle of water then sat across from me and started eating.

"This is good. What do you call it?"

"I don't really have a name for it. It's just a dish that's easy and filling. I'm glad you like it."

After that, we ate in companionable silence. When we finished, we both cleaned our dishes and returned everything back to its proper storage place. Unfortunately, there were no shower facilities but I could carry water from the hydrant close by. I brought water back to camp and heated it for bathing. I had plenty of soap and towels. We would do a basic washing then turn in. Tomorrow night I might take a dip in the lake. Though there were no other campers near, to be on the safe side, I would wear my swimming suit, as I bathed. This time of year, the lake water would be a little chilly but a sudden total immersion would soon acclimate me to the water temperature. I didn't plan to stay in for long. OK, I had a plan for a bath tomorrow night. I turned and entered the tent.

Inside the tent, we gathered our bedding, chose our respective sides of the tent and settled down to sleep. I noticed Rann had properly put out the fire, dropped the flap to the tent and extinguished the lanterns. Soon we were surrounded with a deep darkness and the sounds of the night. Those sounds quickly lulled me into a deep sleep.

Chapter 6

Cassamie

I'm not sure what woke me the next morning. It was still dark outside and the tent illuminated only from my phone when I checked the time. I strained to listen for any sound from Rann across the inner flap of the tent. I heard nothing. Outside I could hear a soft, muffling sound in the distance. As I tried to listen more intently, I heard the definite sound of light footsteps coming closer. I peered out of the tent window flap and saw a flicker of light. I could make out the shadow of Rann. Quickly, I stood up and gathered my clothes together. I dressed, ran a brush through my hair, put on my hiking shoes and left the tent.

"Good morning. At this early hour, it seems more night than day. I tried to be as quiet as possible. Did I wake you?"

"I'm not sure what woke me but I don't think it was you. I see you've got the fire going. I'm going to fill the coffee pot and get that started. What would you like for breakfast?"

"Whatever you feel like fixing but I hope it's heavy on the meat side," grinned Rann, as he leaned over to add larger sticks to the now blazing fire. I noticed he had a nice pile of twigs, sticks and small logs stacked neatly a few feet from camp, leaning against a tree.

"I thought I'd fix eggs, sausage and toast. How do you like your eggs?" I turned toward him for his answer.

"I like them any way. My sausage I like cooked well. Do you have any jelly in one of those containers? I like that on my toast. I'll be glad to fix the toast. I'm pretty good with a skillet on an open fire."

"Sure, that'll be great." I began gathering up the food items and utensils from the storage containers. Soon occupied with the usual steps in food preparation and, luckily, it was all prepared within minutes of one another. We sat together on a blanket, eating our breakfast. There was something relaxing about eating near the fire, sitting on the ground. This was better than sitting at the picnic table. The wool blanket kept the early morning dew from penetrating into our clothes. It was nice. I liked that Rann didn't feel the need to keep up a conversation and was comfortable just eating and listening to nature all around us. I wondered what Sarah was thinking right about now. I prayed and hoped she was still alive and, somehow, surviving her ordeal. I imagined many people's thoughts centered on the little girl. I knew she was a fifth grader but to me she was still a child and a frightened child. I wanted to keep focused on her to help me be my best. I only hoped Rann was as good as I'd been told.

Soon after eating, Rann began putting supplies into his backpack. This time he was putting more in the pack such as beef jerky packages, dried fruit packages and several other food items, along with chewing gum. He gathered up two large canteens, walked over to the water hydrant and began filling them. He glanced over at me and asked me to grab the first aid kit out of the trunk of his car.

I did so and asked if I needed to get anything else. He only suggested dressing in layers because we probably would be out late today and the evening could get chilly. I went back into the tent and pulled a sweatshirt over my tee and grabbed my gloves and some earmuffs. I walked out to my rental, picked up a couple travel packets of Kleenex and put one in each pocket of my jacket. I had on thick wool socks so my feet should be fine in my hiking boots. I was ready.

Rann came over with some insect repellent. He told me turkey mites were bad here and so were deer ticks. Therefore, I liberally sprayed myself down, even under my socks and the neck of my tee shirt. Silently I thought the ointment Rann had brought with him would probably do a more effective job but I'd have to live through it, first.

Within minutes, we'd tidied up the campsite and were ready to head out. Rann gave me the lighter pack to carry and we started off. We headed toward the point where we stopped yesterday. Walking for a few minutes without talking, Rann surprised me by asking if I had noticed anything unusual last evening.

"What do you mean?"

"Just wondering if you saw anything out of the ordinary, when I was marking the tracks."

I really didn't know how to answer that question. Yes, I had seen that 'spirit-like' woman but I wasn't ready to reveal that bit of information, so I acted dumb. I told him I didn't know what he meant. I answered what I saw him doing was unusual. He never replied but kept walking through the forest. Every now then he would stop and look up in the trees.

I was looking in the trees too but I didn't expect to see anything. Boy was I ever surprised when I looked over my right shoulder and saw good ole' 'Mother Nature' sitting on a tree branch waving at me. The next instance she was gone. OK, this was going to get interesting.

When I looked back toward Rann, he had stopped and was watching me. His head angled as if deep in thought.

"See something interesting?" he asked, as he turned and started on. Now I was surprised. Could he see Mother Nature? Something was going on here and I intended to find out but I had to be careful on how I went about it. This would be a challenge.

"No, not really. Did you?"

Either he chose not to answer or he didn't hear me. Once again, I had to hurry to catch up with him. Did the man never slow down when he was on a mission? Of course, his long legs could cover a lot more ground than mine. Anyway, I put it in high gear and took off after him, stubbornly refusing to ask him to slow down for me. When I had just about caught up with him, he stopped and I ran smack dab into him. He quickly turned to steady me so that I wouldn't fall to the ground.

"You in a big hurry all of a sudden?"

"Well, I was trying to catch up with you. Why'd you stop?" I was struggling to catch my breath because I had it knocked out of me when I collided with him. The way he was looking at me, he must have realized it. I pushed his hands away and steadied myself. Recovering, I noticed he was looking at some kind of rope knotted around a tree. It looked as if it'd been used to tie off some animal. In fact, there were some hairs clinging to the hemp of the rope.

"What is it?"

"I'm not sure but it hasn't been out here long. The rope isn't discolored or frayed badly. It was used probably to restrain a dog, I'm guessing. I'm going to put a piece of it in my pack and take it with us. As soon as he said those words, an ominous growl penetrated the air. When I looked up, I saw a menacing-looking dog watching us from the small rise to our left. Actually, it was some kind of large mongrel I had never seen before. It was a dog but I didn't know the breed.

Rann whispered to me, "Don't move. Don't look it in the eyes. Just remain perfectly still, don't talk and maybe it'll move on."

I noticed he was standing quite still and was facing downward, so I did the same. I could see Rann reaching behind his back, slowly and returning with a huge Bowie-like knife. The animal seemed to calm somewhat, raised its nose, must have smelled the air for our scent, turned suddenly then darted deeper into the woods.

I could finally breathe and I turned to Rann and asked, "What was that? It was a dog, right?"

"I'm not sure what kind of a dog. It looked something like an Ibizan hound, only much darker than I've seen. They're usually red or brown. It may have been a mix. The questions are: Why was it tied up out here and who had tied it?"

"Do you think it'll come back?"

"Possibly but we won't be here much longer. I've picked up the trail. Come on follow me."

We walked faster than I would have thought. Rann must have had keen eyesight or an innate insight because he never lingered long in one spot and seemed to pick up the trail. Interestingly, we made it to the area known as Fat Man's Squeeze but, instead of going up and through it, Rann continued on the lower trail running near the creek. At one point, he actually walked out onto a fallen tree extending over the water but backtracked and came back onto the trail. He didn't volunteer any reason for going onto the fallen tree and I didn't ask any questions. We left the trail and hiked back into the forest at a tangent to the lower trail. Evidence of many animal tracks was obvious with some disturbance to the vegetation. Even I detected it.

Rann spoke for the first time in almost an hour. "It looks like someone stopped to rest here. There were at least two adults and a small adult or a child. We'll take a few minutes to rest. You might want to eat some of the beef jerky while we rest. He handed me one of the canteens as I was taking some jerky out of the pack.

"We didn't go up through the squeeze. I thought it was the way the abductor took the child according to the police report."

"You're right and I think that's exactly what the kidnapper intended for the investigators to think. In fact, they did go up that way but my feeling is they came back down off the trail. At this spot, someone else met up with them. You notice on the grassy area there are three places where the vegetation is bent over and some even broken off. For the grass to still be smashed down, they had to have stayed there for a good bit of time and carried some heavy weight. I haven't figured out what they did in this spot. Three bodies stopped here not just the two. I'm wondering what they were doing for enough time to pass to have made these impressions. Their audacity to not be on the run for worry of being caught amazes me. Two sets of tracks are the same ones we've been following but I don't know where this third set came from and it's an unusual track. In fact, there's not much of a track made at all.

This third person, definitely a person of interest, is clever. I'm guessing this one is the mastermind behind the kidnapping. Something went on here. It was something that required the child to lay prone on the ground for a good bit of time."

After making those comments, Rann knelt down on the ground paying a great deal of attention to the place that probably was made by Sarah Bennington. He reached into his pack and took out another magnifying glass. He was looking intently at something in the grass. He sat back on his haunches, reached inside his pack and removed some tiny tweezers. He gently brushed them across the grass and slowly moved the blades of grass covered in the dark spots. He paused, stared at the grass then looked over at me.

"I think these dark spots on the grass are blood stains. I'm going to mark this spot and call in the sheriff's team to come and check it out but, before I do that, I want to finish up in this area. I need to follow this trail to its ending point."

I was listening to him but my mind kept going over a comment he had made a few minutes ago. "What do you mean you don't know where this third set of tracks came from? Can't you find where those tracks came from by working backwards to find the point of origin?"

Before Rann answered my questions, he took a deep breath. He seemed to be gauging something before speaking. He took his right hand and brushed his hair back from his forehead. "That's the tricky part. This is the point of origin for these new tracks."

Chapter 7

Sarah

My captor was tall. I don't think I ever saw anyone that tall. When he took off his sunglasses, I could see he had strange eyes. *They are different colors. One eye is blue and the other one is a light brown. They make me feel funny because it is as if he can see through my head and knows what I'm thinking. Is that possible?* The odd thing was he wasn't "mean looking" really but he was always frowning or crinkling up his brow as if he were thinking all the time. He didn't talk much and when he did, he never said much except what needed to be said, such as asking a question or telling me to do something. I wasn't as afraid as I had been. I didn't think he was going to hurt me but I didn't know that. I didn't know anything except I wanted to go home. I wanted my family and friends. I even wanted to go back to school. Maybe I could talk him into taking me home.

"Where are you taking me?"

"I'm taking you to a place where you will be more comfortable than riding in this car," the man looked at me for only a moment then faced the road again.

"I would be comfortable at home. Are you taking me there? Are you going to untie my hands again?"

He chuckled and shook his head no. I almost started to cry but I told myself not to because that didn't do any good. I needed to pay attention to where we were going. Maybe something would look familiar because my parents had taken me on many trips. I even traveled way up north to a place called Mayo Clinic. I think it was in Minnesota. That was when I was little and sick, often. My parents had talked to me about my illness and all the hospitals to which I had been. What I had was unusual for someone such as me and made me really sick at times but I was getting better at dealing with it. It was something about my blood being different from most people's blood. I had all kinds of blood tests and I still went every three months to St. Louis to get it checked. It wasn't getting any worse, so that is good, except for the times when I get really tired from a surge of energy. Does that even make sense? Anyway, most people don't know I'm sick. It's hard to tell by looking at me. You have to know about blood to be able to tell I'm sick.

For a while, I daydreamed then I remembered something that happened right before he put me in the trunk. We had gone up to that parking lot but then we went across and back into the forest. We walked for a little bit then sat down in the grass. He gave me something to drink from a canteen and I got real sleepy. I must have fallen asleep because the next thing I remember was he carried me and put me in that trunk. I wondered if he had put something in that drink. Had he drugged me? I've read about that before and seen it on television. People can do that without you even realizing it. I think that must be what he did to me but why? Was there something he didn't want me to see?

Something brought my attention back and I noticed we had pulled over to the side of the road. He turned around and faced me. Then he handed me a bag filled with clothes.

"I want you to change into these clean clothes. There are some cleaning towels in the bottom and a hairbrush. I'm going to get out of the car and walk a few feet away to give you some privacy. I'll give you a few minutes."

I watched him walk away and turn his back on me. I reached into the bag and brought out jeans and a blue and yellow top. Those were my favorite colors. Wasn't that strange? As I hurriedly changed clothes, I noticed they fit me perfectly. The jeans looked new but they were comfortable, not scratchy as new ones usually feel, until you wash them. They didn't even feel itchy. They smelled fresh, so they must be clean.

I reached in the bag again and pulled out a brush and a mirror. I brushed my hair. I was getting ready to call him when I noticed he was heading back to the car. Strange he seemed to know things. He opened my door and reached in and gathered up my old clothes. He picked up the brush and mirror and put them back in the bag. Then he closed my door, popped the trunk and placed the things inside. He came back around, got in and started the car. We drove a short distance and I noticed we were turning onto a larger highway. It must be an interstate highway because it had four lanes. I would keep watching and maybe I could see a sign that told what number of interstate highway it was. When I looked out the side window, I could see many trees along the road.

"Are you getting hungry?"

When I looked back toward him, he was watching me through the rearview mirror. He was patiently waiting for my answer.

"Yeah, kind of."

"Well, there's a town not too far from here and I thought we could stop and go in for some pizza. Would you like that?"

"Sure but aren't you afraid I'll say something to somebody?"

"No. I have a way of persuading people to believe certain things. I think we'll be fine. We'll have a talk before we go in. How does that sound?"

It didn't sound too good to me but I wasn't about to say that. What did he mean he had a way of persuading people to believe certain things? I didn't have time to wonder much more because he took an exit. We didn't drive far before we saw a Pizza Hut. He turned left then pulled into the parking lot. He opened his door, got out then opened mine. He got in next to me and untied my hands. He rubbed them a little until the red marks went away then he looked into my eyes and said something I didn't understand but then he smiled at me and told me I could call him Jim. He said I needed to have a name to call him. It wasn't his real name but it was close enough. Maybe one day he would tell me his real name. Jim also told me he had a daughter. That surprised me and I wanted to ask him more but he was ready to go inside.

As we walked into the Pizza Hut, I saw a police car drive by. For some reason, I never even thought about screaming or trying to get the policeman's attention. I just followed Jim into the restaurant. We sat down in a booth close to the door. The waitress came over and took our order and Jim asked me what I wanted to order. I told him pepperoni pizza on thin crust.

"That sounds good to me. I also want the salad bar. Would you like a salad, Sarah?"

I was surprised he used my name but I answered I didn't want one, only pizza. We both ordered a Coke to drink then sat back to wait for our order. There weren't many people in the restaurant but the drive-up window was busy.

Jim looked at me and asked if I needed to go to the restroom. I told him yes and he pointed in the direction and I got up and walked to it. No one else was in there. When I came out, Jim was waiting for me outside the door. We walked back to our table and our pizza was already there. I sat down and took a piece. It was delicious. Jim told me I could have as much as I wanted. He said he wasn't hungry. So, I ate four slices of the pizza while Jim ate his salad and drank his soda. He did eat one piece but I noticed he took the pepperoni off and laid it on his plate. He was different from my dad, who would have eaten the rest of the pizza with the pepperoni left on it.

He really has pretty eyes even though they are strange because they are different colors. I've never seen anyone with different colored eyes. People's eyes were usually blue, green, or brown. I wonder why his are different from one another. In science class, we had talked about recessive and dominant genes and how eye color was determined. I wish I'd paid more attention in class. Maybe I can ask him about his eyes. No, I better not. He might not want me to say anything about them.

Jim looked at me and smiled. There was something about him that made me want to talk to him. I thought it weird I would feel that way, considering he had kidnapped me. He was observing me and giving me time to get my thoughts in order. He asked if I needed anything else to eat.

"No, I just want to go home."

He smiled again, patted my hand and said, "I know you do but it'll take a little more time before I can take you back. Don't worry. I'm not going to hurt you."

He got up, left a tip on the table and told me we needed to go. He stared at me for a few minutes then we walked up to the counter to pay the bill before walking back out to the parking lot. Instead of returning to the car we had been in, he walked over to a white SUV, walked to the front right tire and pulled out some keys. He opened the back door for me and reminded me to fasten my seat belt. I did. Then he pulled around to where we had parked the car, got out and transferred the bag into the SUV. He opened the trunk of the car and threw the keys into it then closed it. We pulled out of the parking lot and drove for a long time. He pulled off the main road and drove down several country roads. He slowed down and pulled over to the side of the road. He got out and opened my door.

"Sarah, I'm going to tie your hands again. I'm also going to put a blindfold over your eyes. We are getting close enough to our destination that I don't want you to know how to get there. It's best you don't know the location. You'll be here a few days then you'll be returned to your home."

"Why did you take me?"

Jim looked at me for a few minutes. He hesitated, seemed to want to say something but didn't. Then he tied my hands and put the blindfold over my eyes. I heard him close my car door and get back up front. We started back down the road and we rode for a while. He made several turns. I had tried to count the number of turns and whether it was to the left or the right but there were too many to keep track of and besides, it gave me a headache. Then he stopped and opened the door. Someone was walking toward us because I could hear the crunch of gravel. I heard a woman talking but I couldn't tell what she was saying because she was whispering. I heard closer footsteps, my car door opened and I was picked up. I could tell that it was Jim because he had a certain smell. It was a good smell but I couldn't really say what it was. It was somewhat familiar but not really. I just couldn't identify his smell. He had a scent that made him stand out from the rest of the people I'd been around. It didn't really smell as a perfume. I guess that wasn't right. Men didn't wear perfume. What was it called? Oh, yeah, it was called cologne. Nope, it wasn't that kind of smell. Maybe I could figure it out later.

I heard several sets of footsteps. Then I think I was carried into a house or some kind of building. It was quieter and I couldn't hear the footsteps any more. Jim must have been walking on carpet. After a few minutes I was placed on something soft. It felt like a mattress. Jim took my blindfold off and I could see I was in a bedroom. Well, it looked akin to a bedroom but it also looked similar to a hospital room. There were machines all around. One of them was an I.V. machine. I knew that machine. Doctors had used those on me many times. There was also a sink and a small refrigerator. I saw another door inside the room with a walled off section, so I thought that was probably a bathroom. I started to get nervous. Had they brought me to a fancy hospital? What were they going to do to me?

I started hitting at Jim and screaming, "Let me go. I don't want to be here. Take me home. Liar. You told me you would take me home."

"Calm down, Sarah, we are not going to hurt you. They will run some tests on you, let you rest then it will soon be over," Jim said.

I heard a small chuckle coming from behind me. I turned around and saw a woman standing in the doorway. She was the most beautiful woman I had ever seen. She walked into the room but it was more as if she floated into the room. She was so graceful and tall. She put her hand on my forehead and it felt so soft and warm. She was talking to me in such a soothing way, although I didn't understand what she said. Her touch was so tender. One moment I was looking into her eyes and next I closed my eyes for just a second. Everything seemed so peaceful and quiet. I wasn't worried any more. My eyelids felt so heavy. I was drifting off.

Chapter 8

Cassamie

What did Rann mean the new tracks had originated in this spot? Oh, not that. Surely, we weren't going to have to deal with yet another being that wasn't human. Besides Malitar, I'd never come across beings other than humans; however, with Mother Nature introducing herself to me and that I actually saw her in these woods earlier along with a transparent form of another woman, what was I now going to learn? Asking myself these questions wasn't going to get me any answers. I looked at Rann. He was still watching me. Hey, he was the one who seemed to know more than what he was letting on.

"What exactly are you saying?" I asked him.

"Something I think you already guessed. We are not just dealing with ordinary people. There are other forces or other beings involved in this kidnapping. It wasn't a usual abduction. Maybe we should be honest, totally, with one another by speaking frankly. Are you willing to do that? You haven't exactly been talkative about yourself. I know you have some special gifts you've not been upfront about and you see a lot more than you let on. So how about we go on back to camp and have an open and honest discussion?"

"Are you finished here?" I asked, to give myself a little time to think. I wasn't ready to reveal too much until I found it absolutely necessary. What I was wondering about was the extra skills that Rann had and how he was truly involved. Malitar must be aware of all of this. Thinking of Malitar, I wondered where he was right now. Where was an angel when you needed one?

Rann walked over to me and took my hand He looked at me as if he were seeing me for the first time.

"It's time for you and me to have a heart to heart talk. A life is at stake here and we need to combine all our resources to find that child. We aren't dealing with ordinary people. The sheriff should be here soon to take samples of the blood to take to the lab and to use the investigative team to comb these woods, looking for any additional clues and evidence. We don't need to be here when they arrive. I'll talk to them later after they've had time to analyze and process this evidence. We need to head back to camp then take a drive around to another section of the forest. You said something earlier about the Garden of the God's area. I want to go there. We'll grab the map and head over. Is that OK with you?"

"Sure. You can tell me on the way exactly why we're headed there."

I gathered up the backpack I was responsible for carrying plus the smaller canteen and followed Rann back to the lower trail. I looked back over my shoulder but I saw nothing except the woods and the trail markings Rann had left. We retraced our entry into the forest without any other mishaps. I was preoccupied with wondering what happened to that huge, wolf-like animal. It was a mystery and one I was happy not to solve; although I am a little surprised, we didn't encounter it again. I knew when I had access to a computer with an Internet connection, I would research the characteristics of that animal. Cell phone reception was quite sketchy in this area, so that research would have to wait. I was curious to find out more about it but from a safe distance and in a secure location.

I wasn't all that fond of dogs, especially one such as that. As a child, I had always been a bit leery of them and had never spent much time around them. Grams always said it was as if I'd been programmed while in the womb not to like or trust dogs. Many of my friends laughed at my aversion to dogs. Even little chubby puppies didn't hold an appeal for me. When I was in the third grade, one had followed me home from school. During the last hour of school, I looked out the classroom window and saw him standing underneath a tree. He was dark, I think black or dark brown and he didn't stand out well in the shade of the tree. Why I noticed him I don't remember because he would have been difficult to spot under that tree. Anyway, it had felt strange, as if he were waiting for me. It was as if he were staring directly at me. I remember feeling goose bumps form on my arms. I don't know why he had affected me in such a way.

When the school bell rang and we were dismissed for the day, I went out into the schoolyard and saw the dog. In fact, the dog came walking up to me. For some reason, he didn't look so dark and big now that I had met him face-to-face. He wagged his tail while nudging my hand He wanted me to pet him. I remember doing so with the constant prodding of my friend, Zeke, who told me the dog only wanted to be friendly and I should pet it. I did then the dog began following me. He followed me all the way home but he never got real close to me again. I went into the house and called to Grams, put down my book bag and started to go out again to see if the dog was still there; however, Grams came into the hallway and told me she needed me in the family room. She had bought some toys to deliver to the charity center and wanted me to help her decide which ones would be more suitable for the older children. After about an hour of helping her, I went back out to look for the dog but the dog was gone. I remember telling Grams about him and she said she was sure he probably belonged to someone and had returned home.

The dog of my childhood had looked friendly, unlike the one I saw today. Today's dog wouldn't have followed me home. He would have probably had me for dinner. I really didn't care to come across that animal again. I hate to admit it but I was a little curious about him. Why would someone tie him up in the middle of a forest? Also, I remembered the texture of the rope used was a little strange. I had never seen anything similar to it. The hemp was thicker than usual with some type of metallic sheen to it. It wasn't thick but it looked extremely strong yet the huge dog had somehow managed to break it. The dog had to be powerful to break such a rope. I noticed even Rann had been a little intrigued with it because he put a piece of it in his bag. Now that I think about it, saving the rope was a little strange. I was beginning to have many questions about Rann and his techniques. Maybe we did need to have our talk.

Chapter 9

The "man" stared into the mirror scrutinizing how the light cast an illuminating sheen on his skin. Throughout the years, the glow diminished somewhat from its initial reaction when he first came here. Now the only time he could really detect that aura was when directly under artificial light. Daylight never seemed to penetrate or accentuate his skin the same way these man-made light fixtures did. He was careful when he entered buildings with a high concentration of intense, bright lights. When someone looked at his face, their first observation was his different, color eyes. No one ever noticed anything beyond those eyes. Of course, they weren't too unusual because sometimes humans did have different color eyes. They were noticeable but not alarming.

Normally, even in high heat, he was careful to wear long sleeves when he knew he would be inside and under scrutiny of artificial lights. Temperature fluctuations didn't bother or even affect him. He felt no consequences based on the environment. He was immune to the constant temperature variations. He felt the same whether it was 2 or 110 degrees. He often thought it must be quite uncomfortable to feel the effects and to constantly have to make adjustments, according to the temperature or the weather. In this, he felt sorry for humans. It must be terribly inconvenient to constantly monitor the weather or the conditions of the environment.

He smiled once again and noticed the way his blue eye tended to reflect the light more dramatically than the brown one. When created, the intent was for him to see much more deeply with the blue eye. He could actually see the intent of motion before the movement even began. For instance, he knew Sarah was going to strike at him before she made any detectable movement. Something in the slight stretching of her skin above her forehead alerted him to her next action. Indeed, he was sure Giselle had known what Sarah was going to do because her skills and strength were intuition and perception. That was why she found so much amusement in Sarah's actions. She had been waiting for the outburst and satisfied somehow to gauge the intensity of Sarah's reaction and any discomfort I had in fending off her strikes.

Thankfully, Giselle didn't allow the child to get too distressed before calming her. Of course, he could have done the same but Giselle's technique was much gentler and more soothing. Sarah would find peace for a few hours. The child needed some rest. He had no enjoyment for this part of the work. He felt a deep empathy for the child and her family. Hopefully, he would be able to return the child to her family as soon as possible. Then he could continue on with the work that needed to be completed to finish this journey that had started so long ago, eons ago and entire civilizations ago. Funny how one or two wrong actions caused such unbelievable chaos, the chaos that should never have occurred. Chaos had no place in the plan, the order of things yet, it happened and there had been no going back. How could one with such authority and honor veer so far from the intended path? He would never understand what caused such total betrayal and the onslaught of utter destruction.

As he turned away from the mirror, he sensed Giselle on the other side of the door. He opened it willingly because he knew they had much to discuss, although he dreaded what would inevitably come about as a chain reaction from all the previous events.

"Well, I wondered how long you were going to brood into that mirror. That is what you were doing, wasn't it, my dear friend? You were brooding, thinking and remembering. You know that doesn't really solve anything. Thoughts can create actions but actions must bring about a solution. Thoughts are not always enough. That's why we're here at this time. Are you ready or do you intend to meditate some more?"

Giselle looked at him for a few moments, not really expecting a response then motioned for him to follow her into the back section of the house. Before he could ask, she told him the child was resting peacefully and would do so for another couple of hours. The tests were finished and all the equipment had been removed from Sarah's bedroom. The child would not remember any of the equipment when she awoke. Giselle affirmed the celestial antigen permeated throughout Sarah's body.

As Grinstead walked beside Giselle, he noticed the surroundings of this house—large by most standards, luxurious but downplayed and located in a highly secluded area. Most of the windows in the house were in the front, the older part of the house and this section, a newer addition, was free of any windows except for the ceiling glass that allowed plenty of light into the space. Convenient, especially because, in the back of the house, there were no trees close enough for climbing and detecting what was going on inside. Someone had put a great deal of thought into the design of this house. It wasn't the usual rural home.

"How did you secure this house?" he asked, as he continued to critique the other characteristics of their sanctuary.

"You know we have our resources and plenty of strategies in place to accommodate all our needs, wherever we go." She gave him a warm smile and thought of how things had changed since the first time she had met up with him again in this realm. Even though she knew it would happen, when she saw him for the first time after so long, it had been a mixed reunion. It had taken decades before they became comfortable again with one another. Too many unanswered questions to be dealt with before she was at ease with him and that had taken some time.

Giselle ran her finger, teasingly, across his cheek trying to relax any misgivings he might have. She was always so sure of herself and never showed any doubt or remorse about what was to transpire. She moved with a grace that was even surprising to him. Her shining, blonde hair seemed to frame her face and enhance the beauty found there. Although tall by human standards, she was not considered tall for a celestial being. She never seemed to care or question that fact, although she was older by many years than he yet she had not obtained the additional height her maturity should have provided. In her own way, she seemed to compensate for the lack of height by carrying herself in such a way that demonstrated both speed and agility.

They both knew she could outrun any of them, filter through the multiple layers of the universe without resistance and, thereby, change into any form of life she chose, whether it be human, animal or plant. One of her favorite phasing forms was of a mighty oak, although she sometimes preferred the small, insignificant weed. She found an amusement in her skills and took full advantage of them, when necessary. Giselle was not to be taken lightly and never to be underestimated. As far as he knew, she only had one equal to match her skills perfectly and that was one of her triad celestials, Terrene. The third member of the triad had her own impressive skills but in a more sublime way. He would see her soon enough. For now, he would deal with his favorite, Giselle.

Now that would definitely upset Giselle if she knew about whom he thought. Her anger would be immense. Two of the triad had a strong rivalry and Grinstead knew Terrene would be insulted if she thought they were similar in any way. Actually, it had been a long time since he had seen Terrene.

He was quite unsure of what would happen when he did come across her again but one thing could be counted on, somewhere, someday, somehow, they would meet again. It was inevitable. The plan dictated it. All a matter of time but their reception of one another would definitely be interesting. Time would tell and he had a lot of time, or at least he had for centuries. He learned patience through eons of time; as the humans were apt to say, "Sooner or later, your time will run out." To put it more plainly, "Time would definitely tell."

Chapter 10

Cassamie and Rann

"Why are you in such a hurry to get to the Garden of the Gods? Cassamie asked, as Rann sped along the winding, paved roadway toward the rock formations. "It's not really that big a deal or that's my impression from the brochures I've read and the pictures I've seen. What's the connection anyway?"

"I'm just going on a hunch I had earlier. Look, doesn't the name, "The Garden of the Gods" sound a little intimidating to you or, if not that, at least a little presumptuous? Come on, why is the area given any connection to the Gods? I mean for goodness sakes, this isn't Greece, Rome or even Egypt, for that matter."

"Interesting you should mention Egypt. Actually, from what I read in the tourist information online, there is a region not too far from here known as "Little Egypt".

Rann whipped his head around to look at her. "Are you kidding?"

"No, I'm totally serious. So what? I'm sure many small, rural towns throughout the United States claim some connection to the earlier civilizations. In an area as remote as this, they have to have some sensationalism to attract tourism."

"That, in itself, is not odd but it's the combination of both being named in such a small radius. Evidently the beauty of this area is what caused it to be called the Garden of the Gods; yet, what does such a small, out-of-the-way area have to do with Egypt? I can't think of any connection. What'd your research tell you?"

"First of all, I've not investigated fully the region and the little I've read says southern Illinois has some of the most productive farms in a three-state region. During the winter of 1830-1831, it was a long and harsh one with a great deal of snowfall. Farms in central and northern Illinois were delayed planting until June. Then an early September frost killed most of the crops in those parts of the state; although here in southern Illinois, the temperatures were milder and crop production wasn't hampered. Much grain was shipped to central and northern Illinois. Wagons traveled to the area to purchase grain. A similarity was drawn from this occurrence with the story in the Bible of Jacob's family traveling to Egypt to purchase grain.

The geography of the region also has some similarities to the Nile Valley, with the region of southern Illinois being located between the Ohio River and the Mississippi River. The town of Cairo, Illinois, was named because of this comparison. In fact, the confluence or joining of the Mississippi and Ohio Rivers, is at Cairo, Illinois. I could go on with other connections, such as Southern Illinois University's mascot is named the Saluki, a dog similar to the Egyptian pharaoh's pets."

"OK, OK, I get your point. This is a special area. So, I want to check it out or, at least, some of it."

Following the roadway signs, Rann and I were able to find the parking lot for the Observation Trail, the trail closest to the unique rock formations. We went down some steps and walked on a winding, hilly, narrow, combination stone and dirt path for around a half a mile or so. Reaching a rocky cliff, an overlook, we saw several formations. Many of the rocks extended out into the valley and were formed in such a way as to resemble objects. The online information discussed the most notable rock formations, which were known as Camel Rock,

Monkey Head Rock, Table Rock and Anvil Rock. Indeed they were well named and I recognized them immediately. Surprisingly, there were no guardrails and absolutely nothing posted that restricted your travel. It was too tempting to just remain on the path and many ventured out onto many of the rocks. The overview was breathtaking. From my viewpoint, I could easily see the shapes. When I glanced over at Rann, he had climbed out onto the Camel Rock formation. He stopped at the edge and peered out at the wide expanse of trees. According to the information on the website, there were 3,200 acres of beautiful old growth forest that can be seen for miles. An old growth forest is an ancient forest with unique ecological features. The data states "The Wilderness area" is over 320 million years old. This part of the region has sedimentary rock over four miles deep. That's deep rock.

Not far from where Rann gazed, the huge dog quietly surveyed the man on the rock. For a moment, the dog thought about launching from his spot and knocking him from the rock face. He knew the fall would probably kill him, even this man with his added skills. He was sorely tempted but the woman was of more interest to him. She sedately waited on the trail for the man to return. The dog recognized the scent of this woman. It had been a long time since he had found her, oh, so many years ago. His drool began to foam around his mouth and he allowed a small growl to escape. He quickly checked himself and looked up through the trees to see if there were any sign of celestials. Yesterday had been an aggravation because of their interference. The wispy spirit had managed to surprise him and with the help of Myriad Dupree, they had tied him to a tree with that infernal rope. He had lost valuable time working to get free, time he could not afford.

Rann heard something as he stepped back onto the path but was distracted quickly by the sight of Cassamie looking longingly toward the cliff. He joined her, took her hand and led her back down the trail. As they walked, they noticed interesting shaped trees seemingly growing into the massive rocks. It was amazing to see such natural resources displayed along the trail.

Iron deposits could be seen filling hollowed-out cavities in the rocks. Unusual indentations weathered into the limestone created centuries ago. Everywhere the eye settled an assortment of wonder was revealed.

Cassamie felt a deep connection to this place. There was something beyond this place, beyond this time and she could sense it yet she couldn't fathom what it was. As she looked across at Rann, he, too, seemed enthralled with the view and was unusually quiet, as if he were communing with something out of reach. When he became aware of her watching him, he nodded to her.

"It is beautiful, isn't it?" Cassamie asked him.

"Yes, I can see why it was given such a name. I doubt we can see it all in a few days. I might have to return sometime on a vacation when I don't have such an important job to do." He turned toward her and waited to see if she had anything to add.

When she made no response, Rann noticed the position of the sun and suggested they return to the parking lot. They could come back tomorrow. For now, he wanted to get back to camp, clean up and fix something to eat. He added they would head to the sheriff's office in the morning. Cassamie was hesitant to leave but knew Rann was right. They did need to get back. Returning by the same path, Cassamie noticed the steep incline required more effort and exertion to reach the top. Her curiosity had been piqued and soon she knew she'd be delving more into the history of this spot.

Rann drove more slowly as they returned to the campsite. He was deep in thought on the ride back. Rann needed to talk to the sheriff to determine any ideas they might have about the abduction of the child. He knew the longer the passing of time, the colder the trail. Knowing some unusual factors were in play, especially from his and Cassamie's experience in the woods today, he realized the sooner the child was found the better.

The Dog remembered the woman from earlier times, though she was only a child then. The first time he saw her she had been a frail newborn. She had no inkling of his presence nor did the others in their pathetic group. The second time she had been aware of him when he followed her home from school. Of course, he had looked more approachable then. He had waited for her to come back out that day but her grandmother kept her occupied too long inside. The dog couldn't afford to wait any longer but yesterday he had tracked her scent. He would have liked to sink his sharp canines deep into her throat; however, the others had been close by in the treetops. They wouldn't have allowed the attack. Just recently, the celestials had tried to subdue him by tying him with the Nyatary rope but it was unable to hold him for long. He had broken the rope and hid in the forest, waiting. The wind had picked up and he knew Myriad Dupree and the spirit were nearby. He spotted her where she settled high in the treetops above the woman and man. Being powerless to do anything then, he returned to the protection of the forest and bided his time. There would be another opportunity. Now that the woman was in the vicinity, she would not be difficult to find again. No need to take a foolish chance now. He would wait. He had perfected his skill of waiting. Resigned to this, the dog turned and darted deeper into the forest.

As the Dog ran, his anger brewed within him creating an unbelievable energy. This energy channeled throughout his form and penetrated quickly by reforming his image. He seemed to pick up speed and became nothing more than a blur in the evening shade. A demonic scream burst from the vibration of the being. The blur began to vibrate, shimmer then fade into an indistinct outline. Soon there was nothing of the outline left, only the coming darkness.

Chapter 11

Sarah

When I awoke, I felt rested and hungry. I sat up in bed and looked around. The machines were gone and I wasn't hooked up to anything. I felt fine. The room was nice and bright. Its curtains were opened and it looked to be an ordinary bedroom. Maybe I had imagined or dreamed the machines. I'd been so tired but I was rested now and looked around the room. Outside the window, I could see trees surrounding the house but they weren't real close to the house. I climbed out of bed and walked over to the window. Beyond the trees, I could see a huge fence. It was as a solid wall around the property. The driveway wound around and passed through a gate. The gate was a large, fancy, iron one. It had to be at least twenty feet tall. I guess these people must be rich.

I heard a sound from behind me and turned around. I was shocked at what I saw. There was a little person standing inside the doorway. He wasn't a child because his face looked older but not real old. He was about my height and he had real curly hair.

It was light blonde. He smiled at me, waved then exited down the hallway.

I wondered who he was. Just then, Jim came into the room. I could tell he'd cleaned up. His face was shiny and his hair looked freshly washed. He smiled at me and asked if I was ready to eat. I nodded and he told me he'd be right back.

It didn't take him long and he came in carrying a tray with fruit, cereal, toast, orange juice and milk. He placed it on a table over by the window and asked me to join him there. I walked over and sat in one of the chairs. He handed me my napkin and placed the spoon and knife on the table. He told me the cereal was already sweet and I wouldn't need any sugar. I noticed it was Honey Nut Cheerios, my favorite. Mom always said it was good for me, so she bought it often. She even ate it. She said it helped her cholesterol levels, whatever that meant. The fruit was in a bowl and it was strawberries, bananas and blue berries. I tasted it first and it was delicious. I reached over and picked up my toast. It was already buttered and spread with grape jelly, another one of my favorites. How did they know so much about me?

"Jim, how did you know what I liked for breakfast?"

"Oh, it wasn't hard. Most children like sweetened cereals and toast with jelly. Grape is the most common found in grocery stores. The fruit is colorful and sweet. Everyone either drinks orange juice or milk for breakfast. That is, kids usually do. Am I right?"

"Yes, you're right. You know so much about me."

"It's deduction, primarily, and the elimination processes that have helped us decide what would please you."

"Still, it seems more than that but I don't guess you'll tell me." I leaned in, poured the milk over my cereal and took a taste. It was just right.

"Giselle wants to meet with you after you finish breakfast, so eat up. It's not nice to keep a lady waiting." He stood up and walked over to the window, looking out across the yard. He stood so quietly he almost looked to be a marble statue. I think he would make a beautiful model for a tall statue in a museum. He was so noble looking. It's funny I think of him as a marble statue. Wonder what he would say if I told him?

"Are you finished eating?" asked Jim, as he turned toward me. "If you are, you may want to freshen up and I'll come back to get you in about thirty minutes."

"OK. I'll take a bath or a shower. Do you have any other clothes for me?"

"In the bathroom you'll find everything you'll need. There's an inner closet as you walk into the bathroom. The bath products are under the sink and the towels and cloths are in a large cabinet near the bathing section. If you need anything else, just ring the buzzer near the sink and someone will assist you." Jim smiled at me then left the room.

I was curious to look at the bathroom. I'd never seen one with a closet inside. I walked to the door and opened it. The room was huge. As soon as I entered to my left were two sliding doors. I opened one and saw beautiful clothes organized by pants, skirts, shirts, tops and sweaters, anything that I could possibly need. There were even pajamas and robes folded on the shelves. I took a pair of jeans off the hanger and grabbed a lavender top with four buttons at the neck and three-quarter-length sleeves.

I turned around and noticed another door on the right side. When I opened it, it had shelves filled with all kinds of shoes and even different kinds of boots. I looked at the shoes and they were my size. I picked out some slip-on tennis shoes. When I turned the knob on the center door, it opened into a huge bathroom with a shower and a deep tub. There was a tall wooden cabinet with fancy handles close to the tub. I opened it and found towels and washcloths on one side and on the other side were panties, bras and even camisoles. I'd never had any camisoles. They were so soft and smelled so fresh.

I decided to take a bath. On the long, double-sink vanity, there was a basket filled with wonderful smelling soaps and shampoos. There was even a bottle of bubble bath. I chose that and poured some in the tub and turned the water on. Water gushed out and in no time, the tub was half-filled. I went back and locked the bathroom door before taking off my clothes and getting into the tub. I noticed a soft, thick towel and washcloth folded on a table near the tub. I reached for the washcloth and a bar of soap then stepped into the tub. I quickly washed my hair using the bubble bath because I forgot to get the shampoo. I hurried and finished my bath. When I stepped out, I noticed a thick, cushiony rug by the tub, so I stepped onto it. Quickly I dried myself and went to get a smaller towel to wrap around my hair.

I searched under the sink and found brushes, combs, hair products and a blow dryer. My hair was short so it wouldn't take long to dry. I also found toothpaste and a toothbrush near the hair products. There was even deodorant, lotions and some wonderful smelling perfume. I tried a little on my wrist. I was careful not to use too much. Mom always told me too much would make me stink. After that, I brushed my teeth and dried my hair. I went back to the large cabinet and looked for socks. I found some in the bottom drawer on the left. I chose lavender ones to match my top. Then I sat in the chair across from the tub and began to dress. Everything fit me just perfectly. Weird.

OK, I was ready. I picked up my dirty clothes and put them in the hamper. I knew I should clean up after myself. At home, I always kept my room looking neat because I wanted things to be orderly. OK, so I was a neat freak, or at least that's what Jenna always said about me. She was my best friend. We spent many weekends together and she stayed all night with me often. We usually stayed at my house because my room was bigger and cleaner.

After straightening up, I used the toilet, washed my hands and went back out into the bedroom. I wasn't there but a few seconds when Jim knocked on my door. I told him to come in. He sure had perfect timing.

"Are you ready to go talk to Giselle?"

"I guess so."

"OK, come with me."

We walked out into the hallway. There were large paintings on the walls. The floor had real thick carpet because you couldn't even hear us walking. Of course, I had on tennis shoes but Jim had on boots and they were still quiet on this carpet. We walked toward the back of the house. The carpet stopped and there was some kind of stone floor. It was made of large tiles. In this part of the house, I noticed the only windows were the ones from the ceiling. It really didn't feel closed in because of all the light coming from above. Then we entered a huge room with a stone fireplace at the end. It took up the whole wall and I could have stood inside it because of its size. This Giselle must be rich. I saw her standing at the other end of the room next to a counter. She was looking at something. When she glanced up and saw us, she put it in a drawer and walked over to meet us.

"Well, Sarah, I see you look rested. How do you like the clothes we got for you?"

"I like them. Thank you."

"You're welcome. You may wear anything you want and you can change as often as you like. Lamechial has already told me you were neat and put your dirty clothes in the hamper. I am pleased with that."

"Who is Lam, Lam-a-cell, or whatever his name is?"

"You may call him "Lam" for short. He saw you from the hallway when you first awoke and after you left your room, he checked in the bathroom and noticed your cleanliness. He phoned to tell me you were on your way and how mannerly you were. You'll like him. He's here to be a friend to you."

"Will he take me home?"

"No, that's not his purpose for being here."

"When can I go home?"

"Soon, soon but first we have some things to talk about. Now, let's go sit down on the couch and visit awhile. We can get to know one another. Gr…I believe you call him Jim. Jim, you can go now. We'll be fine here together. Giselle turned her full attention on me.

"Sarah, you don't mind if Jim leaves us alone for some girl talk, do you?"

"No, that'll be OK."

"Good. She turned around and faced Jim. "I'll call you, Jim, when we're finished with our visit."

Jim looked at me and gave me a reassuring smile then walked out of the room. This time he went a different way, passing the huge fireplace. There was a wooden door, matching the mantel built on the fireplace. I hadn't noticed it before. The door closed quietly.

When I turned back around, Giselle was sitting patiently waiting to begin our conversation. I I wondered what she was going to say. I should probably thank her for my nice room and bathroom. Before I could say anything, she began to talk. At first, I didn't really pay much attention to her. I wasn't really listening until she reached out and touched my cheek. Then I listened to her.

It was hard not to stare at her face. It was so beautiful. Her skin was smooth and I couldn't find any wrinkles. She had a type of glow around her head. It must have been because her hair was so thick and healthy looking. I'd never really seen any hair that color. It was blonde-like but also had a type of brownish red mixed in. She had a terrific mouth, in a way similar to Angelina Jolie but more heart-shaped instead of the puffiness. I couldn't tell how old she was. She wasn't a teenager but she wasn't as old as my mom, either. She was probably around thirty.

She was smiling at me now. "You're wondering about me, aren't you? That's OK, because I would do the same thing. You can ask me questions, if you like."

I cleared my throat and asked if this was her house.

She laughed aloud. "No, it doesn't belong to me. I'm just borrowing it for a while. It belongs to a friend of mine. She's away right now, so she told me I could use it for as long as I needed. Wasn't that nice of her?"

"I guess so."

"I wanted to talk to you about some things, some important things. Are you ready for answers to why we brought you here?

"Yes."

"OK. I want you to relax and get comfortable on the couch. Can I offer you something to drink? Would you like a soda?

"Do you have any Dr. Pepper?"

"I'm sure we do. I'll have one brought right out. Is there anything else you'd like?"

"No, just a Dr. Pepper."

Giselle reached into her pocket and brought out something that looked like a cell phone but it wasn't. Oh, yeah, it was like a walkie-talkie. She spoke into it and ordered a Dr.

Pepper and a tall glass of ice. It was only a little while before that little guy brought it out. What was his name again? Lam something. Oh well, I would just think of him as Lam.

He smiled at me as he brought it to me then he turned around and left.

Giselle faced me and said she was going to tell me a story, a rather long story, so she wanted me to get comfortable and ready to listen. I nodded my head signaling I was then she began.

"A long time ago, in a place far, far away, there was a special land It was the most ideal place anyone could imagine. In fact, it was perfect. It never rained during the day, only a light mist at night. So, there was always bright light during the day. The inhabitants were continually comfortable. They had no worries. The temperature didn't affect them, though it was always the same, no fluctuations or changes. One could hear soothing music playing throughout the land and you could hear melodious singing any time you wanted. No one had to make someone else happy or comfortable because there was happiness and satisfaction everywhere. The inhabitants had responsibilities they enjoyed doing, so it wasn't really work. No one felt pressured, just satisfied in doing what needed to be done. Everywhere one looked, one saw tranquility and beauty. Every possible need was met, without having to ask.

"For a long time, everything remained perfect but then, one day, things began to change. Actually, someone decided he needed more; he should be praised more, given more authority. He became consumed by these feelings and began to plot and meet secretly with others to share his discontent. Oh, he was a wonderful speaker and a beautiful being, long admired by many. In fact, he had been held in such high regard by the Mighty One he had been given the name, "The Morning Star," but even this special meaning hadn't been enough for him. For you see, he wanted to be seen as an equal to the One who had created all.

"This realm was no longer perfect, for disharmony had entered into the great heavens, the supreme bliss and it was serene no longer. Turmoil began. A third of the population chose unwisely and sided with the leader of the discontentment. A great battle followed for many days until the peace was all but destroyed. The One, who belonged in charge, unleashed his great power and threw out those who had revolted against the harmony and peace of the land. These dissenters were destroyed or thrown out from the highest realm. They fell a great distance. Most were sent to a terrible, lower realm and could not live in the light. The only illumination they had was from the eternal burning flames of the underworld. The Morning Star was stripped of his title, denied access to the highest realm and made to reign in the underworld: the lowest realm made of beings that could never be a part of the perfect world. They would never again know peace and tranquility, only turmoil and strife.

"The True Maker created this realm, as well. With his great power and knowledge, he formed the earth that we are now on and the vast universe beyond. He created all of the life that lives here or brought about the beginnings of their creation. Out of the dust of this land, he created man and woman in his own image. They were prized more than any other life form. He honored them by placing them in an area almost as beautiful as the highest realm where he dwelt.

"He gifted them with everything they could possibly need or want. For a while, things were perfect for the two but then, the prime dissenter, the Evil One, the being that had given up his home above because of his great jealousy and greed, began to plot against the just leader and all he had made on this middle realm. When he looked at the man and woman, he was consumed with envy and jealousy. He coveted all the Great One had done. He didn't want the two humans to be happy, to be content with the Maker of all, so he once more interfered with the plan. He went to the woman and, by use of his greatest weapon, deception, he coaxed her into going against what she had been told and tricked her into disobeying one of the few rules the Creator had given them. Then she was able to persuade the man to try something forbidden. Because of their disobedience, all was changed forever.

"No longer did man have everything given to him. Now, he had to work for his food and shelter. He and the woman were driven from their paradise and cast out into the world. The woman would bear children in pain and work alongside the man. Things changed when they dissented from the only restriction that had been given them. The Evil One planted disobedience in the woman's thoughts. He wanted to destroy creation. In this world, disharmony started to grow and spread as the weed found on the ground will thrive and grow. Pain, misery and sorrow took the place of peace, contentment and great joy."

Giselle ended her story and turned to me.

"That last part of the story sounds almost the same as the story in the Bible, the one about Adam and Eve."

"Yes. Do you know much about the Bible?"

"I know only a little bit, just what I heard in Sunday school and what my parents have told me."

Giselle nodded her understanding then told me there was much more to the story but that was for another time. She said Jim would be coming back in and he would take me for a walk around the grounds. She needed to do some work but would see me again at lunchtime. She asked if I had any requests for what I would like for lunch. I told her I really liked cheeseburgers and French fries. She said she would see what she could do.

Jim came back into the room and took me outside for a walk. When we were walking, he was talking to me but I could only wonder about why Giselle told me that story. Was she some kind of a preacher? If so, why'd she help to kidnap me?

Chapter 12

When Rann pulled into the campsite, I had mixed emotions. I was relieved to be safely back and anxious about the conversation that was coming. *How much should I tell him? I really don't know him but I'm beginning to depend on him and trust him yet many unexplainable things have happened in the past few days. How do I reveal this to him without making him think I was absolutely, completely insane? I'll need to be cautious in what I say yet there is something not quite "normal" about him, either. He seems to know things and perceive things that are over the top, not quite explainable. Whatever comes out, I'll let him lead the conversation. Maybe he'll reveal something to tie all this together; still, how could I truly explain or understand the encounters I've had lately?*

Rann turned off the engine and turned to me. "Well, back again. I think I'll gather some more firewood and sticks and start the fire. If you want, you can go down to the lake and freshen up. No one else is nearby so you should have some privacy. I'll whistle if I hear someone coming."

"OK, that sounds wonderful. I'll just pick up a few things out of the tent and head down there." I climbed out of the vehicle and walked into the tent. At least this gave me a few minutes to collect myself. It always relaxed me when I bathed and put something comfortable on. I hurriedly found my scented soap, shampoo, lotion, cloth and towel. I snatched a clean tee shirt and underwear, scooped up my flip-flops and left for the lake.

It wasn't far to the water. Darkness had arrived so I really couldn't tell how clean the water was but it would still feel good to get out of these clothes and feel the water on my skin. I shimmied out of my dirty clothes and quietly dived into the lake. The water was cold but refreshing. I came back to shore and gathered up the soap and shampoo. I decided against the cloth. I would use my hands. I felt the cool night breeze on my skin so I hurriedly finished. I walked out and picked up my things and went over to a large rock to sit and dress. I already felt better. I wrapped the towel around my head, slipped into my flip-flops and walked back to camp.

Rann had a roaring fire going, so I went to get my brush and sat down near the fire to brush out the tangles and dry my hair. He was roasting some hot dogs and had put out condiments and chips. He had also brought out a couple of apples. I snagged one and took a huge bite out of it. I hadn't realized how hungry I was.

"Hey, that's dessert."

"I'll have my dessert first. My stomach's growling."

Rann grinned and told me dinner would be ready in a few minutes. He asked if I had a nice swim.

"Yes. I'm not so sure how clean the water was but it had to be cleaner than my hair, with all the forest debris in it." Noticing the aroma, I added, "That smells delicious."

"You're just hungry but I'll agree outside cooking always appeals to the senses," he added, while forking one of the hotdogs onto a bun.

"What would you like on your hotdog?"

"Oh, everything you've got."

He loaded the bun then handed it to me. I got up and went to get a diet soda from the Yeti cooler. I noticed the ice was just about gone.

"We're going to have to make a trip to buy some ice and other supplies," I reminded him.

"Tomorrow we can do that when we go into Shawneetown to meet with the sheriff. He said they had some leads. Something about a camera picking up a young girl in a Pizza Hut that looked like Sarah."

"Did they get the abductor on film?" I asked.

"No, evidently something was wrong with part of the film, a bad section on the roll but they have a pretty clear picture of a young girl."

"Is that all he told you over the phone?"

"Yep."

I sat quietly and thought about all this. I must have meditated for quite a while because Rann tapped me on the shoulder.

I jumped then apologized for daydreaming. "Do you think it was Sarah?"

"It could be. It was within the hundred mile radius, which sounds about right. I don't think her abductor wants to get too far from this area."

"Why? What makes you think he wants to stay close to this area?"

"It's just a hunch. Look, I think it's time for us to lay all our cards on the table."

"What do you mean?"

"Cassamie, I know there's more to you than what most people see. I'm a good tracker because I'm also observant. I'm perceptive and sensitive to certain…situations. I know you saw something in the treetops. I saw her, too. I don't know who she is but I think you might. So, the sooner we discuss our extra abilities, the better we'll be in combining our resources to find the child. Why don't you start by telling me who was in the tree and how she is connected to the missing child."

"First, you tell me how you saw her."

He let out a low sigh then ran his hands through his hair. "OK but first I want to give you a little background information."

"OK, I'm listening."

He began.

"About ten years ago, I was involved in an accident. I was on one of the new quarter horses at Matt's farm. He was a young gelding, firmly attached to another horse and used to staying in the pasture near the barn. I took him out alone to break him from his dependence on the other horse. He didn't want to leave the corral and he tried to buck me off. I kept making him turn small circles in the paddock until he calmed down. I rode out through the gate and onto some open land Dream Doc was full of himself but he wasn't too much for an experienced rider. We had galloped about a half-mile from the barn and we were approaching an overgrown fence line with tall bushes and saplings. Suddenly, out of the bushes, jumped a dog that startled Doc. He shied and leaped to the left. I went sharply to the right and was nearly unseated. I remained in the saddle by gripping tightly with my knees, grabbing the saddle horn and leaning the other way.

"What I didn't know at the time was that strong jerk of my head had torn my right carotid artery. When I returned to the barn, I felt a little tired but I figured it was because of the incident with the dog and holding the horse under control. Two days later I was hauling a bale of hay into a stall when I had an excruciating headache. Unknown to me then but the inner branch of my right carotid artery had completely dissected. I felt dizzy, my vision was blurred and evidently my face had dropped on one side.

"Matt was in the stable corridor and asked me a question. When I answered, he couldn't understand what I said because my speech was slurred. He came into the stall, took one look at me and took me to the hospital emergency room. Unbelievably, I had suffered a stroke at age twenty-two. When an angiogram was performed, they found the dissection of the inner wall of the right-side carotid artery. The artery had filled up with blood clots, which kept me from bleeding out. Strangely enough, my high levels of cholesterol had probably saved my life by helping to form those clots.

"They put me on blood thinners and kept me in the hospital for five days. I was fortunate and the only residual I had from the stroke was the loss of part of my peripheral vision and some short-term memory loss. I have learned how to deal with that with accommodations and, actually, my short-term memory improved; however, the vision defect remained and I've become accustomed to it. At least it's the upper left-hand quadrant of each eye and it doesn't interfere with my driving.

"Evidently the blood and oxygen supply found alternative access to bypass the blockage preventing any further damage to my brain, though, the 're-wiring' of my brain did make some changes in my brain, mainly my vision. I may have lost some of my visual field but my insight certainly increased. I was able to see things and perceive things I had never been able to see before. Some unusual and unexplainable things have developed from that incident and I have dealt with them for almost ten years.

"After a time, I adjusted to it and used the skills in my work. I was young, so the stroke was much easier to overcome. I no longer have to be on blood thinners but I do take an aspirin daily to prevent any other clots from forming and I do take cholesterol medication; however, the accident was the reason for the tearing of the artery and that caused the blood clots. So basically, I'm healthy if just a little abnormal."

I sat there absorbed in Rann's story. It was a miracle he had survived the accident. I mean, come on, the carotid artery? From what I remember from an anatomy course, the carotid artery is a big deal. There are two, one on each side of the neck. Their main function is to supply blood to the brain, blood with valuable oxygen for the brain. Then I remembered one of the other details in his story.

"What do you mean you saw some unusual things? Why are you a little abnormal?"

"Out of all of that, that's what you picked up on? OK, the unusual part is I see angels. You heard me, good ole celestial beings from above. I think you see them too. Am I right? Are you ready to talk about exactly what you saw in the woods, in the top of the trees?"

"What makes you think I saw something?"

"Come on, Cassamie, are we going to play games? I just told you I can see angels and you took it all in stride. Your eyes are giving you away. You weren't shocked about it. You didn't call me crazy or a lunatic. Come on. Admit it. You didn't find it unusual that I can see angels because you share that same characteristic. What I'm curious about is, why? My gift came about because of an accident and an adjustment in my brain, an activation of a usual but dormant part of the brain. Where does your ability come from?"

I took a deep breath and prayed I was right in sharing my carefully, guarded secret.

"I've been able to see angels since I was a little girl. It's just a gift I was born with. My grandmother has a similar gift but she doesn't see angels or spirits. She is able to perceive some things before they actually happen. She doesn't really have much control over it. It just comes to her in visions and she can't just call it up at will. She is highly perceptive and intelligent. She never had a head injury or anything that brought it about. It's just a trait that many in her family have had. She keeps her gift well-guarded so I expect confidentiality in this discussion. Agreed?"

"Agreed."

"OK. Anyway, I see angels, at least some angels. I have one who has been a part of my life from the beginning but, of course, I wasn't aware of that fact until I was older. He's like my guardian angel. He knew my parents and my father quite well. He was present at my birth. My mother died giving birth to me and my father, well, I'll just say, he didn't stick around. I've never seen him. I wouldn't know him if he were standing right beside me. I know nothing of him and I don't want to know anything about him. He must feel the same way because he has never been a part of my life. Malitar is the angel I know best and he is the one who first informed me of this abduction. He wanted me to help and he told me about you.

"The spirit you saw in the treetops, I met her for the first time when I left the airport in Marion, Illinois. I drove across the highway and went to buy some pizza. I literally ran into her when I walked in the door of the pizza joint. She told me she'd been waiting for me and asked if I would please order some pizza for her. She said she'd wait for me at the back booth. When I took the food to her and sat down beside her, she introduced herself. She said she was Myriad Dupree but better known as 'Mother Nature."

"Who did you say?"

"That's right, 'Mother Nature'."

Rann just sat there for a few moments. Looking straight at me but not really seeing me. He must have been as surprised as I'd been. Then he burst out laughing.

"Well, I'll be, in the flesh, or better yet, in the spiritual flesh."

"Do you really find it funny?"

"Yep, I do. I sure hadn't considered that side of it. It makes it much more interesting; don't you think?"

"Well, that depends on what you know or think you know. You said earlier you had a hunch. It had to do with the abductor not wanting to be too far away from the area. I remember when I first told you the abduction took place in the Shawnee National Forest, not too far from the Garden of the Gods area, you found that a little startling. What do you know about this area that I don't?"

Rann took a deep breath then plunged in.

"It's not so much what I know as the connection to this area and its ancient status. You know the forests near the Garden of the Gods area are an old growth forest, right?"

"Yes, I read that on the website."

"Well, then you know that means it's an ancient forest and those rock formations have been there for millions of years. The land has history of use. It has served purposes that make it important to this particular situation. Nothing in this case seems to be coincidental. I think everything has been carefully planned and orchestrated for some reason. There's more to this than merely a child's abduction. That's a hunch, a gut feeling. What do you think the area was used for thousands of years ago? Any guesses?"

"I have no idea. Do you?"

I looked at Rann and wasn't expecting the answer he gave when he said, "Maybe."

Chapter 13

Sarah

The land around us was hilly. It seems the ground near the house had been leveled for the building site. For a few hundred feet it was mostly clear of trees and the ground was flat. When one walked away from the house and fence, it became really hilly and full of trees. Actually, it was part of a forest. It rather reminded me of where we had been that day on the field trip. It wasn't the same place but it had lots of trees and underbrush and was quite secluded. I couldn't see any other homes and I had been looking for them. We walked for quite a while then Jim asked if I wanted to continue walking or turn back.

There was a higher ridge just a few hundred feet away and I wanted to get there so I could look out. I told him I wanted to walk just a little farther. As we approached the ridge, I could hear what sounded to be water. Yes, it was water. When we got to the edge, I could see the water. So, we were near a river or a large creek. I had been to the Ohio River many times and the Mississippi but this part didn't look familiar to me. There were no houses or buildings nearby, no boats in the water; just an expanse of water with a strong current but if it were a river, then surely there would be some kind of travel on it. Near Shawneetown and Cave-in-Rock, there were always barges moving on it. This must be just a branch off a river because it wasn't wide but then, in science class, I learned the width of a river didn't always determine its depth.

Jim nudged my arm. I looked at him. He was staring at me, patiently. I wondered if he could tell what I was thinking; probably guessing I would be thinking of a way of escape.

"I'm ready to turn back now. I'm getting a little hungry."

"Sure. We'll head back now."

We didn't talk much as we walked back. I did ask him the name of a plant that was growing against a tree. It had three leaves. He told me it was poison ivy so to be careful of it.

Yikes. I got that once when on a picnic at Cave-in-Rock. I thought I'd itch to death. My face even had places on it and I looked akin to a monster, with red welts all over my cheeks. My eyes were almost swollen shut. I most definitely did not want to get that again. On our field trip, Mr. Orr had pointed out some to us so we would know what to avoid. I thought I recognized it with Jim but I wanted to be sure. Later I would look in my bathroom medicine cabinet and see if there was any lotion or spray for poison ivy. It never hurts to be prepared; at least that's what my dad always says.

I wondered what he was doing. Were they still looking for me or had they all given up? I'd been gone for a while but I didn't really know how long. I didn't know what day it was because I had slept so much and lost track of time. Maybe I could find a newspaper somewhere in the house. I know that house must have a television somewhere but I hadn't seen one yet. That would be my next mission, to look around the house without them noticing me. I needed to find a television. I hadn't seen any phones, either. Not too many people kept landlines anymore because everyone used cell phones. It made me think of mine. I wonder what happened to it. Maybe someone would find it. Much good that phone did me. It was in my bag when I had been taken. I think I remember Jim picking it up but then later he stuck it in a tree, between the base of the tree and the bottom limb. At the time, I didn't think too much of it but now I found it a little odd. Why would anyone just leave it in the forest? Maybe I would ask him but not now. I didn't want him to know I was even thinking of phones. It might make them watch me more closely.

We entered the house from the back-patio door. I didn't see anyone but I'm sure they were somewhere nearby. Jim led me into the kitchen where there was a plate with two cheeseburgers and fries. A Dr. Pepper was beside it with lots of other stuff like mustard, pickles, catsup, onions, salt and pepper. Everything you could possibly want to put on a burger sat before me. I went over to the sink and quickly washed my hands and grabbed a paper towel. I sat down and reached for a fry. It was great. Then I bit into the first cheeseburger and it was still warm. I added pickles and mustard to it and finished eating. I ate most of the fries but I couldn't eat the other cheeseburger. I asked Jim if he wanted it and he told me he wasn't hungry. Strange but I rarely saw him eat anything. Even at breakfast, he just sat there and watched me eat. He didn't eat a thing. Maybe he ate a big breakfast before he brought me mine, or maybe he was on some kind of a diet. I can never figure out adults and their eating habits. I eat whenever I'm hungry or have a craving for something. It's just easier that way.

After a while, Jim got up and walked out of the room. I looked around. I was alone, or it looked as if I were alone. I got up and went around to the other side of the counter near the appliances. Nope, there wasn't a phone or a television. I opened a long cabinet door that reached almost to the ceiling and down to the floor. I only found can goods, some kind of spices and boxes of food. That must be what they called a pantry. I was just closing the door when I heard something behind me. I turned around and there was that little person, just watching me.

For a while, we just stared at one another. Then he came around and sat down on a barstool. He just smiled at first then he seemed to be thinking about something. After a few seconds, he started talking.

"I'm sure you want to find a way to communicate with your parents and I'm sure you want to go home. Believe me when I say we are here to help you and will bring you no harm. We want to protect you from those that may want to harm you."

"Who wants to harm me?" I started to breathe really hard then it felt as if I couldn't breathe. Next, I felt clammy all over. It's when you feel cold then hot almost at the same time.

"Now, calm down. That's not going to happen. You are safe with us."

"Why can't I go home? I just want to go home. I want my mom."

"I know this isn't easy for you but you can't go home right now. You are safer here with us. Your home and parents could not protect you from what is seeking you."

"What are you talking about? What's seeking me? Who are you? Why do you look different? You don't look like a child and you don't look like an adult."

He smiled and touched my shoulder gently. Surprisingly, I did feel calmer.

"You're smart," he said, after removing his hand from my shoulder.

"So, that doesn't answer my questions."

He nodded then told me he would answer my questions this evening when we would all meet together. For now, he told me I needed to go to my room and rest. He took my hand and led me back to my room.

When I got there, I closed and locked the door. I was a little frightened. What did Lam mean I couldn't be protected at home? What was seeking me? Would my parents be safe? How could I sleep with that on my mind?

Just then, I heard a knock on my door. Before opening it, I asked who it was.

"It's Giselle. I've come to check on you. Are you OK?"

I opened the door and Giselle came in. I was going to ask her about what Lam had told me but when I looked into her beautiful eyes, I suddenly felt tired. I started to talk to her but nothing would come out. I felt so sleepy. Actually, I could barely keep my eyes open. For a moment, I thought I might pass out but then she reached for me and helped me to my bed. I sat on the edge; she turned the covers back for me then took off my shoes. I climbed in, Giselle moved up beside me and began softly rubbing my forehead.

"Now you have nothing to worry about. You're safe and your family is safe. Lamechial told me you might be upset. There is no need to worry. Just close your eyes, rest then we'll all meet together later. That's it. Just close those eyes and in no time you'll be asleep."

Long after Sarah had fallen asleep; Giselle sat beside her and sang a soft chant. *"Nom lay shan, shu naut to nawgh. Nom lay shan, shu naut to nawgh."*

She rested her own forehead against Sarah's and whispered into her ear the same chant then covered the child with a blanket, left the room, closing the door behind her.

Outside in the hallway, Giselle took a small vial out of her pocket, dipped a few drops from the vial onto her fingers and rubbed her fingers across the door lintel, going over it several times. As she did this, the chant was repeated three more times. She wasn't concerned about the outside windows or doors. They had been taken care of earlier and were secure. She turned and slowly walked away.

Giselle was wise to take extra precautions. Nearby, in the shadows of the trees lurked an animal of tremendous strength and cunning; one that could have ripped a human in half with one strong clamp of the jaw. The dog paced back and forth smelling the air for any discernible scent. He was poised for attack and ever vigilant on his mission. Soon, soon the time would be right for his move but, for now, he would bide his time allowing them to gain a false sense of confidence in their tactics. When they were comfortable in their fortress, feeling safe and secure, he would make his move. Giselle and her allies would feel his full wrath and be powerless to stop him.

Slowly the dog turned and bounded back into the woods in route to his safe haven away from any prying eyes. No one, man, beast, or spirit could find him in his sanctuary. He knew he was invincible. All their foolish plans and precautions would not be sufficient to stop him. The feeble attempt to suppress him using the Nyatary rope was pointless. It held him briefly but was unable to contain him for long—fools, all of them. They could not comprehend the full range of his powers. He had waited too long and prepared too carefully to be defeated. He would take care of them, finally he would continue until he had erased every trace of mankind from this realm. He would not spare any living thing and it would be total annihilation. It would be a blur of nothingness with no past, no present and certainly no future.

The creature pushed his thoughts deep into the void of his being. For now he would concentrate on reaching his haven and resting to regain strength for the tasks ahead. The day was nearing closure and soon it would all be finished. Finally, he would take his rightful place and all would be as he had planned. The dog started to weave back and forth; he started to tremble and vibrate. His image became blurred as he sped along the path to his resting spot. In an instant, there was nothing remaining of the huge mastiff, only a slight flickering of oncoming darkness.

Giselle trembled slightly, which startled her. What were her preceptors picking up? What was nearby? She walked over to the large bay window that looked out into the meadow flanked by heavy foliage and trees. Something was out there or had been. She could feel her skin begin to tingle at the base of her neck. Should she go out in pursuit or was it better to stay here near the child?

She would remain here. It's better to guard what you have in an environment you control rather than forfeit it all on a hunch or an intuitive feeling. She would wait where she was in control, soon all would be in place and the battle would begin in earnest. The battle must be won at all costs. This time there would be no negotiating, no concessions, only a pure, clean victory was necessary, their only option.

She heard someone approaching her from the back, the left side of the room. She closed her eyes and scanned its perimeter. It was a faint smell, something similar to cotton candy or warming caramel, an innocent smell but one with such unique power. She turned and smiled at Lamechial as he came closer. His company was to be appreciated and sought. He had skills far superior to many of hers but he lacked many of the attributes she possessed. His skills were defined and geared for one purpose, to seek out the great deceiver, to keep those powers of corruption at bay and to redeem what he had cost so many. Lamechial was good at his role because he had been created for just this purpose. Giselle had no doubts in that area, for she knew his capabilities. She had known him for a long time and had been witness to the precision and range of his strength and perceptions. He would keep the child safe though it would not be an easy task. It could well be the last task he performed. This thought brought sadness to her and she hoped it did not prove to be true. She would do everything within her powers to keep all of them safe, while gaining victory.

"So, noble Lamechial, did you sense his presence?"

"Yes, he was quite close but he chose not to show himself. He is waiting and observing all that goes on to assess the situation. He is looking for any weaknesses in our defenses. I'm sure his patience will run out soon. He has never been known for patience, especially when dealing with those such as us."

"I agree with you. We must allow for no weaknesses. The child, Sarah, how is she?"

"She is sleeping now. Jim said she was investigating her surroundings when they were outside. He is sure she is planning some type of escape. He sensed it. She's also trying to find a means of communication. We did well by removing the televisions and phones from the residence. I agree with Jim's assessment of the child. She is extremely bright, more so than the usual ten or eleven-year-old. Interestingly, she is also wise for her age. She has some extra skills she hasn't yet become aware of or has never tried out. Her sheltered life has prevented her exploration but here, she may learn to tap into them."

"She may have to learn to use them quickly. The 'dog' will not wait much longer. Therefore, we will meet with the child in two hours and start our own assessment of her. The blood tests affirmed her celestial trait. She is getting stronger and there was no need for any medical intervention. That's why the machines were removed from her bedroom. We'll determine what she is capable of. We may well need those skills to help us in this battle. Inform Jim to meet with us in the family room in two hours. I'm going into the basement for a while. Was there anything else you needed to say to me?"

"No, that was all."

Lamechial turned and left the room as Giselle headed through the door leading down into the basement of the house. It was a hidden door that had to be opened by a lever under the wall panel near the hallway. Giselle tripped the mechanism as soon as she finished speaking to Lamechial. In its day, this underground room had been used to hide runaway slaves and to provide a sanctuary for them. It was more a cellar than an actual basement but it had been improved through the years and was modestly comfortable. It had all the perks of modern technology, with communication devices.

Only the previous owners of this home had known about the existence of this hidden room and most had died keeping the secret. Dark, underground passages led to various areas of the property and had been strengthened and maintained through the years. As far as she knew, there was only the one family member and the trusted caretaker who were knowledgeable about the secrets of the home. The owner of the property was not presently in the area, though the house would have made an important tourism feature. The family, through the years, had shunned the idea of disclosing the characteristics of the property and had held the secret. This had been instrumental in Giselle's mission. She and her allies used all aspects of life, human and celestial.

Giselle sat at the computer desk and booted up the machine. It was a current model and quickly opened. She would scan the local newspapers and see what information was available about the child's disappearance. She was particularly interested in any details about the parents and any new experts or departments brought into the investigation.

She quickly found one article about the parents' continued desperation in finding their child. Authorities had spent a great deal of time trying to make any connections to anyone who might want to cause trouble for the couple but no leads had been found. The parents were well-respected people in the community and had no prior legal problems. As she skimmed the article, she found what she was looking for. The couple had adopted Sarah when she was an infant and had never told the child. Authorities were investigating the possibility of abduction from the birth mother but there was nothing about a possible link. Giselle knew there would be no threat from the birth mother.

In another article, there was mention of two outside, independent individuals who had been brought into the case. One was a well-known tracker from Kentucky and the other was an investigative reporter from Montana. The name of the reporter caught Giselle's attention. A slow smile formed across her face. She was astute enough to realize their chances of success had just gone up by several percentage points; however, it was imperative she make contact with the reporter. That would be a delicate operation. She would need to leave this residence to do so. The planning would be crucial. It had to come at the right time when it was safest to leave the child. Giselle had no doubt in her ability to find the woman but her fear was in leaving the others with the beast nearby or in, perhaps, leading the beast to the woman. By her acknowledgement of this woman, it could put that woman in danger. This would take careful consideration and she would need to plan carefully with the assistance of someone else. It had been years since she had made contact with the one she was considering but it was a desperate situation and she had no choice but to make the contact.

In addition, she would need to send Jim on another trip. When she told him who was involved, his loyalty would be sorely tested. He would be in a delicate and difficult situation. Would his fear of the unknown or his love of the known prevail? She would soon have the answer to that question. The instant she told him the name of the reporter, he would realize the extent of his involvement in this mission and he would know why he had been chosen. His loyalty would be determined by the answer he gave. Hopefully, it would be the right answer and one that would prove their mutual commitment. She would seek him out.

Giselle knew she'd probably find him in the bonus room off the three-car garage. This was his sanctuary, where he went when he needed some alone time or down time. The room was comfortable with a huge mahogany desk, a large leather, sectional couch, book-lined wall and state of the art exercise equipment along the far wall. Jim often used the weights and equipment for working out, although there really was no need. His earthly form was lean and strong just as he had been in his celestial form. He had held an important position in the highest realm and was a trusted confidante of the One Most High. His love and devotion had never been questioned until the Day of Destruction and even those details were sketchy and incomplete. Only the One highest along with Grinstead knew what had actually happened. Giselle only knew Grinstead's life, since that day, had held a great deal of turmoil and unrest. He had disappeared for eons, believed cast into the bowels of Hell but then he had resurfaced one day.

She had been sent to meet with him, make a connection and build a bond between them. It had been a fragile bond for decades but over extended time, she had come to rely on and trust him again yet she had never felt the all-encompassing love she had felt for him during their tenure in the heavens above. The same love they all felt for one another until the "Evil One" presented himself. His change had caught most of the heavenly beings off guard and totally unprepared for what was to come. She, along with many others, including her triad, had found strife and discontent with one another. Even here there was not the perfection of undisputed trust that had existed before yet, she had been given an earthly job to do and she would fulfill her quest until there was no longer an essence of "life" within her, if the Holy One ever decided to terminate it. She hoped Grinstead would feel the same. That answer would soon be known.

"I thought I'd find you here. We need to talk and there is no longer any reason to address you as anything other than exactly who you are, Grinstead. So, we'll use your given name from here on out. Understood?"

She waited for him to give acknowledgment. Even as she spoke the name bestowed upon him at the moment of his creation, she noticed a change in him. Before her eyes, his appearance intensified and evolved into a stronger, more powerful force. This acknowledgment redirected all he was and an internal glow seemed to emanate from him as in the days before "all hell had broken loose". She smiled when she saw this transition to his prior self. She knew the Great Maker had reinstated this heavenly gift and returned all Grinstead had been before the terrible event had occurred. This was the stamp of approval she had hoped for and her confidence in the battle ahead grew once more.

Giselle felt this gift would help to buffer their forces and she smiled in recognition of her old friend as she said, "You are going on another trip tonight. Events are speeding along more quickly than I had thought possible."

"Yes, I, too, have detected his presence nearby. That presence doesn't surprise me but there is another I'm detecting and these feelings confuse me. I have a great deal of anxiety and it's not because of the Evil One being nearby. It's something else, someone else and I believe you know what's causing this alertness inside me."

"Indeed, I know who it is in our vicinity causing these mixed emotions in you. Prepare yourself for what I am about to tell you and the mission that will take you away from here to protect another besides the child, Sarah. The rest of us will be keeping Sarah under our protection. We'll all be leaving this place tonight through the tunnels; however, you will be traveling alone to fulfill your responsibility. You must gather all your strength and gifts within you so those who wish to fool you won't be able to deceive you again. Strengthen and fortify yourself so none can compromise what you were made to do. Your redemption and destiny are one and the same. Are you prepared to prove yourself worthy of this task, a task given as a means for you to regain what you lost so long ago? Do you accept your mission?

"I will not pledge a commitment until I'm aware of what this mission is. I will never again be sucked into something of which I've not been given full disclosure, no matter who proposes it. If I have learned nothing else during this time of trials, I have learned to gauge all the circumstances before making a decision. So, are you prepared and willing to give me full disclosure?"

"Yes, it's your right. Let's sit on the couch so we can be at eye level when I tell you what must be told and what must be done."

Chapter 14

When Rann pulled into the parking space outside the county courthouse, he glanced over at Cassamie. She seemed intent on staring a hole through the windshield. She was deep in thought and he hated to disturb her but she needed to become aware they had reached their destination.

"Are you ready?"

"Oh, sure, I was just daydreaming. I'm ready. So, this is the courthouse. Not big, is it? I'm always amazed with how much a small town seems to surprise me. Let's go." Cassamie grabbed her bag and opened the door.

Rann came around to the side of the SUV and waited on her. He smiled at her and turned to allow her to walk in front of him. He reached ahead of her and pushed the door opened for her as they entered the courthouse. They walked through a metal detector then asked for directions to the sheriff's office. The guard told them it was on the second floor, exiting the elevator to the right.

They quickly rode the elevator to the second floor, exited and found the sheriff's office. When they walked in, Rann told the secretary who they were. She said to go on in, the sheriff was expecting them.

A middle-aged, balding man stood from behind a desk appearing to be absorbed in reading some report. He quickly put it aside and reached across the desk to shake hands with them both.

"Please have a seat. I'm Sheriff Ralph Patton but most people just call me Sheriff. I was just looking over some of the notations I made from our conversations over the telephone. That was good investigative work finding those additional impressions off the path. Your securing the evidence was commendable. I have to tell you, I'm a little thrown by some of your techniques and some of the evidence you found. We'd been all over that area with a fine-toothed comb and I completely missed the cell phone up in the tree. For some reason, the phone's internal GPS did not function, so we wouldn't have found it. When this case is closed, I'd be interested in learning what led you to its location."

"I'd be glad to discuss it with you. Have you found any leads to where those last tracks may have led?"

"Nope. It's as if they disappeared into thin air. One funny thing that probably has little to do with the case but I've had several reports from residents in the area that a large, black dog has been seen running in the vicinity. Nobody seems to know much about it and no one has gotten close to it to make a more detailed description. It just seems to appear out of nowhere then disappear totally, again. Did you happen to see it when you were out tracking? Also, we found what was left of a rope that was tied to a tree." He said this as he opened the top right-side drawer and began rummaging around inside for something.

"Unusual material. Can't say I've ever seen anything like it. Thinking about sending it off to the lab in Carbondale to see what they make of it. It probably has little to do with the case and would stretch our already limited budget but just a thought."

Then the sheriff bent over and was peering inside the drawer. A pure look of puzzlement crossed his face as he pulled out what looked to be a thin strand of some kind.

"What in God's name happened to that rope? It...it shriveled up to nothing. Now, how in the hell did that happen?" He disgustedly dropped it on top of the desk.

Cassamie looked over at Rann and was surprised to see he was hiding a smile before quickly looking away. She would definitely ask him about that rope but it would have to wait.

Rann finally said, "I wouldn't worry too much about the rope. We did see the dog or a large, black one while we were in the woods. It didn't come close and ran off when it realized we'd noticed it."

Cassamie could remain silent no longer. "How are the parents holding up? "

Sheriff Patton turned his attention to Cassamie and said, "They're pretty upset. The mother looks terrible and the dad doesn't look much better. I guess that's to be expected. Both are worried about the child's health. Seems she's had several medical problems and the girl was never made aware she was adopted. Alan and Rachel, the parents, always intended to tell her but they kept putting it off. I guess, if the child is ever around a TV or radio, she'll have another shock to deal with. It would have been much better to find out from her parents but, hey, too late for that now."

"Have you found out any more about the child that was spotted on camera at the pizza place? On the video, did you find someone to clean up the image of the man with her?" Cassamie inquired.

"Yes, it was Sarah but we couldn't do anything about the tape footage. It must have had a weak spot in it and that was our bad luck that it'd be on that part of the tape where the man's image was recorded, however, we have the location and the Kentucky state police are investigating it now. Hopefully, we'll hear back from them shortly. It might even be while you're here."

"Let's hope whenever we hear back from them, they've found the child," added Cassamie.

"Yep, that would be great news," responded the sheriff, "But I wouldn't put too much stock in that happening. We're not dealing with your run of the mill abductor. I'm not so sure that weakness in the tape footage was a random occurrence. I think he knows just what he's doing and how to manipulate the recording of those cameras. If I had a look at the tape, I could be sure. He probably spotted the camera right away and navigated to an area where his face would be caught in the glare from the windows or doorway. Let's face it, he nabbed the child with seventy or more people within a few feet and made a clean getaway."

Just then, the desk telephone rang. The sheriff reached over and answered it. He was talking to one of the troopers. The sheriff asked several pointed questions, listened for a while then ended the conversation. You could see the excitement on his face.

"Well, they have one kid who works in the pizza place that noticed the man and girl. He said he'd finished his shift and pulled out of the parking lot right behind them. He remembered them because of the vehicle the man was driving. Some luxury SUV; he thought it was a Land Rover. Anyway, the good news is they turned off the main highway and went down the same blacktop road that the teenage boy lived on. He followed them for quite a while before turning down his own drive. So we have a lead on the direction they were headed; finally hitting pay dirt."

Rann looked impressed. "How far is it from here?"

"That's the good news. It's only across the river from Cave-in-Rock in rural Kentucky. Maybe you're familiar with the area near Marion, Kentucky."

"I've been there a time or two," answered Rann.

"I'm getting ready to head over that way. You two are welcome to follow me. I hope you're driving something that can navigate some rough roads."

"We're in my rented Ford Explorer. I think we'll be able to keep up," answered Cassamie.

"Sure, sure, that'll work. I'll let Susie, my secretary, know my intended 10-20. I'll meet you out front." The sheriff left the room.

"10-20. I haven't t heard that expression since CB radios were all the rage and my grandfather used one. I guess it's not just a trucker phrase but a real phrase for location or destination," Cassamie stated, as she got up to follow the sheriff out of his office.

Before Rann left the room, he picked up the tiny strand that was left on the sheriff's desk and surveyed it more closely. It was literally disintegrating before his eyes. When the sheriff returned, there would probably be nothing left of the strand. He wasn't surprised by it. They had left the rope in the forest, not realizing the sheriff would find it so interesting. Rann was re-evaluating the sheriff's level of expertise. There was more to him than what Rann's initial impression had been. He just wondered how much flexibility the man's brain would have to comprehend the seemingly impossible forces at work in this case. Well, that revelation would all come in good time. He placed the strand back on the desk and followed behind Cassamie.

"In response to your question about the sheriff's use of 10-20, I think it technically means your location. It's actually a police code. The '10' codes were developed in the 1940s at a time when police radio channels were limited to the use of the AM frequency. In the early days, radios were of lower frequency; close to the same frequency as the CB radios and there was a lot of static on the channels then and you could get a code through quickly when a sentence might be broken up. Of course today, with FM, satellite and digital channels available and other means of communication, the transmissions are clear and understandable; but it's hard to change people when they're accustomed to a way of doing something, especially when it comes to a bureaucracy. So, the '10' codes are still in use with law enforcement agencies."

"Well, thanks for the history lesson. You seem to have a broad knowledge base."

Rann chuckled, as he steered Cassamie out front to their vehicle.

"Not at all, just typical adolescent interests in anything having to do with police work. My best friend and I memorized the police code years ago in grade school; I think it was fourth or fifth grade. His dad was our local police chief and we spent a great deal of time listening to their home scanner on the weekends. I'd actually thought about going into law enforcement when I was young but then I got involved with Matt at the horse farm and that all changed."

They waited in the vehicle until the sheriff climbed into his white Chevrolet Tahoe before starting it up. The sheriff waved for them to follow him as he pulled onto the highway. Rann looked at the gas gauge to make sure he had plenty of gasoline. He was skeptical on how much investigating they would get done this afternoon. If they didn't get much covered today, at least they'd know where to begin the next day.

Chapter 15

The starless night sky blanketed the land with pitch darkness. A clustering of clouds blocked all moonlight. It was a night suitable for all that was evil in the world to congregate and, indeed, at this place, many were doing just that; though the normal, human eye would not be able to detect all that was gathered here. The noise of bickering could be heard if anyone dared to venture this far into the depths of the forest and, if anyone did venture in, it was unlikely they'd ever venture out again, or at least not the way they'd come in.

Leaning against a huge boulder stood a creature of such height and girth the boulder began to crumble around the edges. A single movement of its hand pulverized the limestone. The creature noticed its effect on the stone and smiled with amusement. It loved to destroy, for this was what it was best at doing, destroying the helpless or unsuspecting. Pure evil did exist and it lived within the frame of this being. It was not human, had never been human and it was definitely not of the heavenly realm. It was Death waiting and biding its time until the exact moment when there would be no recourse. Many unsuspecting humans and spirits had come onto it without realizing its danger until it was too late. It always introduced itself in disguise with only the slightest bit of notice; and when one became enamored with it and here was where the danger lay; it pounced and started the gradual demise of that being.

Chernobog was in his element. He had earned the rank as a "black god" of the world of demons. He alone in the "Council of the League of Demons" had the power to bring all things evil out at night and he had been busy this night. He was good at what he did and had defeated many throughout the millennia. This night's work had been fruitful and a great crowd had assembled at this place. Just to his right lay Apophis, the demon serpent that stalks at night. Chernobog could feel the evil spirit within Apophis trembling with excitement. Apophis would be useful in the nights ahead, slithering stealthily toward the unsuspecting and annihilating them. Looking around, Chernobog acknowledged that it had been centuries since such a group had come together. Balan, a high prince from Hell, had positioned himself near the flattened rock and waited patiently. Chernobog, called by the one being that held reign over him, the only one he feared and he was not reluctant to admit that to the crowd here tonight because most of them could not face that one.

Soon the battle would begin, the one stretched through the centuries. He practiced throughout the years on the less fortunate, the lower ranks of the enemy. This next phase would be more challenging because he would be facing the highest echelons of the enemy's battalions; however, he did not fear the outcome, for his own leader would be with them in this campaign. Defeat was not an option and that he knew without the slightest doubt. Timing and planning, with all the precision of the elements of evil, were in their favor. He was beginning to shake with excitement and anticipation in thinking of those they would massacre finally.

He heard a slight noise behind him and the hair at the base of his head stood on end. The others hadn't detected anything yet but Chernobog knew whose presence had joined them. The multitude, except for Balan, would soon cower before the latest arrival but Chernobog was ready and turned to meet his maker's approach.

The huge, black dog walked into the midst of the crowd and jumped upon the flattened rock as Balan moved aside. Soft gasps and murmurings could be heard. Apophis quickly coiled into his tightest circle and raised his head trying to sense the mood of their maker. Balan reclined on another nearby rock and appeared somewhat bored with the tension that was building. Next to Balan stood Elathan, a lord of darkness that belonged to the ancient Celtic tribe and was known for his prowess in trickery and debauchery. He had purged many innocents of their sanity. His appearance was the most beguiling of all, for his face was one of beauty and serenity. He used both with great skill. Elathan had worked with their maker for many centuries, though; he did not feel comfortable with their leader and was continuously wary of what the great one would require of him. He watched with a degree of terror while struggling to keep it hidden. Close by to Apophis, stood the only female in their midst but more would soon arrive. Jezebeth, a demon of falsehoods, had an unusual face with vibrant thick strands of ebony hair flowing down her back. Her beauty was well known throughout the demon world, for she had been irreplaceable to the leader throughout time. Her face had caused many to falter in their decisions and she had been instrumental in causing the damnation of many human souls. Though her countenance showed no emotion, Chernobog could detect some reluctance in her mood. He would delve deeper into those emotions later, at a more opportune time. For now, he would pay homage to the one on the flattened rock.

Before the assembled, the dog began to vibrate with movement and soon the dog was replaced by a man-like being of undisputed beauty, one with no visible defect or blemish. The noble face displayed eyes of the deepest blue imaginable set beneath a beautifully carved forehead; the nose perfectly formed without weakness to the lines and shape. His mouth formed flawlessly and positioned and bordered with slight dimples at the corners. The cheekbones lifted highly and honed elegant cheeks that tapered to a strong jaw line and chiseled chin and his hair was the color of burnished waves of gold hanging to his shoulders. He was beautiful beyond description and it was easy to see why, long ago, he had been given the name, "the Morning Star."

There was a loud rumbling and the earth began to pitch violently, the trees swayed wildly and the flattened rock, supporting their leader, began to shake causing a large crack to appear down the middle of the rock. His image began to flicker and fade. The earth would not accept or tolerate him in this form. The Holy One would never again allow the presentation of the beautiful countenance awarded eons ago through love and trust. That gift had been betrayed with a challenge of authority. The Morning Star no longer existed in the books of record. Only the look of the beast or the monster was permitted. Therefore, this beautiful image was unable to remain for long.

Soon, what was left behind was a creature so hideous the pores of its skin seemed to ooze pus and other vile smelling substances. It emitted a horrific stench, causing even those of his ilk to step back. Many in the group looked away and shielded their faces. The eyes of the creature were serpentine with the diamond-shaped pupils of putrid brown. The nose was hooked and large for the face and the lips were nonexistent except for a continual sneer that spread across the reddened, pock-marked face. When the mouth opened, razor-like teeth could be seen. The shape of the head was of a goat with raised horns protruding through the forehead. The body was huge and draped with long strands of black hair, tangled and crushed against the strong chest and back. His legs were massive with thick, beefy calves connected to shins leading down to cloven hooves. When he turned, there appeared a long tail with spiked nodules covering the entire surface. There was nothing beautiful about this being and his presence revolted even this assembly, though none dared to entertain even a thought of this truth.

The rumbling ceased; the area around showed major damage. Many trees had fallen and a new fissure had formed separating some from the rest of the group. The group could relax somewhat but a few kept a wary eye on the one standing before them, while most looked away in fear. Even Chernobog had been affected by this display. Simultaneously, they all kneeled and bowed their heads to the ground or surface where they stood. Total silence prevailed, for none dared to be the first to speak or draw attention. They waited silently for "him" to address them. The clouds above had separated briefly, while the earth revolted and the light from the moon streaked through before momentarily receding back behind the approaching clouds. Once more the night submerged into pitch-blackness.

The diabolical one looked out at those trembling before him and he smiled with great satisfaction. Euphoric from their fear, he spoke.

"Welcome. We have come for an important reason. The battle is that reason and the one building for centuries, the one that brings you all to gather here because of your skills and strengths, the one battle we must win. None in your legions can outrank you or defeat you. You are the best of our world. So stand and recite with me our common cause."

In unison, the group stood and voiced their pledge to their leader and all they represented. They enunciated loudly and fluently in their secret language.

"*Ogra lamu tu sunj delah. Enchi unkle dafar. Bugento sal gar. Omar lamu tu sunj dehah.*" The chant was recited six times, as the creatures moved in a circular pattern, swaying from side to side as they rotated around. Each totally absorbed in the rhythm of their chanting and their hypnotic stares connected to the one in the middle, the one that birthed all that was evil. That hideous creature gained strength from their chanting and seemed to pulsate with spasms of energy. This energy continued to build until the chanting stopped then, with a surge of force, the monster pulled some of the energy within itself.

Instead of the chant carrying across the night air as sound does, it floated downward to penetrate into the ground where they stood. With its passing, the earth quivered in revulsion and the underbrush spreading across the ground withered away leaving only barren soil in its place. The stench of burned earth remained for several minutes, as the sulfur smell dispersed. Nearby, a small rodent burst into flame as the essence of the chant penetrated its fur, a split second before totally consuming it and leaving no trace behind.

Using the gifts given so long ago in the beginning, Mephistopheles began building up his army's confidence. He sat within the circle and reviewed, with each demon, his or her particular skills and where they would position themselves for the onslaught. Each was given a name of an adversary and briefed on his or her strengths and weaknesses. After a short time, the assembled were filled with excitement and anticipation. For now, all their fears had been erased. They marveled at the cunning and depth of intelligence their leader displayed. The battle had begun but only in the strategies and plans that were forming. The group would await the arrival of additional allies. They would now travel to another location that had been secured and prepared for their training and to provide sustenance to bolster them for what was ahead; however, first, they must clear the woods of anything that would give away their presence. All were given instructions on what to do. This area of ground would never be the same again, for the soil had been tarnished in such a way nothing could or would grow here, only the rock from below would remain and it would be reduced. They removed all traces of the force that had caused the change, hiding all evidence of their gathering.

Chapter 16

Rann and Cassamie returned to their campsite. It was dark and starting to rain. Both were tired from the day's events and interested in getting to bed early but they still needed to put up their supplies. They'd purchased a small generator and refrigerator to use for some of their creature comforts and mainly to run the small refrigerator. They'd decided running back and forth for ice was not time efficient or convenient. Although many of the campsites were wired for electricity, they'd chosen one off the main track and more secluded for privacy, therefore, no electricity. The small refrigerator and gas generator should be adequate for their needs.

Their excursion with the sheriff had been informative but the state police had lost the trail a few miles outside of Marion, Kentucky. The Illinois State Police and the Kentucky troopers were working together to try to locate the child. Cassamie came away with feelings of helplessness. It was going to take more than the resources of the law enforcement agencies to find that child.

After putting away their supplies, fueling up the generator and hooking up the refrigerator, they sat down for a long, anticipated talk. Cassamie placed the coffee pot on the fire and waited for it to brew. She leaned back into her camping chair and stared into the roaring flames of the campfire. Rann sat in a seat nearby. He had grabbed a beer from the refrigerator and took a long drink. She hadn't seen him drink any alcohol before and wondered if he ever became intoxicated and how he behaved when he did? She had never cared to drink anything that might influence or impair her judgment. Coffee and Diet Cokes were her preferred drinks along with lots of good, natural water.

"OK, Cassamie, what unique skills do you have?" Rann looked her straight in the eye, allowing for no postponement of this conversation.

Cassamie took a deep breath and wondered just how transparent she should be. Perhaps she should lay all the cards on the table; after all, Sarah needed them. Much more was required than the ordinary means. She looked down at the ground, took a deep breath and began her story.

"When I was a small child, I climbed up high on a rock formation above a cave, actually not too far from here and got scared. No one was nearby and when the storm clouds rolled in I really started to panic. I began trembling, closed my eyes and when I opened them again, Malitar, an angel, was beside me. Of course, at the time, I didn't realize what he was and strangely enough, I wasn't afraid of him. He comforted me and carried me back down to safety. Now the journey down in his arms terrified me but that's beside the point. Since that time, I've met with him on many occasions. It's usually when he has something that he wants me to do. I guess you could say it's when he needs a good deed done by a human and you're looking at that human."

"OK, why you? Why not some other human?"

"Because," she paused briefly before continuing, "I have a connection to angels, at least a direct connection to one in particular. My father is an angel, an important angel that was compromised. It's unclear if he's a "good" angel or one on the wrong side, one in league with Satan. When I was born, Malitar was there with him and my mother. She died right after I was born. The delivery was too difficult for her. There is an abnormality in my blood that doctors can't recognize and I was monitored for years. It's not life threatening but an oddity to modern science. My grandmother tells me it's because I have a combination of my mother's blood and whatever makes up my father's composition. So, I have a gift of being able to see through and beyond some forms of energy and I'm able to see angels and converse with them."

She looked at Rann for the first time since beginning her story. He was steadily watching her, not turning away in disgust. He seemed to take it all in, without thinking she was completely mad.

"How'd your mother meet your father?"

"I don't really know. I never asked. Malitar really doesn't tell me much. I think they must have an unwritten code from above that you don't give away secrets to humans. Anyway, it's not really what Malitar says that bothers me but what he doesn't say."

"I can understand that. What about your grandmother? Does she know?"

"I think she knows more than she's willing to tell. You see, my grandmother has gifts of her own. She can sense things about most people, things likely to happen in the near future. She's never really talked much about her gifts but she doesn't deny them, either. If I ask her a question, she'll answer it. I've just always been super sensitive when it comes to my mother. I've felt guilty because of her death at the time I was given life."

Rann reached over and took Cassamie's hand, squeezing it softly, before speaking.

"I can see why you'd feel that way as a young, insecure child, growing up but surely, as an adult, you realize you were innocent of her death. Even with today's modern medicine, with the best hospitals and doctors, there are still deaths because of complications during childbirth."

"Yes, I know all that but still it's hard to accept that for you to live, your mother had to die."

"What makes you say she had to die instead of that she died?"

"I don't know for sure but it's just something I've always felt. It's odd. I hear this voice, not aloud in the room, just inside my head. It gives me warnings. Not often but it has happened several times throughout my life. It's not a conversation and it never lasts for long. For instance, there was a time when I was ten or eleven years old and I was riding my bike. I was headed over to my girlfriend Beth's house. She lived a few blocks away. As I pedaled along, a quiet voice told me to turn around and go back home. It told me to stay calm but to go back home. I was so surprised I did exactly what it told me to do, without giving it a second thought. I didn't find it frightening or annoying but just took it seriously and turned around. As I rode into our yard, grandmother came running out to meet me. She grabbed me and hugged me to her chest. She said there had been a gas line explosion close to my friend's house. The house had completely blown up and damaged nearby homes, including Beth's house. Fortunately, the widow that lived in the house was away visiting her daughter when the gas line erupted and none of the neighbors were hurt. If I'd continued on the bike ride and went to see Beth, I might've been in the path of the explosion.

"I thought your grandmother could sense things? Didn't she have any inkling of what was going to happen?

"I'm not clear on the range of her intuition or skills but from what I can remember, that sixth sense never really applied to me. At least, I don't remember any others except for that one time. Actually, I think it was simple deduction on her part. She knew I went out to ride my bike and I usually rode over to Beth's house. I don't remember telling her specifically where I was headed, just I was going for a bike ride."

"OK, that makes sense, now back to Malitar. Has he told you anything about your parents, particularly your father?"

"He only tells me generic things, such as how important my father was in the decision-making processes then it's as if Malitar hits a stone wall and stops talking altogether."

"OK, tell me more about this voice you hear inside your head."

"Are you beginning to think I'm a little touched in the head?" Cassamie said it in a joking manner but she was actually quite serious. She couldn't blame him if he did.

"No, I think you're sane and extremely gifted, with a special ability that couldn't have been easy to deal with for all these years, especially as a child. I'm also impressed with your intelligence and generosity in helping people, people you don't even know. The compassion you showed today, when we were searching for the child, was obvious. I admire you, Cassamie, and I like you for it."

Well, what could she say to that? He had just given her a compliment and he showed an innate sense of perception. She liked him for that, in fact, she was finding many things she liked about Rann Steward and quite a change from her initial opinion of him. Even with these thoughts, she struggled to suppress a yawn and realized how bone tired she was getting.

Rann noticed her fatigue and suggested they call it a day and get a fresh start in the morning. He stood up and poured Cassamie another cup of coffee then went inside the tent. He returned a few minutes later with his toiletries, towel and clean clothes. He headed down to the lake.

The rain had stopped altogether and Cassamie went inside to gather her things and head down to the lake. This time she slipped into a two-piece swimsuit, pulled a long tee over it, went back out to the campfire to sit and wait for his return. She might take a longer swim. Her thoughts immediately drifted to her childhood and an old memory emerged. She had been here before, with her grandparents, although they had never camped out. They always stayed in a hotel when they visited the area or rented a cabin. Strange that this search had brought her back to a place where she had spent a great deal of time as a child.

The one reunion she thought about had been a strange one for Cassamie. She met many people that summer and most of them she never saw again. The one "cousin" who had taunted her so much on the cave adventure had been a few years older than her. She never saw him again after that and was glad. Some people you just don't seem to get along with no matter what you do. That day, when she'd been taken back to the picnic area, most of the people had already left. He was one of them. Strangely enough, later that night when she said something about him to her grandparents and described him, neither one had any idea about which relative she was talking. When they returned home, they pulled out all the old family photos and never found a picture of him or anyone with any resemblance to him.

Her grandparents thought he was probably from another picnic shelter and had joined their group for the excursion through the cave and playground area. Cassamie never really accepted that theory because he had known her name and seemed to have some kind of a grudge against her. You usually didn't get that kind of reaction from a complete stranger. She often wondered how she had come to the conclusion he was her cousin. It must have been because he seemed to know her and called her a "Momma's baby". That would do it. That was the fuse that would set her off. Just like tonight, there were many times her thoughts went back to that day but she had no clarity of the details.

What did she expect? She was young then and hadn't yet developed her inquisitive, reporter's mind. That mind had sent her on many wild goose chases. She had solved most of them but her early experience was still a great mystery to her. At one time, she had thought about being hypnotized but always declined from actually going through with it yet it had always puzzled her and she had never forgotten the experience.

Cassamie heard Rann whistling, as he was returning from his bath in the lake, so she gathered up her things from the chair and headed down. She met him on the path and noticed he was still toweling off and hadn't put on his shirt. Though it was getting dark, there was light from a nearby light pole illuminating the path to the lake. She could see the expanse of his chest and most definitely he had a distinct, six-pack across his abdomen. Rann definitely kept in shape.

As he came closer, he said, "Let me give you some advice. Jump in. The water is cold and full emersion is the best way, otherwise you'll find it a bit uncomfortable."

"Sounds like good advice. I think I'll follow it. It is a little chilly tonight."

"OK, I'll see you back at the campsite." Rann moved on up the pathway as Cassamie headed to the lake.

She slipped out of her tee shirt, revealing her swimming suit and dove into the water. It was deep in this part of the lake. They were camped away from the main area and the drop off was more abrupt. She came up with a bracing stroke and headed out toward the center of the lake. It was really getting dark now. No moon to give any illumination. She only took a few strokes then headed back to shore. She sat on a rock against the shore and rubbed scented soap across her arms, torso and legs. It was her favorite scent, Coconut Lime, a Bath and Body product. When she found something she liked, she stuck with it unless it was discontinued and, usually, her favorite products eventually were discontinued. She took a shallow dip and shampooed her hair. She cleaned her face quickly then stepped out of the water. That was when she noticed him.

Chapter 17

Lamechial knocked on Giselle's door before entering. When she looked at him, he seemed somewhat agitated while waiting for her to address him. She knew immediately what was wrong.

"So, he's come?"

"Yes, he's nearby and not alone but has gathered many of his most trusted allies. They are planning an assault. The young girl, Sarah, is having difficulties this evening. She's been pacing in her room and I've heard her crying several times. She's ready to go home and is no longer satisfied with waiting here. I fear she's planning to strike out on her own, so we'll need to watch her even more closely. This is not the time for her to go out on her own, unprotected from what stalks in the forest."

Giselle nodded her head in agreement. "Call all except the perimeter guards and we'll gather in the basement. Bring Sarah along with you. Let's meet in fifteen minutes; I'll change into battle gear. All should do the same before meeting together. The child must pack some articles of clothing. Tell her to dress in blue jeans, a long-sleeved tee, thick socks and to wear the hiking boots in her closet. I will get her a waterproof jacket from my closet. You are now solely in charge of looking after Sarah. I've sent Grinstead ahead on another mission. Pack enough food and water to last for at least a week, add the first-aid kit and a blanket. We leave tonight. We can wait no longer."

"It will be as you wish," voiced Lamechial, as he turned and left the room. He headed out the back door to convey Giselle's instructions. There were over thirty on the property perimeter to be notified, so he quickly changed into spirit form and floated through the air. When he had instructed all outside, he changed back into his earthly form and entered the house. First, he went to those at their posts inside and relayed the same message. Then he gathered the supplies, as he had been instructed. Finally, he went to the child's door and knocked gently. He could hear her rummaging around in the back of her room and it was a few minutes before she answered the door.

"Oh, it's you, Lam. Come in," Sarah beckoned for him to enter. She looked tired but maybe it was sadness he saw in her eyes. Lamechial could sense her deep loneliness and felt empathy for the child.

"Sarah, I have some important instructions for you and you must follow them exactly as they are given. Do you understand?"

"Yes, what's going on?"

"The only thing I can tell you now is we are all meeting in the basement in about ten minutes. You are to dress in jeans, a long-sleeved tee, thick socks and hiking boots. There is a light pack on the top shelf of your closet. Pack a few pieces of undergarments, two or three pair of socks, a few tee shirts and two pairs of jeans. You might also want to grab a sweatshirt. Get all of this together and I will be back for you in a few minutes. We are moving out and we'll eventually be returning you home. So dress and pack as quickly as you can. Will you do that for me?"

"Yes, I'll be quick." A large smile spread across her face.

Lamechial felt a little guilty for misleading her but he knew this would speed along her preparation and secure her cooperation. He left and went to dress in his own battle gear. What would she think when she saw him next? He would be in his true form, his created form. He'd have to deal with that later. For now, he needed to prepare. The child would adjust because it was what she had to do. She would be made aware of many things as they traveled through the tunnels and into the night air. The earlier planned detailed "talk" would happen, just in an abbreviated form and in a different setting. They would condense the most important information and concentrate on what needed to be said. Somehow, he had faith in the child; she would adapt well to their traveling and accept her vital role in the battle before them. Incidentally, Sarah would be getting closer to home and she'd realize it in time. She might even recognize some of the landmarks as they traveled closer to their final destination before returning her home. It would be difficult for the child in all that she'd face. This adjustment would not be possible by another child. Sarah had the blood consistency to help her adapt and survive this night and several more difficult nights ahead. She wasn't aware of her unique strengths or even how she would use those strengths but she would soon learn.

Lamechial entered his own room and began putting together what he required. Actually, he would have to gather relatively little for himself because his true form supplied most of what he would need at any given time. He removed most of the clothing but didn't bother to put on others. He only took a long, hooded tunic. The clothes he had worn were necessary for this earthly lifestyle and his acceptance without drawing unwanted attention. He and Giselle had worked diligently to disguise his true identity. Celestials were adept at controlling their flow of energy and forming various shapes to hold their essence. It merely required constructing an image in the brain then transforming into that image. Nevertheless, tonight Sarah would see him as he truly was but for now, he would hurry and meet with Giselle in the basement to make sure nothing more was needed before going back for the child.

As Lam turned to head toward the door, his reflection was captured briefly in the mirror but could not be held long because of its brilliance. No longer a man-child reflected in the mirror but a creature of such fierceness and surrounded with a shining aura encompassing unchecked strength yet he would weaken this form for the child. When he faced his strongest enemy, he would call forth this ultimate façade. Now, he would modify it to prevent frightening Sarah. He wanted to console, comfort and protect her. She was a good child and an innocent, so the adjustment would hold for the next few days. Lam was now of medium height for a celestial with a much broader shoulder width than a human and able to support a head that carried four different faces. The additional faces were hidden under the hood of the tunic. The frontal face was one of a man, Lam's face with lines of maturity. The face toward the East was a lion's symbolizing the strongest of the wild beasts. The face toward the West resembled an ox, symbolizing the most powerful of the domesticated animals. At the rear of the head was the face of an eagle, symbolizing the mightiest of the birds. Lam also had two sets of wings folding in for compactness while he navigated his strong body. The torso was that of a man having straight legs tapering down to the feet of a calf and the hooves gleaming of burnished bronze. As Lam moved, he became part of a translucent cloud surrounded by penetrating light. This too would intensify when facing the enemy. For collecting the child his resemblance was surrounded by a subtle, gleaming mist.

In the basement, a highly unusual gathering was assembled. For such a large room, it was now dwarfed by the physical size and presence of those in attendance. Large individuals dressed for battle flanked the perimeter of the room. These beings were at least fifteen feet tall and varied in their appearance with human resemblances, while others didn't appear human at all but formed with a combination of animal-like attributes. Their faces obstructed by the helmets and protective, facial guards. This group numbered twenty-three. In the middle, were seventeen others standing at attention. Their appearance undetectable by the human eye, for they were in spirit form and could only be seen by those with the brain power to navigate the energy force around them and penetrate that energy for recognition of what the eye was relaying back to the brain. Only the celestials and a limited number of humans could see them as they actually were. The child, Sarah, would be able to see them, if she allowed herself. If she became frightened, her brain would close off this recognition and delete the images from her memory. Soon, they would know how she would react to their unique group.

In the center of the group stood Giselle, Myriad and one other who had not been in attendance before. Next to Myriad Dupree, known as "Mother Nature", stood the third triad spirit, Terrene. The entire group was uneasy with her presence because she had been declared a traitor for eons and none felt comfortable with her in their midst. She was blamed for much of the damage that had occurred because of her association with the one who held their upmost contempt. Although, their leader, Giselle, did not appear disturbed by Terrene's company and this somehow seemed to ease their apprehensions. They all owed their allegiance and undisputed trust to Giselle. She would not betray that trust. For whatever reason, Giselle had accepted Terrene in their presence.

As Lam entered the basement, all moved aside to let him pass. He went to the right of Giselle and paused briefly, as he studied the one beside her. He nodded his head and turned to Giselle.

"Do you need anything else before I bring the child?"

Giselle answered, "No, all is as it should be. Go ahead and bring the child to us but first, you need to place the supplies I requested near the hidden doorway leading to the tunnels."

"I will do as you say," Lamechial answered and moved back through the large group. Many stepped out of his way to allow for his passage. The entire group had been silent as Lamechial spoke with Giselle and bowed their heads in respect, as he moved among them. He could feel their unspoken support by the expressions on their faces and their respectful manner. He hoped Giselle had chosen well in this mix of beings, for their mission ahead would be a difficult one. This mission would determine all of their futures. He could only put his faith in her orchestration of the plan and that she was following the Omnipotent One's Will.

Lamechial paused outside Sarah's room. He would talk to her through the door first so she would recognize his voice. He would warn her about his change in appearance and assure her he was still the same being, only in a different guise. He knocked.

When he heard her walking toward the door, he spoke. "Sarah, before you open the door, I must prepare you for a bit of a shock. I'm not going to look the way I did before. It's still me but I'm in a different form. So, I want you to be prepared for this. I am still your friend and I will not harm you. Remember that. Now please open the door."

"Huh? I don't know what you mean but…Oh my God," Sarah said, as she opened the door and shockingly saw what was waiting in the hallway. She stepped back into her room but didn't try to close the door.

She stood quietly looking at him. Only a few moments passed before she asked, "What are you? I knew there was something strange about you."

Lamechial laughed before bending down and lightly cuffing her chin. He was pleased with her reaction and felt better about the other adjustments she would soon be making. Sarah had just proven she was made of a strong constitution and not one to panic easily. These were good qualities, indeed.

"Do you have all I told you to bring?"

"Yes, it's all stashed in this backpack. It's kind of heavy but I can carry it."

She turned and picked up her bag. Before stepping out of the room, she paused and looked directly into Lam's face. She took a deep breath, brushed her hair out of her eyes and joined him in the hallway.

"What are you exactly, some kind of an angel? You've got wings poking out from that cape."

Lam couldn't help but be impressed with her guts and bravado and he smiled at her. "Yes, I am an angel, more specifically, a cherub. I will explain it all to you more thoroughly later. Now we have to join the rest."

"Are they all angels, too?"

"Most are."

"What about Giselle? Is she one?"

"Yes, an important one. May we go now and talk later?"

"OK but I want to know everything. I don't want you leaving anything out, OK?"

"Agreed." Lamechial grinned, reached down and easily picked Sarah up and her bag. Before she could say anything else, he floated down the hallway, with her.

Chapter 18

Cassamie stood still on the edge of the water. Even though it was pitch dark, she knew the man could clearly see her because she could see him. He was motionless but she could feel his eyes on her. Something calmed her. She wasn't afraid and didn't feel the need to call out to Rann. He would hear her if she did and would come quickly to her aid. For some odd reason, she knew there was nothing to fear. In fact, all of her senses told her there was something special about him, something extraordinary then it hit her. She knew. He wasn't a man. He was another angel. He had the same look about him as Malitar: the tall frame, the alert and all-knowing eyes, the patience and tolerance that Malitar had always exhibited; the unbelievable beauty. Yet, this angel wasn't similar to Malitar. This angel was broader of shoulder with a larger frame. He had the build of a warrior with his angled cheekbones and broad forehead. His eyes were set wide apart and his chin was square and firm. He looked older than Malitar and much more powerful. Strange but as she continued to stare at him, she began to recognize something and she could feel a connection bridge from within her. There was a vague awareness of him, a glimpse of something just lingering below the surface of full recognition. What could it be? She had never seen this one before but something within her knew him. How could that be?

As if he sensed her thoughts, he began walking toward her. Cassamie stayed where she was still puzzled by the nagging feeling she should know him. Something, maybe intuition told her this angel was important to her. Here in the night, she could see him as clearly as if it were broad daylight and he could see her. How was that even possible? He continued to walk closer, as if he had knowledge of whom she was and had purposely come to find her. She could read the recognition in his eyes. The eyes, that's what had captured her notice. Even from this distance and with the darkness, she could tell they were different colors. The eye on the right was blue, while the one on his left was a mottled brown. Both were framed by long, sweeping eyelashes; amazing that her eyes were able to detect all of this from at least fifteen feet away and in the pitch of night. A shock coursed through her and she knew beyond a shadow of a doubt, who stood before her. So, he had finally come. Why? Why here? Why now, after all these years? Oh yes, it finally dawned on her. She knew who he was, his appearance should have been a shock to her system but strangely, it wasn't. She stood up straighter and walked out of the water to meet him head-on.

He stopped only a few feet from her and seemed to be evaluating her, gauging her and taking some kind of a measurement before he spoke to her.

"So, you know who I am?"

"Yes."

Grinstead admired her response to him. She didn't look away from him and didn't feel the need to say anything other than her affirmation that she recognized him. She was only a newborn the time he had been fully in her presence, though she would've been too young to be aware of him. Grinstead looked at her with longing and had to fight the urge to enfold her in his arms, to feel her warmth against him and to listen to her beating, human heart. He wanted to look deeply into her eyes, the same eyes of her mother, the love of his existence. She so looked as her mother but she wasn't human entirely for she had part of him inside her. It was her celestial attributes that allowed her to see him, especially in the darkness. These characteristics had helped to keep her alive and protected from the evil forces of Mephistopheles and all his minions.

She wouldn't know of the sacrifice he made when he walked away all those years ago, when her mother had stopped breathing. Even with his celestial powers, he hadn't been able to save Shelby, for he was not God. Her small, weak, human body was unable to tolerate the childbirth. She had struggled to bring Cassamie into this world, through immense pain and suffering but with the birth of his child, his seed had ripped Shelby apart; the midwife and he couldn't stop all the bleeding. Though an ambulance had been called earlier, something had gone horribly wrong and the ambulance hadn't arrived until Shelby had already lost her flickering flame of life. Her smile remained on her face as she drifted off from him, knowing her child had survived and would live. He had known no pain as the pain he felt when she died.

He thought those senses and feelings were not a part of him, the mighty Grinstead but he had been wrong. He grieved, as any human would grieve and was still grieving today; though he knew, without a doubt, Shelby would be in Paradise, a place off limits to him now. He still had much to do to gain full redemption. Even though so much time had passed, the pain of his loss hadn't diminished through the years; although he learned to cope with the emptiness and to find some solace in watching his child grow through the years, watch but always from a distance, always undetectable to her and those near her.

When Shelby died, he couldn't accept it. He held her close, shook her, willing her to wake, until Malitar had come and pulled him away. Giselle was also there and the two of them forced him to leave. He had to leave. It would be safer for the babe. Malitar would watch over her and see that she was taken to her grandparents and he became Cassamie's guardian angel always staying close by to provide protection and guidance. It was too risky for the child to be found by the Evil One, so he would have to disappear and not make contact with her. He could have no involvement in the child's life. It would be too great a risk. In the red miasma of his grief, he agreed to those terms but what a sacrifice he had agreed to. To protect his child, Grinstead would have to always keep his distance from the child given to him by Shelby and by his holy maker.

He knew Cassamie would grow up wondering about him, her father and would learn to despise him for his absence and see this as a total abandonment. If these steps would assure her safety, then he had agreed to leave and only watch, always from a distance, ever vigilant for those suspecting eyes that were looking for any indication a child had been created from his loins or was important to him. Now, he knew the Evil One and his cohorts had ferreted out the truth and would seek her out to destroy her. For in doing so, they would also be destroying a part of him. Little did they know a part of him had already died with Shelby and he had become nothing more than an empty shell.

"Why have you come?"

Cassamie watched a multitude of emotions cross his face. In seeing his reaction to her, she wondered what he was thinking but then she quickly told herself she really didn't care about his thoughts. He was nothing to her, only a stranger in her midst. Where had he been for all those years, all those years of uncertainty and loneliness? Why did he wait until she was a full-grown woman before appearing in her life? She had never met him though Malitar had told her her father had been there throughout her mother's pregnancy and her birth. Cassamie had pieced it all together and reached her own conclusions. Her father had seen her but had never held her. He could not bear to look at her after her mother died. He had turned away from the one who'd caused her mother's death and had chosen to abandon her. Yes, the one being who might have made a difference in an infant's life, in her entire life, had chosen to desert her. Well, she was grown now and owed him nothing. She turned her back on him and walked back to the water's edge to retrieve her towel, soap and other bathing supplies. She would have walked right by him if he hadn't stepped in front of her and put his arms on her shoulders to halt her progress.

"Stop. I know there are many things you do not understand and I realize you're angry with me. Those feelings are warranted but the cause for my distance was necessary. I had no choice but to leave you in the care of those I trusted most.

Your life would have been in jeopardy if I had stayed. It was too great a risk. You don't understand that now, in time you will but for now, you must listen to me. You are in grave danger. The one I had so carefully hidden you from so long ago now seeks you. He will not stop until he has destroyed all we have worked so hard for through the years. Surely you trust Malitar and know he is close by as are many others you can depend on and trust?"

I could remain silent no longer. *Grave danger? What was he talking about?*

"I'm sure Malitar is nearby, as he has always been when I've had need of friendship and companionship. For the "others", I have no idea who you are talking about. I do not know you but I recognize you as being the one who fathered me. Now step aside and let me pass."

"Cassamie, is everything OK?"

I looked over my father's shoulder and saw Rann standing a few feet away from us on the path. His face showed he was uneasy with the situation for he must have overheard much of our conversation. I could tell he saw my father, so his ability to see angels was true. My father turned to look at Rann. He was probably a little surprised Rann could see him but his face did not register that surprise. He continued to hold me in place as he glanced toward Rann.

"No problem, Rann, I was just getting ready to come back to camp. There's nothing more for me here. This conversation is over," I said, as I pushed my father's hand off my shoulder. I turned my back on him, walked to Rann taking his hand and led him back up the path toward the campsite. I never bothered to turn around and see what my father was doing, though I knew Rann had looked back.

"You can't get rid of me that easily, Cassamie," my father called out. "We will talk soon but for now I'll remain close by. Your companion will need to be vigilant to keep both of you safe. Be warned, the vilest of evil is about tonight and moving in closer. I repeat you are in grave danger and must be ready to move at a moment's notice."

When I spun around to address him, he was gone. Nothing. Rann put his arms around me and led me back to camp. I felt numb, as I struggled up the hilly path, stumbling as we ascended to our campsite. A cold sweat beaded across my forehead and I could feel the beginnings of what was probably a panic attack, though I had never had one before. Rann reached down and swooped me up in his arms and carried me the remaining distance to the fire.

Chapter 19

The wind had calmed and the leaves outside the cave were rustling gently. Trees surrounded the cave and the river gently washed against the limestone ledge that bordered the entrance to the cave. At this spot, the river was at its widest and the current its strongest. The cave was embedded on the west side of the Ohio River on the Illinois shore. The massive cliff of the land jutted out several feet over the river's edge. Trees and vegetation occupied the outside roof of the cave. Pathways led down to the entrance with stone steps carved from the limestone descending to the bottom. A wide expanse of rock-paved frontage ran along the mouth of the cave providing ample flooring into it. The rock fell away to sediment and muck as you entered deeper into the cave unless you climbed along the limestone edges carved by the river however, both could be slippery and perilous if not careful.

During late spring to early autumn, the entrance to the cave was partially hidden by thick foliage and brush. It was a deep cave meandering back into the land for miles and most of these tunnels remained unexplored. The space constraints and deep recesses were too dangerous and limiting for people, though many creatures of the night found refuge there; however, man had used parts of the cave and many families in nearby communities visited the cave during the spring, summer and autumn. Children found it fascinating to climb over the outside roof of the cave and to venture down the path into the cave to where there was still light, before the darkness began. Still, children have an innate intuition to stay away from the dark, from anything unknown, although they could be persuaded even if in the company of those that would bring them harm. Many had suffered broken bones and injured pride while climbing along the rocky ledges. Some had found death but those were few and the bodies remained undiscovered in the dark, dank pits beyond. If one listened carefully, the wails and screams of troubled spirits announced unrest and loneliness, untethered souls proclaiming the remains of their bodies. Unfortunately, these screams were ignored or those with the ability to actually hear the wails would attribute the noise to wind whirling within the many recesses of the cave. It was so much easier for people to deny the horrors and possibilities.

It was vacant today and had been for a while. Mephistopheles, the Dog, had made sure of it by sending out an aura of warning that penetrated for miles around. Humans were vulnerable to many of these manipulations and subconsciously avoided traveling to the cave until the Evil One called back the aura or its duration was spent. He used tentacles of persuasion to ferret out any individuals with a weak conscience and could easily manipulate those thoughts. Whenever he needed to discourage others from coming near a certain location or even to coerce them to go to a certain place, he would send out an aura. Through the years, he perfected his skill, yet he could not use it on celestials or humans with a strong, steadfast, unquestionable faith. At times, he could tempt them but he couldn't control their thoughts long enough to influence their actions for his ultimate purpose. A disappointment but he continued to persist in breaking them down, emotionally. Sometimes it worked but never for long then they became even stronger against his efforts. He had learned to hate them, as he had the ones left on the highest realm. Regardless, for now, he didn't want any interference from curious humans.

The cave had been quite useful to him throughout the ages and now allowed for his temporary residence. Of course, humans utilized the cave throughout time. There was an influx of river travelers to the area. From 1768 until 1770, between 4,000 and 5,000 settlers traveled on the river. They had dreams of beginning a new life with better living conditions and many headed to Illinois and Kentucky. The cave became a sanctuary for the early pioneers but because of Mephistopheles's influence, it quickly became a nefarious site. He had chosen it as his safe haven because of its evil history, a prime ingredient for his ability to remain on this realm for an extended time.

The past occurrences of this location were almost as evil as the Dog, almost. It had harbored much bloodshed, torment and suffering caused by those that inhabited it for a time, the unscrupulous river pirates. This unsavory and merciless group had quickly claimed the cave for their personal gain. The cave was located at the southeastern part of Illinois on the Ohio River and had provided shelter and a wide view up and down the river. No one could travel on the river without the outlaws knowing of their arrival. The river pirates plundered the flatboats traveling down the river and murdered or robbed the unsuspecting travelers. One early pirate, Samuel Mason, had operated a tavern and gambling parlor in the cave. He used whiskey, cards and prostitutes for enticing weary travelers. Many of these were beaten, robbed and even murdered after docking at his crude and cruel wharf.

Ferryboat passengers were also preyed upon. In fact, the local ferryman, James Ford, later given the nickname, "Satan's Ferryman," was said to take up where the river pirates left off and harmed many travelers on the river. While operating the ferry, he built and maintained a road on either side of the ferry, upstream from Cave-in-Rock. In time his misdeeds were well known by the locals. Not only did he operate Ford's Ferry but he was also a "slave catcher" hired by John Crenshaw near Equality, Illinois, where Crenshaw's home, Hickory Hill, the legendary "Old Slave House," was erected. Many tales of woe and heartache were forced on the fleeing slaves as well as the free blacks, for it was rumored Crenshaw disregarded the law and sold them back into slavery, destroying their legal papers of freedom.

Because of such avenues of behavior, Ford eventually lost his life by a vigilante attack on him, while dining in the home of a local woman. He was shot to death with seventeen bullets found in his body. His funeral attendees were: his widow, a few family members, even fewer neighbors and a small group of slaves. At the time of his burial, a terrible thunderstorm came up just as the slaves lowered the coffin into the ground. With a flash of lightning and a loud roar of thunder, one of the superstitious slaves accidentally dropped the rope holding the coffin and the coffin dropped into the hole headfirst and became wedged securely in the ground at an odd angle. A deluge of rainfall further hindered their attempt to move the coffin, so it was covered over exactly where it lay. Ford's body remained fixed with the corpse standing on its head. There were many who thought it a fitting burial for one such as him. The Dog had found this amusing, while gaining strength and energy from this environment of evil.

Today, the Dog awakened from his resting place in the deepest recesses of the cave away from any prying eyes. He stretched as he clambered up and out of his hiding place. Surveying the area around him, he sent out sensors to detect anyone's nearby presence. The air felt bracing and awoke a deep hunger within him. His energy recharged and filled him with added strength and a stronger determination. As he assessed his surroundings and was satisfied he was alone, he jumped across the interior of the cave and landed on a small boulder. When he climbed to the top surface of the cave, the chilly night air and the coal black night sky greeted him. If a dog could smile, you would see one form across his muzzle. He was pleased with the conditions of the night. No moonlight to illuminate the path he would take. Before he sought out the others, he would check again on the woman in the woods, the one the celestials had protected through the years.

Grinstead had been so clever in his ruse to keep her hidden from him and what a sacrifice he had made in denying himself the joy of getting to know his one and only child. By now, she would only harbor feelings of animosity toward him. Mephistopheles had made sure throughout the years the child wondered about her father and had come to the conclusion her father cared nothing for her. Knowing his greatest skill was to pounce on the wary and vulnerable and manipulate those thoughts so their beliefs became futile and hopeless. Even with all of that, it was still amusing to him, after all these years, she had turned up at the exact time when he would require her presence. This was no mere coincidence, no fluke, or chance occurrence. No, this was one of the many puzzle pieces falling neatly into place. In fact, a main piece of his "puzzle" was to destroy cohesion and bring about total destruction.

He stepped behind a large outcropping of rock. For a moment, he felt the strong pull of the underworld. His time here was running out but it should be adequate enough to complete the mission. Long ago, when he had been cast out, his ability to leave his domain for long had been established. If the pull became too strong, he would return briefly to recoup his strength then come again at the most crucial time. He was confident his "army" would be invincible against those gathered to fight him. Foolish league of angels. None matched him, not from the beginning of creation. He acclaimed superiority above all celestials. His anger boiled at the thought of the one who had cast him out. Yes, in this battle the Dog would concede nothing and claim all. His hair stood out as he thought about the past.

Sent to the inner bowels where magma, molten lava and steam surrounded him, his only light came from the fires and fumes that penetrated the entire area of his environment. Heat of unbelievable temperature surrounded him but never consuming him. He wasn't affected by the extreme heat because he was immune to the elements as were all celestials but he missed the beauty and tranquility of his past life. Where once he dwelt in serenity, beauty and harmony, he now must dwell engulfed in darkness decorated in scarlet red, orange and black. His home filled with sulfurous gases and endless gurgling sounds of molten rock flowing along the entire surface. The total loss of beauty festered within him, until he was totally consumed with hatred for all celestials remaining in the highest realm. The archangels drew his greatest wrath along with the cherubim and seraphim perpetually in the presence of YHWH. This jealousy knew no bounds and fueled the prime stimulus that drove him. He shared this hatred with mankind, who usurped what should be his alone, his importance.

His punishment was banishment to the pits of Hell, Hades, the Underworld, whatever you chose to call it. YHWH intended for him to suffer from loneliness and despair but he had learned to tolerate his home. Loneliness was not a problem for him because many other celestials had been cast out with him and some had stayed connected to him. When YHWH created man, Mephistopheles visited the earth from time to time and caused as much havoc and disharmony, as possible.

How easily mankind had been swayed, so gullible and trusting. Their weaknesses were nectar for his strength. The renegade celestials were not the only beings drawn to his domain. The imperfect and ignorant humans became easy prey for him throughout time but still the anger lived within him. That he was so callously thrown from the place where he was created, thrown out like chattel, had continued to spawn hatred within him. It gnawed away at him for millennia. He never thought his banishment possible but it had happened.

Now it no longer mattered for he had gained strength from his new domain by harvesting many souls to do his bidding and to suffer through punishment given because of his control over them. So be it. He learned through the ages and gathered thousands from the ranks of these humans, so inferior to all celestials. He gained strength and power from their misery and suffering. The cave where he claimed his resting place had held such earthly monsters throughout the years. They were easy prey for him, so greedy, so blood thirsty. His role had been quite simple. Just standing in their company for only a few minutes and he easily discerned their fears and needs. A weak human is so easily controlled. Why had the mighty one even bothered to create such beings? They were no match for him and his legions of demons. Perhaps the all-knowing One had made a misjudgment.

No more time for pondering. He would seek out the woman and if the opportunity arose, he would destroy her tonight. That would make things so much easier with her out of the way and the ever-vigilant Grinstead would be distraught and incapable of being at his best. The mighty Grinstead would feel the wrath of the one he had challenged so long ago. Grinstead had always been an adversary, thwarting his plans during the initial meetings with other celestials, those who were easily swayed by his appearance and beguiling voice.

Remembering back, Grinstead had dared to mock him and discouraged others from listening to him. Grinstead had unknowingly ventured into an area of the highest realm where the dissenters were initiating their move. Now, that was a juicy memory and an inspiring thought for this time, to finally have the chance to bring Grinstead down. It would be satisfying to see him falter before the complete assault against the One above. These thoughts helped fuel the Dog's energy as he sought out the woman, Grinstead's child. Somehow, she always escaped him in the past. Her crafty grandmother had seen to that. Soon enough, he would see the grandmother again and end her meddling once and for all. In a great leap, the Dog became a blur in the night as he journeyed westward toward the unsuspecting woman and her fate.

Chapter 20

Sarah

I never experienced anything similar to the ride I had on his shoulder. We moved so quickly I didn't even realize we were moving. My eyes couldn't keep up with the movement and it was as if I were in a fog moving ahead then we slowed and stopped. Lam lowered me to stand and walk beside him.

I really didn't have long to appreciate the ride before more surprises came. Walking down the stairway into the basement, I could hear much talking. I recognized a few of the voices but most of them were new to me. We turned the corner and I had the shock of my life. Tonight was a night for surprises. In front of me, all kinds of "creatures" were assembled and dressed to do battle. The height of some required sitting or stooping to fit into the space. Out of the corner of my eye, I saw Lam watching me for my reaction. Surprisingly, I wasn't too startled, for I had figured out earlier I wasn't with normal people. I guessed immediately, especially when Giselle told me that Bible story, I knew they must be some kind of angels. Why else would she tell that story? They were just too slick for everything that happened. For instance, they always knew exactly what I liked whether it was food, sodas, or clothes. Everything fit perfectly. The one thing that puzzled me though was why didn't Jim carry me as Lam did today when I was kidnapped? It would have saved a lot of time when we walked on the trails and, specifically, when we went through that "Fat Man's Squeeze". It didn't make sense unless he wanted the police to think he was a normal guy or he wanted to be tracked. That must be it. I think they knew how to plan for everything but what did I expect? They were angels, right?

Giselle noticed our arrival and moved toward us. Naturally, all eyes simultaneously focused on us. I felt a little uncomfortable but no big deal.

"Hello, Sarah, we're glad you joined us," Giselle said, with a smile.

"Thank you." I kept looking around the room at all the beings gathered. Some of them without a helmet over their faces looked just about normal, or I mean, they rather looked to be regular people, except for being almost giants. Then there was another group that definitely didn't look human. I don't know what they were because they looked to be a combination of animal and human. Surely, they were not angels because I always thought angels would look like God. Now I know God made man in his own image, so these beings did not look to be God because God must look the same as man. All I could figure out was these beings were special, heavenly creatures that probably helped to fight God's battles. They definitely looked like soldiers then I wondered what kind of battle they would fight. As a heavy weight, it hit me I might be in the middle of this battle. Would I be involved? How could that be? I knew nothing of battles except what I saw on television or at the movies.

Giselle stood quietly, giving Sarah time to take in and process what she saw around the room. Outwardly, Sarah appeared calm while looking at each group before her. She hadn't yet noticed the less observable group but Giselle was confident their presence would soon register in Sarah's brain. Hofniel was an important steward of the highest realm, a Seraphim and walked over to Sarah. "Hello, Sarah, I'm Hofniel and I'm pleased to meet you." He gave a slight bow and smiled at her, warmly. For one that looked so fierce, he was not frightening to her. He had a friendly expression on his face.

"Hello," addressed Sarah. She was looking at him intently. Now he did look to be an angel because he had wings, actually six wings. His face was bright and it was hard to look at him for long. She had to look away. She glanced down at his feet and they looked normal. Except for his great height, those wings and those intense, orange, glowing eyes, he could almost look human. He had wide shoulders and big hands and arms. He was massive. She thought he was probably strong. He sure took up a lot of room in here.

As she glanced around the room, something caught her attention. She noticed a sudden movement, a type of cloud-like reflection or a folding of air. When she looked closer, she could make out some type of figure. It wasn't a person and it wasn't one of these angels. It rather looked like a ghost, a spirit. When she began to focus on it, she realized there were numerous ones, all clustered together and just floating around the room.

"What are those ghost-like things, Giselle?"

"Oh, so you finally noticed them. Good. They won't harm you. They're spirits, celestial beings that help to look after people and relay information back to the highest realm. Not many humans can see them but I thought you would. The spirits, or Naymers, as they are known in our realm, are here to help us. They can cushion you against harm and reverse some natural elements and forces on Earth."

"Oh, I get it. They're like buffers and contacts for the above place."

"That's exactly what they do. Now, how do you feel knowing we're not an ordinary group, not human at all?"

"Oh, I figured that out a long time ago. You were just too ready for everything. What I really want to know is why did Jim kidnap me and bring me here? What do I have to do with this?"

Giselle admired the child for her strength and her curiosity about her situation. Sarah was strong and exhibited no hysterics, a good trait for what would come.

"Of course, you want to know and I'm going to tell you but first we're going to take a journey. All of us are going, except Jim. He has already left to meet up with someone else then we'll all come together at a place that's not too far from your home. Soon you'll get to go home. Will that please you?"

"Yes, but why did Jim have to go ahead? Is he going to be OK?"

Sarah had become attached to him and would want nothing bad to happen to him. Even though he was the one who actually took her from the school group, she had never actually feared for her life because he had always been gentle with her and concerned about her comfort. She knew he was doing something he felt had to be done. She didn't really understand the part she played in this whole thing but she would find out. They would be leaving soon because she had packed a lot of stuff to take with her and Giselle said they would be traveling to another place close to home. She was getting excited. She missed her parents and friends. She couldn't wait to see them all again and didn't even mind the thought of going back to school. It was late April, so there really wasn't that much school before summer vacation. The thought made her stop and think. *I wonder if they will make me forget everything I've seen and all the angels and the special beings. They probably will. That's what usually happens in books and the movies.*

Giselle spoke again, "Jim had to go protect someone else. He'll join our group as soon as the situation is resolved. Don't worry about him but I do think it's time you knew his real name. It's Grinstead. We thought that "Jim" would be a normal name for you to hear and use."

"Grinstead sounds more like an angel's name."

Giselle laughed as did many of the others standing nearby. She turned to me again and said, "I'm glad you've faced everything with such openness."

Then she turned to the others and told them it was time to head to the tunnels and soon they would be engaged in the reason they'd all been called together. She urged them to have faith in their mission for the glory of the One above. The crowd parted to make room for Giselle, myself, Lamechial and the other woman standing beside Giselle. I didn't have time to notice much about her except she seemed to be surrounded by a purplish mist. I really wasn't able to see her face because she had a deep hooded cape over her body and her face was shielded in darkness from the folds of the cape.

We exited the room and moved to doors that looked ancient to me because they were made of some kind of old wood and heavy metal. As we came to them, a large man-angel opened them. I felt a rush of damp, musty air hit my face then I saw that it led into a tunnel, a high ceiling but narrow tunnel. Giselle turned to me and told me to stay behind her and Terrene. As she said this, she pointed toward the cloaked one. I nodded my head and we began our trip through the tunnels. I wondered why the tunnels were here and why we were using them but I didn't bother to ask anyone. Before I got too far into the tunnel, I looked behind me and saw Lamechial right behind me. Giselle stopped and turned toward me.

"Sarah, it's going to get dark in here. We don't need the light but you won't be able to see. Let Lamechial carry you so we don't have to tread so cautiously and slowly."

"OK," I answered because that made sense to me. As soon as I agreed, Lam scooped me up. He sure was quick and strong. We went deeper into the tunnel and it became completely black. I think Lam noticed me tense up a little, so he started talking to me. I couldn't see his face but I could easily hear him above the muffled noise of our large group moving deeper into the tunnel.

"These tunnels were originally built as part of the Underground Railroad to help hide and protect runaway slaves during the mid to late 1800s. As you know from your history books, slavery was not legal in Illinois but, because this region is so close to Kentucky, a former slave state, many people wanted to help the slaves. Of course, there were others like John Crenshaw, the owner of Hickory Hill; you would know it as the Old Slave House, who found personal gain in capturing blacks to sell for a profit or to return to former owners at a price. He was even known to capture freed men and women and throw them back into bondage. He was a wealthy man but not a good man and he brought about much pain and suffering for the slaves."

"Is that how he made a living, selling slaves?"

"So, you don't know that much of your local history? I guess most fifth graders aren't yet interested in it. While we navigate through these tunnels, I'll give you some background information. Do you want to hear about it to help distract you from the pitch darkness?

I looked around me but all I could see was blackness. It really was a little creepy. "Yeah, I think that would be good."

Lamechial began the story of the local history.

"Although the Civil War was never fought in southern Illinois, it had a great impact on the area. Many local towns played a vital part in the war. Southern Illinois supplied weapons, iron products and major grain supplies to the North. Cairo, Illinois, not too far from here, at the southern tip where the Ohio and Mississippi Rivers join, served as a strategic point for Union Army expeditions into the territory of the Confederacy. In fact, Cairo was an important Union supply base with protection from nearby Camp Defiance. On the other sides of the rivers, those states, Kentucky and Missouri, were sympathetic to the South and supplied troops for their cause, putting Cairo in a unique but dangerous situation."

He continued, "Workers in various factories and mills, the port and shipyards of Chicago helped provide a steady stream of material, food and clothing to the Illinois troops and the general Union Army. Foundry workers in Mound City converted river steamboats into armored gunboats and put them in Union service. The southern markets were cut off from the North because of the war. The port of Chicago rose in prominence and grew because of trade with the Great Lakes region."

"What's a foundry worker?" I had never heard of that kind of worker.

"A foundry worker is someone who works with metals to melt and mold it or cast it into different shapes for various uses."

"Oh, OK I get it. So, we were for the Union's side."

"Well, not exactly. Let me explain. At the time of the Civil War, the residents of southern Illinois were first- and second-generation Southerners and most of the region was loyal to the Democratic Party, so the Civil War caused mixed feelings in the region. Most young men here joined the Union Army but a few joined the Confederate regiments in the South."

"OK, if we were mostly for the North and they were against slavery, then how did that man have slaves at the Old Slave House?"

"Good question, Sarah. You're using that fine brain of yours."

He added, "Although Illinois was a free state and opposed to slavery, John Crenshaw, a wealthy businessman and huge landowner in Gallatin County, operated the salt works near Equality, Illinois. In those days, salt was in high demand and valuable. Salt was vital to the early American frontier economy because it was an important nutrient and a means for preserving food. In fact, salt was often used as currency or as a bartering tool for purchasing goods and supplies. With this demand for salt, Crenshaw was permitted to use slaves for the difficult work of hauling and boiling the brackish water to produce salt.

Few white men, only the desperately poor, would touch the job; so, slaves were brought in and housed on Crenshaw's property and near the salt mines. He was the only Illinois resident legally permitted to keep slaves and he became remarkably rich. He owned thousands of acres of land, leased 30,000 acres from the state and had more than 3,000 slaves. At the time, slaves could be leased for one-year terms in the mines. Later Crenshaw became greedy and started another clandestine or secret operation. He began kidnapping former slaves that were now free and illegally pressed them back into service as slaves in the South. Thus, his home, before known as "Hickory Hill," became known as the "Old Slave House".

"So, were these tunnels used to hold those slaves before being taken to the South?"

"No, just the opposite. These tunnels were used to help the slaves get to freedom in the North. The early owners of this property believed in helping the slaves and secretly built these tunnels. The secret of their existence has survived for generations. That is one of the primary reasons we chose the property for our base."

"Well, slavery is not used today, so why did they keep the secret?"

"Another good question, Sarah. I don't know the answer to that but the family probably values their own privacy and would not want the government or tourists to get interested in the historical role the property played. They don't need the money, so they kept the secret. Most of the family has died out now or moved away and just the one relative maintains the property. The relative doesn't reside here but does return periodically to check on things. A trusted caretaker maintains the property and is paid well for his loyalty and discretion. If you had traveled outside the security fence, you would've seen the home site is surrounded by farmland. Some of the acreage is used for livestock but most is planted in corn and soybeans."

"I know that Gallatin County is a farming area so that doesn't surprise me. My parents also own some farmland but my dad is an attorney and my mom is an accountant. They don't farm but rent the ground out to a local farmer."

We stopped talking for a while and I could tell it wasn't quite as dark; in fact, I could see some things around me. We were getting closer to the end of the tunnel. Ahead I could see benches sitting against the walls of the tunnel and Giselle had lit some lanterns. Lam reached them and sat me down on one of the benches. Giselle and the other "lady", Terrene, remained inside the tunnel with Lam and me, while the rest went further down the tunnel to the exit.

Giselle smiled kindly at me and said, "Sarah, now is the time for us to have that talk. There are many things I need to explain to you and many things you need to embrace to accomplish what must be done. I want you to remain on the bench across from me and listen to the amazing story I will tell. It's a true story about who you really are. Are you ready to hear that story?

Chapter 21

Rann helped me back up the hill to our campsite and sat me in a chair. I trembled uncontrollably and couldn't seem to focus on anything. I was still in shock realizing I had actually seen and talked to my father. Rann poured me a cup of coffee and brought it to me.

"Here drink this, or would you like something a little stronger, like beer or whiskey, if we have any?"

I finally looked at him and saw the concern in his eyes. "No, I'm OK. The coffee will do nicely. I'm better. I guess it was just a shock to me."

"Yeah, I would think so. Why didn't you call out for me? I would've been right there," he leaned down close to my face then kissed me. It was a gentle kiss, a sweet kiss, not one that demanded anything, just a warm pressure to bring me around. He gently pulled away and continued looking at me.

"I really am OK but that was nice. Maybe we can try it again sometime." I smiled at him then got up and walked around the campfire with my coffee cup in hand. After taking a few sips, I returned to my seat.

"I guess I was a little overwhelmed about finally meeting my father after so long. I recognized him right away. He was just standing over to the side when I came up out of the lake. He was about fifteen feet away standing near the tree line. The strange thing was even though it was pitch dark, I could see him as if it were broad daylight. He wasn't frightening or anything. He just stood there patiently watching me, waiting for me to acknowledge him."

"Why do you think he revealed himself to you, now? I heard him say something about you being in grave danger."

"Yes, I heard that, too. I won't deny it makes me a little uneasy. I don't think anyone could ignore that statement; however, for whatever reason, I feel protection is near. I'm sure Malitar must be in the area but I'm a little surprised he hasn't made an appearance to me by now. It's been a while since our last contact. Actually, I haven't heard from him since I left my home in Scobey, Montana. Also, a little unusual is my grandmother hasn't contacted me by phone since the time in the hotel in Marion."

"Well, I can't answer for your angel but I know for the most part, especially here at the campsite, we don't have good cell phone coverage. Looking at my cell now, there are no bars on it for receiving or sending messages. How about yours? Have you checked lately?"

"Oh, I'll check." I went inside the tent and looked at my cell. He was right. There weren't any bars on mine either. I went back out to where Rann was and showed him my phone.

"You're right. No service."

Rann nodded. "I don't know about you but I'm ready to eat a meal out. How about a date to go out for breakfast in the morning? The sheriff told me there's a fine restaurant in Equality, if you like 'plain, good cooking.' How about it? Are you up to sampling some local food in the morning? Then we can swing by the courthouse and see if there are any new developments in the case."

"That sounds like a plan and I can call Grams. For now, I'm ready to hit the sack. Guess the meeting left me mentally and physically drained. See you in the morning." Cassamie emptied her coffee over the embers before walking into the tent.

Rann stayed outside giving her some privacy settling in for the night. He thought about the scene down at the lake. That had been one big angel standing next to Cassamie. He didn't think he was your usual "run-of-the-mill" angel, if there were such a thing. If he were a Bible scholar, he'd say one who held a high rank, possibly even an archangel. When he thought of Cassamie standing there and confronting the angel, he felt a sense of pride in her spunk. He'd say one thing about her; she had true grit, just as that western movie. He'd seen both the original one with John Wayne and the remake with Jeff Bridges. He liked them both and appreciated the qualities of the characters in the movies. If Cassamie and he needed any character traits for what was probably ahead of them, they most definitely needed some grit.

He went around and separated the burning pieces of wood then kicked dirt over them to smother any remaining sparks. As he tossed his empty beer can in the trash, he detected a distant rustle of leaves near the path leading to the lake. He reached over and picked up a flashlight, shone the beacon in that direction but he didn't see anything. Nevertheless, he went to his car and removed a hammer out of the trunk. It wouldn't hurt to take it inside with him. You never knew when it might come in handy. Hank used to sleep with one under his bed and told Rann it was a fine place to keep one. Thinking about what he heard a few hours ago, he decided Hank was right. It would be a handy thing to keep at arm's reach.

As he turned to walk into the tent, he heard someone call his name. He jerked his head around and saw the angel who had been with Cassamie down by the lake, her father. He walked to the campfire.

"If you don't mind, I'd like to talk to you before you turn in. I know Cassamie is asleep and she won't be able to hear us. I really am concerned about her and I need to make you aware of some important events that are about to begin, events which will affect both of you along with many others."

"OK, come on over to the fire." Rann was a little weary as the angel walked toward him. Yep, he sure was a big one, probably over twelve feet tall but then, suddenly, the angel seemed to shrink to a more normal height.

"I thought the adjustment would make you a little more comfortable. May I sit at your fire?"

"Sure, go ahead. Do you need me to rekindle the fire?"

"It might give some illumination for you while we talk but I don't require it." The angel moved toward Cassamie's chair. Even with the adjustment in size, he was still a large one. Surprisingly, I was reminded of Cassamie by his mannerisms, intensity of his gaze and the movement of his head. In the brightness of the rekindling blaze, I could see his unusual eyes. I moved the embers closer together to feed the fire. As the new intensity of the flames blazed, I could see the angel's eyes more clearly. One was blue and the other one was a light brown. I had seen people with different colored eyes before but his were different. The blue was deep and circled by a silver rim while the brown one was light and had speckles throughout. Regardless of their coloring, they were alluring and seemed to see more than just appearances. I could feel something probing within me as if he were reading me to see what my intentions were and to gauge my character. When I blinked, I could feel the power recede somewhat. Either the connection was broken when I stopped staring or the angel had found what he wanted.

"So, you're Cassamie's father and an angel?"

"Yes."

"Why have you come to her now? She told me this was the first time she's ever seen you. I also heard you say she was in grave danger."

"I've stayed away from her to protect her. Now that our enemy has found her, I had to make myself known to her to warn her and to give my protection. She's in danger along with many others but most are other celestials, or angels.

"I was with Cassamie on the day of her birth and the death of her mother. My closest allies, Malitar and Giselle were with me. We were not too far from here in an old deserted train depot where she was born. She told you, her mother Shelby, died shortly after giving birth to Cassamie. We had called for an ambulance but it never came. Shelby was gone and I hadn't been able to save her. She gave birth to our beautiful daughter, held her briefly then drifted off. Her body was unable to survive the birthing. I know Cassamie has always blamed herself but she was innocent of her mother's death. If anyone were to blame, it would be me for getting her pregnant. I should've known she was too small in frame to deliver my child but it was such a miracle she'd actually conceived. Being what I am, I know it was part of the plan and the events that are unfolding are partly because of that conception. She's a vital part of what is to come. You both are and you're here because of that plan. We're all here because of it.

"What is it that's trying to harm Cassamie?"

"Hell itself and all its hatred. This is a battle between good and evil, between mankind and Satan's forces and we're here to protect what is good and just in your world."

I heard him but it was taking me a while to process what he said. It was difficult for me to believe I was actually sitting here talking to an angel, a being sent from Heaven, a being sent specifically to talk with Cassamie and me. He was telling me we were part of a plan, a plan that involved good against evil, just as some of the Bible stories I'd read, only this time it wasn't a part of scripture but a part of Cassamie's and my life.

"Are you saying the abduction of that child, Sarah Bennington, was a part of this plan and we're going to be battling the ranks of Hell?"

"Yes."

I sat there stunned to hear him confirm my wildest guess as to what was going to happen. To think the possibility of Heaven and Earth being involved in some battle against the evil forces of no less than Satan himself was just too much for me to take in right now or to fully grasp the importance of it all. I know I must have been staring at him.

"Look, I don't even know what to say right now. By the way, what's your name? Surely you have one."

He smiled at me and extended his hand; I shook it as he told me his name was Grinstead. His hand felt normal, like any other person's hand I had shaken before. I looked him in the face, before asking, "Well, Grinstead, how're we involved with fighting the Devil? I guess that's who you're talking about."

"Yes, that's exactly who I'm talking about. I'll tell you more about it tomorrow night when Cassamie can be awake to be part of our discussion. I'm going to leave you soon but I'll be close, so you don't need to sleep with your hammer." At this point, he nodded toward what I thought was concealed beneath a rug by my seat. Then I remembered I was dealing with an angel, someone with supernatural powers. I'd have to get used to that.

Grinstead stood, reached and softly touched my shoulder. "All will go as planned. Get some sleep and I'll meet with you tomorrow night. You're not alone in these woods. There are many like me close by. You've already been made aware of one, Myriad Dupree. Cassamie met her near the airport in a pizzeria. She is also known as 'Mother Nature', a title she finds amusing. Nevertheless, she's always near Cassamie and can protect her. Goodnight for now. Get your rest. We'll talk tomorrow. The child you search for is in good hands and will be joining us soon. She hasn't been harmed. She was taken to protect her from the evil that sought her."

I heard a noise coming from the tent and looked over toward it. Cassamie must have stirred in her sleep. I walked to the doorway, moved the flap aside and looked in. She wasn't up. I could hear her soft, even breathing through the tent divider. She was resting peacefully, unaware of the conversation taking place out here beside the campfire. I momentarily wondered what she would say in the morning when I told her about this visit. I'd find out soon enough. When I turned back toward Grinstead, he was gone. There was no trace of him. I walked toward the trees, quietly calling out his name but there was no answer. For now, he'd left. I walked back to the fire, separated the embers once more and threw water over the burning coals. I started to retrieve the hammer then remembered what Grinstead had said. I left it and went into the tent.

Chapter 22

The Dog watched from a safe distance so those who were holding a vigil in the woods wouldn't detect his presence. So they had foreseen his plan or had deduced he would try to get to Grinstead's daughter. No matter, they wouldn't always be around her. He would make sure his forces kept them busy so he or one of his own would get to the woman.

The man with the woman had great skill but he'd be no match for those he would face. After all, he was only human and mortal. He wouldn't stand a chance against those who would come for him. Now the woman, she posed a different challenge. She was not entirely human for she had part of Grinstead's composition inside her and she had survived this long, even though he himself had sought her out on several occasions. She might be stronger than he thought, a stronger adversary. The Dog was unsure just how much of Grinstead was a part of her or even how it would be affected because of her human traits. Surely her power would be diminished because of being human. Previous offspring of angels and humans had either not survived the birthing, or he had found them. He always remained vigilant in his quest to find any human made from a union with an angel and most of them he'd destroyed yet he found a few worthy enough to join his ranks.

His plan to destroy the spawn of Grinstead wouldn't happen tonight but it would happen soon enough. Now he would investigate what other celestials were near to protect her. It was always wise to know the enemy before meeting in open combat. The Dog "grinned" with satisfaction knowing he would be superior to all he'd detected thus far. He would need to move stealthily through the underbrush of the forest to avoid detection. In this form, he could easily pick up their scent. He would begin by going out in ever widening circles until he found them. Though his basic drive was to strike out at the woman, he knew it would be foolish to do so, on his own. He would bide his time but he would make his time useful.

Suddenly, he felt a strong pull from the underworld; he had to root himself to the spot to withstand the tugging force. After a few minutes passed and he could relax, the Dog turned his massive head toward the heavens and emitted a silent growl. So the One above was flexing his might and causing the underworld to try to pull the Dog back to his rightful domain. No matter, for the Dog would not go back, yet. Though the Dog would be much more powerful as the beast, he knew it was too soon to revert to that form. He would conserve himself for the most crucial time when the battle was fully engaged. Frustratingly, the pull became stronger and he decided to forego his search and return to his haven to gain strength from the deep depths of darkness and evil. With one great heave, the Dog freed himself from the pull and surged forward into the night leaving only a mighty rush of wind.

Grinstead left while Rann had been checking on Cassamie. He liked that about the man, his cautionary manner and concern for Cassamie. He knew Cassamie also liked Rann. He thought she'd chosen well but then it'd never really been her choice. It had all been foreseen so long ago and now the events were unfolding as they'd been meant to do. Grinstead knew she would be safe this night, though the Dog was prowling in the area. There would be no strike tonight because he would learn the celestials were well positioned. The Dog would be at a great disadvantage, although he would boast otherwise.

Myriad was now perched high above the tent in a massive oak. She would send warnings if Cassamie and Rann were in danger but she, by herself could deal with the beast as the dog. When the Dog chose to revert back to his true form and call his legions, then all the celestials would be needed. The Dog's time on this realm was running out and soon he would have to return to his domain far below the earth. Perhaps this time he would choose to remain there but that was highly unlikely. Evil constantly had to seek out new victims. Sadly, on this realm, there were plenty to choose from.

The wind began to pick up in the forest and Grinstead detected a strong presence commanding that wind. He looked to the east where he was sure she would be found. Some wayward branches headed his way but he easily deflected them. There was a small tempest brewing in the forest. Grinstead launched himself down from his perch in the tall hickory tree and landed on the forest floor to stop the whirlwind from heading in the direction of the tent. He recognized the aura surrounding the funnel cloud. He reached out and grabbed the funnel as it swirled near. The energy defused, lost all power and dwindled away until the milky form of a woman remained.

"Eurus. I should've known. Why've you come?" Grinstead released her and she changed into a womanly form, except for her inability to look completely whole. She couldn't hold the shape only the line with a milk-like filling within the boundaries of her form.

"Why do you think I came? I've come to help. I've been in these woods long before you came. I've watched the Dog. I was able to lasso him with the Nyatary rope and hold him for a while but he broke free. I should've used something else. He's come quite close to your child before and he was in these woods the other evening, only feet away from her. I revealed myself to him then and he left. Of course, Myriad was nearby as well, so I can't take full credit."

Grinstead knew Eurus was an important spirit. She was a calming spirit and one that penetrated through barriers, both physical and emotional. Because of her unencumbered form, she could travel quickly and secretly throughout the realms. She used those skills to help mankind and to facilitate the directives of the celestials. She was a celestial but with different attributes and powers. There were many spirit-like celestials and all played an important role in the events of the past, present and future. Eurus was the spirit he would have chosen if given a choice. He felt stronger, knowing she was here.

"I'm glad you're here and thank you for keeping an eye on Cassamie. So, the Dog has seen her before and he was near her the other evening?"

"Yes, she was with the man in the woods tracking, looking for clues for the missing child. He's quite good at what he does for he found the spot where you had laid her to rest, while waiting for Giselle to join you. He figured out the child had not been taken by a man but by something more. He's a smart one, though he was concentrating so much on his tracking techniques he didn't notice me in the trees although your daughter did. She's observant and sensitive to those like us. That would be your influence."

She reached out and touched Grinstead's shoulder and smiled. It was easy for her to reach his shoulder with little effort. She had always been especially tall for a spirit and had no problem floating to reach any height of the celestials.

"It's good to see you."

"Thank you. It's good to see you. Until recently, I hadn't realized how much I'd missed my friends. He shrugged off the sentimental thoughts and asked, "Shall we move closer to the campsite where my daughter and her companion are sleeping? I believe the Dog has returned to his lair by now."

"Tell me, Grinstead, do you see your Shelby in your daughter?" As soon as she asked the question, she wished she could take it back. The pain still looked fresh on his face. She wanted to comfort him but felt inadequate, so she waited.

"Yes, she reminds me a great deal of her mother but she is stronger than her mother. Actually, she is quite formidable for one so young. I fear she doesn't have a high opinion of me. I knew that would happen but it was best I stayed away from her. I'm proud of her. She holds a great deal of compassion for the child, Sarah, though she has never met her. Cassamie has goodness within her. She also has her mother's stubborn streak and is too headstrong. We'll have to watch her carefully. I know Myriad is always nearby and Malitar will be here soon; yet, I worry. It appears I have many things in common with human fathers." He looked off into the forest until he could regain his composure before facing Eurus again.

"Myriad says Cassamie has many gifts and abilities. She should be an asset to our cause and the fight that is coming. I know Giselle and her groups are getting close. In fact, they should be here soon. Should you prepare your daughter for the gathering that arrives soon?"

"No, let her sleep. She'll know when it's time. They need their rest to gain strength. Tomorrow night will be soon enough to confront them. I fear she will do something reckless if I approach her before Rann has had time to talk to her about our conversation. All will be well until tomorrow night. I trust Giselle and Lamechial have assessed the strengths of the child and prepared her for what is to come.

"Grinstead, do you know the outcome of the battle? Have you been given additional information I'm not aware of or, perhaps, Giselle does not know?

"No, I only know we fight for the good of mankind and are allied with those who trust in the plan that was set in motion, so long ago. I believe the objective of that plan is about to be fulfilled. We can accept no other alternative."

He looked at Eurus for a few minutes then reminded her she needed to rest. Her form was fading even more than usual. He told her of a small crevice under the overhang of the ridge overlooking the lake and she should find solace for the next few hours. He wouldn't require any rest and would take over her surveillance. He needed to personally patrol the area where his daughter slept.

Eurus was grateful for the offer and thanked him before seeking shelter. She was becoming weaker and floated to the location in a thin mist fading quickly with each passing second. Grinstead was right. She needed to rest and rebuild her own strength. She would be of no use to anyone if she couldn't stay in form. She found the ridge and gladly entered the dark confines of the deep crevice. Right before she settled her energy, she could hear the approaching group of celestials. She smiled with contentment that the elite were now gathered and closed her eyes for a much-needed rest.

Chapter 23

Sheriff Patton drove down the country road headed home after a long, trying day. He was bone weary and feeling the aches in his joints and muscles. His wife, Molly, had probably cleared dinner from the table hours ago. He'd promised to be home in time for dinner but once again, he was late. She was used to it by now or should be after over twenty-five years of his being in law enforcement. He'd raised two sons on that salary and for the most part, he'd enjoyed his job and had been successful. On the other hand, this case was a tough one and he continued to try to figure out the whereabouts of the child. He had a nagging feeling he was missing something. He was preoccupied with the kidnapping case during his waking hours and sleeping ones, although he hadn't been sleeping much. There had been no more leads on the child. It was as if the earth had opened up and swallowed her whole. Though deep in thought, he noticed the evening shade from the trees on either side spread across the roadway then recede back again. As he briefly watched the effect, it hit him. Why hadn't he thought of this sooner? He was getting old or losing his touch. It was simple, investigative deduction.

They'd circled back. All this time and waste of resources looking farther away from the abduction area and the kidnapper had doubled back. He'd led them on a wild goose chase, making sure they were sighted at different places, providing a ruse they were on the run, while being right under their noses the whole time. The sheriff jerked the steering wheel to the right and did a quick U-turn in the middle of the road spewing gravel in all directions. He headed back to his office, while radioing ahead to contact any state troopers in the area. He had a pretty good idea on the possible location of the child. It was a remote and privately-owned compound in the heart of the Shawnee National Forest, close enough to the abduction site the kidnapper or kidnappers could have walked to the location. He was confident that the owner of the property was not connected, that the kidnappers had trespassed on her land, somehow disabled the alarm system and broken into the residence. It would make a perfect haven for them because of its remoteness from prying eyes. The house was a fortress with high walls for security and privacy. The child could walk outside for miles and never be observed. When they'd checked it out, he would notify the property owner. Hopefully the child would still be there.

The sheriff was one of the few people who had extensive knowledge of this private residency. It was an old, pre-Civil War home renovated by a family with strong historical ties to the area. The property was now in possession of a family member from the east; a wealthy, low-key family who preferred to leave the operations to a local farmer, a long-time trusted friend of the family. In fact, the farmer's family had managed the estate for generations. The sheriff had never been inside the home but the security system of the house was linked to his office as well as a private, top-notched security firm based in Evansville, Indiana. As far as Sheriff Patton knew, there had never been a break-in on the property. Conservation officers were familiar with the property because it was in the middle of the Shawnee National Forest. It bordered one of the most scenic areas of the Shawnee and had paved roadway access. The long, winding drive was secluded and private. It'd been years since the sheriff had even been up the driveway when he had been tracking an injured buck. He found the buck in the thicket not far from the entrance of the drive. By then the animal was in bad shape and had to be put down.

As he contemplated the circumstances, he reasoned somehow the kidnappers had known about the field trip and had made arrangements to park a vehicle in the Rim Rock area. The sheriff knew school field trips were popular. Parent letters would have been sent home giving information about the outing. Those children would talk about it and the information could easily be spread throughout the small communities. With his excitement building, the sheriff stomped down on his accelerator and fishtailed down the gravel road. His next call was to Molly to tell her he wouldn't be home for dinner.

Trooper Edward Turner received Sheriff Patton's radio call and he was only a few miles from the Shawneetown courthouse. He would meet Sheriff Patton there and call ahead for some additional back up. The sheriff explained he would fill him in when they got there because he didn't want anything picked up on the radio. They cut off their conversation. The sheriff was deep in thought as he sped down the road and didn't notice the shape lurking in the woods.

Sarah sat in dumb silence as Giselle finished telling her an amazing story, one about herself. Giselle said she was special and had extra abilities needed in the next few hours. Her blood was the reason for her involvement. She had been chosen because of the special antigens in her blood stream and their ability to merge with celestial composition. That was totally awesome to her. She'd always been treated differently but she had no idea just how different she actually was. This "oddity in her blood", as Giselle called it, would allow her to generate and collect a strong concentration of light energy and direct it toward an intended target. She would need to learn how to call if forward and to control it. Giselle and Lam would coach and train her on this and they would begin when they reached their destination.

That destination had surprised her. It was in the Garden of the Gods area. Tonight, they would be traveling to the Glen O

Jones Lake, at the camping area. She'd been there many times with her family and friends. It was real close to Equality, Illinois. Many of her friends and classmates lived in Equality. To think, she had never been far from home all along. Giselle told her Grinstead had taken her on several circular routes throughout the region to confuse those who were searching for her. One thing was for sure; he had most definitely confused her. She never realized, all along, her parents had only been a few miles away. Somehow that was comforting to her.

Lam told her they needed to leave now. The others had scouted ahead and it was safe for them to leave the tunnels. Giselle and Terrene were waiting in the woods. Lam said there were many good celestials waiting for her near Glen O Jones Lake, including Grinstead and they would all work to protect her from the evil that wanted to take her for its own use. They wanted her because of her special blood and Grinstead had kidnapped her before they could get her.

"So celestials are from Heaven, right?"

"Well, they started out that way. Some of them changed and became evil and were thrown out of Heaven a long time ago."

"Why would angels become evil? I thought they had everything they could possibly want."

"You would think so," added Lam, before scooping her up to carry her more quickly through the forest.

The gathering grew restless while they waited for their leader. They'd all come to the spot that had been selected. It was the part of the Garden of the Gods known as the Devil's Smokestack and was located in a spot beneath a high, mossy ledge of the canyon-like region. This exact spot had formed thousands of years ago as a result of the Laurentide ice sheet that covered almost eighty-five percent of the forest. The name given to the rock formation amused their leader and, thus, he'd chosen this location. Those here had little interest in the names given by man. Such things were of no concern to them but their leader knew the importance of the spot and the role it would play in the next few hours. Perhaps, Chernobog also understood the importance but he was keeping his thoughts to himself. He'd spent the last few days with Jezebeth planning their own strategy, in case their leader might choose to neglect their desires in this upcoming war. Jezebeth had visited this region on many occasions and knew it well. She would be instrumental in the strategic operations of their group.

Apophis curled up beside Chernobog and waited until he was detected. He'd found comfort in the wet, mossy covering of the rock and forest floor and enjoyed the permeation of the moisture into his skin. He'd recently fed on a mouse that unfortunately for it had scurried too closely to him. The extra food would prepare him better for the movements he would soon make. Though he hadn't been hungry, he could not pass up the chance to gain more power from the essence of the rodent. Besides, there were many more from where that one came. This region was densely populated with all kinds of wildlife. He could see himself remaining here for a long time after this battle was finished. As he relished the thought, Chernobog noticed him.

"So, Apophis, I see you've enjoyed a meal. I hope you found it pleasing to your taste." Chernobog found his own comment amusing and belted out a laugh; however, his merriment was cut short by the approach of the Dog. All creatures were at full alert and waiting for instructions. The night sky began to unfold her veil of blackness.

Jezebeth was next to Elathan, the Celtic one known for trickery and debauchery and she seemed to draw some of his vile energy within her. She prided herself in secretly stealing from others and using the gain to bolster her own strength. Though Elathan knew exactly what she was doing, he allowed the transaction. Unknown to Jezebeth, he would benefit from her this by having a presence within her now and he would use that force at the optimum time. He turned his head to smile at his own trickery.

Balan was sitting nearby and observing all the interesting maneuvers. He hadn't earned his title as a prince of Hell by being idle. His skills were superior to all here except for their newly arrived leader. Only Mephistopheles realized his full range of powers and all its potential. Balan was amused by Chernobog's over-inflated vanity of his own powers. Soon he would know how limiting his powers actually were. Somehow the comradery of Apophis and Chernobog had formed but Balan knew it too would soon crumble. He smiled in acknowledgment of this. It would be interesting to see how that played out.

Balan would also deal with Jezebeth. He would enjoy that. She had once been a close companion of his for many years but that had worn thin. Her fickle ways would one day be her undoing. Even in the world of demons, a level of loyalty was necessary. Jezebeth had no inkling of what that meant. Perhaps it was a flaw in her creation or, maybe, part of her demonic composition. No matter, he would soon see how they all played their roles. Some demons were just as malleable as humans. Oh, how he'd enjoyed playing havoc in the many lives he had trespassed against.

Remembering so many years ago, he recalled a dark, deserted, old train depot. Grinstead's mate had suffered giving birth to the child they now concentrated on destroying. Shelby, the mate, had endured great pain in the process of delivering her babe. He, Balan, took full credit in the interference that prevented the ambulance from reaching the woman in time and she had perished. The delight he'd felt as he watched Grinstead, a primary enemy, suffer and completely fall apart had been a major coup for him. Many times, he called forth that memory and gained much satisfaction. He would personally take the initiative in destroying the child, a grown woman now. It would almost be as great a bonus as his previous interventions combined.

When he brought himself back to the present, he noticed Apophis looking at him. He yawned to give the impression of boredom. Let him and all the others underestimate him. It would make the game much more interesting.

The breeze increased in the secluded valley where they all gathered. The ageless trees provided privacy and shelter from the large rock ledge above. Only supernatural eyes and senses could find them here and no celestials were in the immediate area. Balan was at peace. He'd suppressed the gentle tug of the underworld as he was reminded of his quickly approaching return. When he closed his eyes, he could feel the bodiless demons on their ascent to this realm. They would come in handy in dealing with the celestial spirits. Soon all would be in attendance and the battle would commence. It couldn't be soon enough for him. Easily bored, he was anxious to finish this job so as to return to his own amusements. As he looked around the forest floor, he felt an urge to tunnel in and find what lay just below the shallow surface but knew it wasn't possible at this time. *Soon, soon, all will progress, as I desired.*

The Dog interrupted Balan's thoughts. He'd entered their circle and was sitting upon the forest floor, patiently waiting for their undivided attention. As the Dog looked around the assembled, he paused long enough to send out his aura to make sure the gathering was secure with no uninvited celestials nearby. When he called back his aura and was satisfied with the security of the area, he began instructing those in attendance of their exact locations to travel and reviewed the names of those who each would be fighting and destroying. None were too surprised with the role they would play or the names of their opponents, except for one.

When Apophis was instructed to travel ahead to the location of the battle, he was hesitant to leave so soon and unwisely voiced his thoughts aloud to Mephistopheles. Surprisingly, Mephistopheles didn't take offense but merely directed his gaze intently on the snake until he rescinded his earlier thought and agreed to head in that direction. He was forbidden to change his form and had to crawl the entire distance as this form dictated. Obediently, Apophis left the circle and slithered toward the determined location. Because of his supernatural abilities, he was able to pick up momentum and glide just above the surface of the ground. The group watched for a few moments and only Chernobog seemed a little uneasy with the fading form of his ally. His strength and confidence were always bolstered with Apophis's presence. Now he would have no one to watch his back. He began to sweat. Many in this group begrudged his strength and cunning. He was sure none would venture to draw closer to him. So be it. He, the great Chernobog, could take care of himself, alone.

Chapter 24

The sheriff's car came to rest at the entrance of the private drive to the estate. He waited for the two state troopers' cars to arrive along with Noah Drone, the caretaker. While waiting, he thought about the last time he had been here. He remembered it had to be about seven years ago when he had tracked the injured deer. A tourist's car had hit it. The deer had run off into the woods, leaving a trail of blood. A deer incident was usually reported to a conservation officer or ranger but he had been in the area, so he took the call and followed the trail. The deer made it only a few hundred yards before collapsing from loss of blood. It was too far-gone for him to be able to save it and as an act of mercy, he shot and killed it. Looking around, he noticed the upkeep of the roadway was in excellent condition. Ahead, he could see the large steel gates and stone enclosure that blocked the entrance. Sheriff Patton knew the caretaker well and had spoken to him earlier. Noah was unaware the owner was in the area and he agreed to come and open the gate.

He heard the crush of gravel and turned to see Noah pull up in his pick-up truck. Noah got out and walked up to the cruiser.

"Hello, sheriff. I got here as soon as I could."

"No problem, Noah. I'm waiting on the state boys. Sounds like 'em comin'. Glancing down the road, he saw them. "Yep, sure is. Can you open the gates?"

"Yeah, sure thing." He pulled out a remote, pushed it and the gates swung open.

"Just follow me." He climbed in his truck and drove down the driveway. The cars followed slowly behind him. They drove a short distance then pulled their vehicles off the road behind a blind made of thick shrubs and overgrowth. They'd travel the rest of the way on foot so as not to be detected by anyone who might be in the house. Of course, if surveillance cameras were stationed this far out, they'd be seen before they ever got close.

As Sheriff Patton looked around, he marveled at the beauty of the place. This family had to have owned the land for generations, because when the Shawnee Forest was designated and lands purchased, he was sure the government would have vied to own this section. Recalling his history, he knew President Franklin D. Roosevelt declared the land purchases as the Illini and Shawnee Purchase Units to be known as the Shawnee National Forest in September of 1939. There were over 280,000 acres of federally managed lands in parts of Pope, Jackson, Union, Hardin, Alexander, Saline, Gallatin, Johnson and Massac counties in southern Illinois. It was a large section of forestland with acreage spreading for hundreds of miles. The sheriff had enjoyed most of the forest throughout his lifetime and had become somewhat of a history buff on the area. He felt blessed to live here with all its bounty and splendor.

The driveway was a long and winding road and they traveled for over two miles before coming to another stone fence with yet another gate made of elaborate ironwork with the letter "T" forged in the middle of the gate. Noah opened it with a remote and they saw a more cultivated and landscaped lawn. The spacious and rambling house could be seen from this spot. It was made of stone, brick and some treated wood. A long porch ran along the front of the structure with beautiful, floor to ceiling windows facing the circular drive that led to the front door. Lush shrubbery and plants bordered the foundation of the house. An ornate fountain peacefully circulated water at the corner of the house. The house was beautiful and the well-maintained lawns added to the tranquility of the place. Trees planted strategically to provide shade and shelter enhanced the serene setting surrounding the well-manicured lawn.

The sheriff surveyed the area for a few minutes. He told Noah and the troopers he was going to the door. The troopers loosened their pistols from the holsters. The sheriff walked up to the front door and rang the doorbell not expecting anyone to answer. To his surprise, a middle-aged woman opened the door. He recognized her then heard Noah call out a greeting to her.

"Ruby, I didn't know you were working today. I thought you usually took this day off during the week," Noah said, as he approached the porch.

Ruby Elder, Noah's cousin, had worked here for over ten years. She was a hard worker and lived only a few miles from the property. Her husband had been killed in a coal mining accident about twelve years before and she had needed a job to help raise her three children and to help her cope with grief. She, too, knew about the tunnels but had held the secret. They were all paid well for their services and their discretion.

Ruby answered, "That's true but the boss is coming in this weekend and I needed to get things spruced up a bit. What brings all of you out here? Is there a problem?"

"Well," said the sheriff, "that's what we've come to find out. How long have you been here?"

"I came in this morning before six and I've been here almost twelve hours. It's going to be dark soon, so I was hurrying up inside. I think I have everything ready. I had thought about cleaning the windows again before leaving but they look fine to me. This house is so well built it doesn't get too dusty. What are you looking for?"

"Did you notice anything unusual? Has there been a break-in or any vandalism?"

"No, of course not. This house and the grounds near the house have an alarm system. If any intruders came, the alarms would have sounded. Gosh, if I thought someone could get in here, I sure wouldn't come out here by myself four times a week to clean and take care of watering the plants. What made you think someone was here?"

"Just a hunch. So, everything's OK inside?"

"Perfectly."

"Sheriff, I'll go inside and check it out, I know how things should look inside because I come out here frequently to check. You all can search the grounds, Noah said. "They're pretty extensive but you might look out by the creek. Head north over that rise and you'll see it. It's a large one that eventually feeds into Eagle Creek then on to the river. I've caught several large bass in that creek. Good fishing."

Noah knew he couldn't allow the sheriff to go inside. With his training and experience, the sheriff was observant. Noah didn't want to risk the chance he might find that secret passage leading to the tunnels. His family helped maintain that secret for generations. He didn't want to be the one responsible for revealing and breeching that confidentiality. He would look the place over thoroughly and if there'd been an intruder, he'd know. Although he didn't know how anyone could get passed all this technology and security.

While Noah looked inside, the sheriff and the troopers walked around the perimeter of the house then headed toward the creek. One of the officers was concentrating on the ground but found no unusual tracks or obvious breakage in the shrubbery. There was no sign of disturbance. Everything looked as if it belonged and normal. After about forty-five minutes of investigating the property, the troopers left and the sheriff rang the doorbell. It wasn't long before Noah answered the door.

"Everything looks normal, sheriff." Taking a chance, he added, "Do you want to come in and look around?" Noah held his breath, while waiting for the sheriff's expected response. If he gave the wrong one, then Noah would have to come up with something to keep the sheriff out of the east end of the basement. There was no way he was taking him into that basement.

"No, that won't be necessary. You know the residence and would be able to tell if anything had been disturbed. I was just certain about a hunch but I've been misled by my hunches a few times before."

"Did you really think the child would be here?"

"I thought maybe the kidnapper had doubled back. It's been done before and this place is secluded. Hey, this is some place, huh? If my memory is correct, some people by the name of Timothy own it. Your family has been the caretakers for generations, right?"

"That's right; my great-great-great-great-great-grandfather was the original caretaker of the property. Of course, it didn't look this way then but taking care of the property has been the responsibility of my family for generations. Kind of special, you know?"

"That's a long span of family connections. This place has been renovated through the years but I can see some of the original structure of the house. It must be nice to be able to afford a place like this as a second home."

"Yeah but the family is real nice and down-to-earth kind of people. They're from up north, New York City to be exact, so they don't come this way too often. There's nothing uppity about them and I know they're wealthy. Anyway, I'm sorry your hunch was wrong but I'm also glad nothing has been disturbed here."

"Sure. Sure. I understand Well, Noah, I guess I'll head on home. Molly's probably wondering if I'm going to show up at all tonight. Take care. Tell Ruby I'm sorry if I worried her any."

"I'll do that. I sure hope you find that little girl. I don't know her but I know her grandparents real well. Good people."

"Yes, they are. Thanks again, Noah." Sheriff Patton reached out to shake Noah's hand then returned to where he had left his car.

Noah felt sorry for him but gave a sigh of relief he hadn't found anything here. As long as he could remember, there had never been a robbery or any vandalism on the property. That could've posed a big problem and one he wouldn't want to happen during his watch. He went back inside to double-check a couple of things and to talk to Ruby about the homecoming this weekend. He wanted to find out what he needed to do in preparation. Seems as if a woman always finds more work. Anyway, usually Ruby was right about these things. Besides, he wanted everything to be perfect. Just as his ancestors before him, he took pride in doing a good job. This property was a big place and took much time to manage. He believed in working hard and earning that dollar. He enjoyed the privilege of taking care of this fine place, especially when he was appreciated and rewarded well for his loyalty. When he turned in for the night, he knew he'd done everything in his power to make the place as inviting as possible.

Chapter 25

Sarah was a little nervous after Giselle and Lam filled her in on everything. Now that the newness had worn off and she had time to think about what it all meant, she started to really worry. Was she actually capable of all they told her? She never had an inkling about what she really was or that her blood was anything more than a rare disease she had dealt with her entire life. She was also supposed to be highly intelligent and told that was evident by the extent of her vocabulary. Her teachers said her broad and sophisticated vocabulary was primarily because of her extensive reading of all kinds of books. To top it all off, now she was going to be part of some huge battle, fighting the Devil, no less, and all his demons.

Yep, she was getting good and worked up. She had to say it flat out; she was scared silly; but then she knew they'd all be with her, her new friends. Jim, or his real name was Grinstead, would soon be joining them along with a couple of humans with special powers. The woman, Cassamie, was much the same as herself, having some of the same blood disorder, only much more potent because Cassamie actually was Grinstead's daughter and he was a big-time angel. That was totally awesome. The man, Rann, was what the celestials called a "perceptor," one with a high range of perceptive powers or one who could connect the dots quickly and form accurate judgments based on that preceptive power. Giselle said some humans could have extra senses such as that but most didn't realize their full potential.

After they joined Grinstead and his group, they were going to move to another location in the Shawnee Forest, over near Vienna. It was a place called Max Creek. She'd been to Vienna before but she had never been to that place. If she had her phone now, she could check it out on the Internet but, she didn't have her phone. It had been placed in a tree of all places. Grinstead had put it there when he took her from the field trip. That seemed so long ago now and she felt so much older. It was as if she'd aged ten years or more since then. She was learning much every day. Soon, hopefully, it would all be over and she could return home and see her parents. She missed them so much and wondered about them, constantly. She also wondered if when it was all over, if she would be able to tell them what had happened? Somehow, she doubted it. She bet they would do something to make her forget everything. That's usually how it went in the movies. She just hoped her side won and she'd soon be going back to a normal life.

They were all gathered in a small valley to rest for a few minutes. She knew it was for her benefit because she was sure the others weren't tired. Lam had given her a sandwich and a bottle of water. He also handed her a banana, her favorite fruit. It was nice to be cared for by the celestials. They took care of everything without having to ask you what you liked because they already knew. While she ate her sandwich, she looked around their group. There were more here than she'd first thought and they were on their way to meet up with even more. Hopefully, they would have plenty to help in the battle.

Sarah replayed in her head all that had been discussed that day.

Giselle had said, "Sarah, you are a special little girl. I know you soon will be twelve but you are still a child. You've been brave in accepting all of us and we admire you for it. Thank you for your maturity in controlling your emotions. This is a testament of your uniqueness and special abilities. Your blood is rare because of its consistency and its ability to control certain elements of nature. That has not been determined by modern medicine because most humans do not have the ability to comprehend the "specialness" of your blood. We, on the other hand, know specifically what you are capable of doing with this abnormality but what we call a gift."

"How did I get this gift?"

"You were born with it. You had an ancestor, who at some time mated with a celestial. This trait was passed down to you. There were numerous relatives to whom the antigen did not transfer but for a reason, you were passed the antigen. You are part of a superior plan instituted many years ago."

"Gosh, when you put it that way, it really does sound like this all was planned a long time ago."

"Yes, none of this has been coincidental. Your blood was not a fluke of nature. Your blood was a gift to be used for a purpose. Your purpose is the skill you can perform because of that gift."

"What skills do I have?"

At this point, Giselle took my hand and led me to a large, flat rock. We both sat on it before she continued. "You have a highly, unusual gift, one that I've only seen once before, by a celestial. He was destroyed a long time ago by an evil so consuming that none realized the depth of its vileness. That won't happen again and it has no bearing on your abilities. What does matter now is you, too, have the same ability to control light energy.

"If you were older and had more education in the physics of science, you'd know light energy you see is actually electromagnetic radiation. This is light you and other humans can see with your eyes. When humans observe sunrise, they actually are seeing something that happened approximately ten minutes or more exact, eight and three tenths minutes earlier because that's how long it takes the light to reach Earth. Light energy is really a broad range of 'packs' of energy called photons. Your eyes have 125 million rods and cones so sensitive some can detect a tiny handful of photons. The 'packs' of photons are different based on the amount of energy it contains. Some examples of different ones are: X-ray light, gamma rays and radio waves and so on.

"Different photons produce various wavelengths of light. For instance, this is why animals have the ability to 'see at night'. They are able to detect alternative light wavelengths the human eye cannot see. Actually, in pure darkness, it's devoid of any light and no earthly animal or human can see; however, the night has a number of different light waves that exist even though humans are not able to process that energy."

"Are you saying I can see in the night like an animal? Because I've never been able to do that."

"No, Sarah, that isn't what I meant. I know it sounded as if I were leading up to that but let me continue. I have just been explaining the different aspects of light. The skill you possess is, with the right training, one where you see the onset of light, when the energy is first formed and when it possesses the most photons. That energy is in its virgin form, its most vital and intense form. You can harvest it and use it to protect and fight against the evil of darkness. When I say darkness, I'm not just referring to the absence of light but the evil that cherishes and depends on dark acts to cause great harm to others. If the light of the world is goodness, the darkness of the world is evil. Do you understand?"

"Yeah, I think I get what you're saying. I'm going to be able to help in the battle by using and controlling light to fight the bad guys. Is that right?"

Giselle smiled and said, "Yes, you've got it. Now we're going to continue on our way so we meet up with the rest of our friends. Are you ready?" Giselle waited patiently for an answer before heading down the path.

In our group, I counted forty-four including me. Giselle left my side to go ahead and speak to the one known as Terrene. According to Lam, Terrene was a big deal. Evidently, at some time, she was believed to be in league with the Devil. Ha, clever way of putting it if I say so myself. But then Lam explained it had all been a ploy to gather information about the former celestials that joined the Devil's ranks along with the monstrous beings he called forth or converted to his side.

Celestials used many of the same tactics as man in obtaining important information; but much more than humans, they had a broader range of knowledge and, oh, so many more secrets. They knew all the secrets of life but guarded them well. I'd been around them for some time now and all they ever really told me were things about the history of the area. As if I wanted to hear that all the time. Gosh, I hadn't been in the classroom for so long but I sure had been taught science and local history. I guess it all had to do with the reason we were here. My home area was much more important than I'd ever dreamed.

Just then, Lam came up to my side and brought me back from my recollections. I hadn't seen him for a while because he had been busy elsewhere.

"Sarah, we are leaving in a few minutes. I know Giselle filled you in a little on some of your skills. While we travel, I'm going to carry you and help you understand how you'll learn to control your gift, especially your ability to gather and control the force of light. I brought you another bottle of water and a bag of pretzels. I thought you might be ready for a snack.

"Thanks, Lam, I'm a little hungry." I reached out and took the bag of pretzels and the water. I took a huge gulp of water then opened the pretzels. I'd eaten them all in about three minutes but I was satisfied and didn't need anything else.

Lam waited for me to finish then picked me up and placed me on his shoulders. "It won't take long before we reach our next meeting spot. We'll be joining the others and heading to an area where we can train you on how to use your skills. Are you ready?"

"Yes, I'm ready to get this all started so it'll soon be over. That way, I can go home to my parents and friends. Let's go."

Lam patted me on the knees and increased his speed. I was beginning to get used to this way of travel. Wonder what my friends would think if they saw me now? I wasn't so nervous any more about what was to happen. After all, I was in the hands of angels.

Chapter 26

Rann and Cassamie woke early the next morning, dressed and drove into Equality to have breakfast at the recommended restaurant. Both were silent as they dressed then climbed into the Explorer for each was caught up in their own thoughts.

Cassamie slept like a rock during the night and suppressed any thoughts about her father. The emotional shock had taken its toll. She knew she would be discussing it with Rann but right now she only wanted to have a big breakfast before settling into the conversation.

Rann, on the other hand, was a little unsure how to begin the discussion on the sensitive subject. He hadn't slept well for continually thinking about the things Grinstead told him and he'd also worried about their safety, even though Grinstead assured him they would be well protected during the night. He was tired and hoped a big breakfast would restore his energy.

It only took about ten minutes to reach the restaurant, The Red Onion, and he pulled into a spot right in front. It was still early but there were several cars parked nearby. He jumped out and went to open Cassamie's door. For a few moments, she was unaware they'd even stopped but she quickly rebounded from her daydreaming and climbed out.

"Gosh, I'm starved. What about you?"

"Yeah, it'll be nice to sit in air conditioning and be waited on," Rann grinned as he helped her out. They walked into the restaurant and were met by a young waitress who led them to a booth near the front windows.

"Is this OK?" she asked.

Rann responded, "Sure. It's just fine. Thank you."

"Can I bring you some coffee or hot tea?"

They both answered in unison that coffee would be good before settling into the booth. Rann picked up the menus, handed one to Cassamie and they started to read over the selections. After making a mental decision on what he would order, Rann looked around the restaurant. Not surprisingly, he noticed black and white photographs of the area. He spied several locations in the Garden of the Gods, Old Shawneetown and the Ohio River. There were even some framed photos of Cave-in-Rock, Illinois. He'd forgotten how close they really were to that small town. There sure was a lot of history in this part of the state with connections to the past and many events coinciding with those connections.

Cassamie was ready when the waitress returned for their order. Starved, she planned to enjoy all the foods she routinely denied herself. She ordered biscuits and gravy, sausage patties and a bowl of fresh fruit. She even ordered a cinnamon roll to take with her. Rann watched her the whole time with an idiotic smile on his face then he ordered the exact breakfast, except he added orange juice. She would stick to her coffee. The waitress, Kelsie, told them she'd get the order right in, gathered up the menus, turned and headed toward the kitchen.

Rann took a deep breath before plunging in. "How'd you sleep last night?"

"I slept like I hadn't slept in years, deep and dead to the world. I don't remember even dreaming. What about you? Did you get a good night's rest?"

"No, not really. I kept thinking about what happened and your father," he looked at her waiting for her response.

"I think that's why I slept so deeply. It really was an emotional roller coaster for me. Although I don't really expect you to understand what it was like for me." She looked down at her lap and took a deep breath.

"You're wrong there. I know it was hard on you and I can certainly understand why. Look, there are some things we need to discuss and I thought we could drive back to the campground and talk. We really need to do that."

"OK but for now let's just relax and enjoy this breakfast. I don't want to think about anything. I just want to act as normal people enjoying a meal together. Can we do that?"

"Yes, we can do that and I think it's a great idea." Timed perfectly, Kelsie brought out their food and it smelled heavenly.

Both ate as if they hadn't eaten a meal in a long time. The food was delicious, the atmosphere was peaceful and homey and the seating was comfortable. The air conditioner purred quietly as the Freon gas did its magic to cool the area. Plenty of customers kept all the waitresses busy and the food was steaming hot when it was placed in front of the diners. Everyone seemed satisfied with the service and no one bothered Rann and Cassamie, as they ate and shared small talk. Rann pointed out the local photographs on the walls and Cassamie commented on the interesting metal ceiling tiles. They both enjoyed their respite from camping and searching. It almost felt to be a normal day, almost.

After they finished breakfast and nursing their last cups of coffee, a woman and man came into the diner and sat down close to Cassamie and Rann. Cassamie heard another patron address the two as Alan and Rachel. She stiffened in her seat and Rann quickly noticed her reaction.

"What's wrong?" Rann asked with a look of concern on his face.

"I think those are Sarah's parents. Their names are the same and that gentleman who approached their table asked if they had any news."

After a few moments, Rann turned so that he could see the table to which Cassamie referred. The look on the couple's faces affirmed Cassamie's conclusion. He knew that look of despair when someone felt powerless and desperate to find an answer. He thought about introducing Cassamie and himself to the couple but decided against it. He knew they, too, needed a break away from their ordeal. It was clear both struggled to hold their composure. Once more, Rann silently prayed the child would soon be returned to her family. He thought back over the assurances Grinstead had given him the night before but knew he couldn't share that information with the Benningtons. Once more, as he glanced back at the couple, he felt empathy for their suffering and knew the ordeal would soon reach its conclusion. Hopefully, the child would be home in her own bed before too many more nights passed. Indeed, he looked forward to being back home in Midway, dealing with everyday problems, such as what the best meds were for treating a horse's minor colic or administering prevention vaccines. Normal would be good.

Rann looked back at Cassamie and noticed she'd finished her last cup of coffee and had pushed the cup over to the side of the table. He picked up the check and walked to the register to pay. As he pulled out his billfold, he happened to notice a newspaper headline, "Old Conservation Trail at Max Creek Closed." The headline caught his attention because Grinstead had mentioned something about them traveling to an area near Max Creek. When he got back out to their vehicle, he would surf the Net to see what he could find out about Max Creek.

The waitress noticed his interest in the newspaper and told him that the paper was for sale out in a box in front of the restaurant. He thanked her and said he'd buy one.

As he walked back to Cassamie, he noticed the Benningtons eating their breakfast; however, it looked as if they were eating only out of necessity rather than actually enjoying their food. He knew they had no appetite but realized they both needed to keep up their strength. Even in their heartache, they continued to have faith their child would be returned. He wished he could reassure them.

When he got back to his table, he said, "Hey, are you about ready?"

"Yes." Cassamie stood up and grabbed her bag. She avoided looking over toward the Benningtons but wished somehow, she could comfort them. For a moment, she actually thought about going over to them and introducing herself but paused long enough to change her mind. She walked out of the restaurant with Rann following closely behind. He stopped briefly to buy a newspaper from the vending box and moved on to the vehicle. He tossed the paper in the back for future reading.

When they climbed into the Explorer, Cassamie turned to him and said, "I don't think this can end soon enough."

Rann looked at her and shook his head before plunging in full throttle. He faced her and said, "She's OK, you know. She's in good hands."

Cassamie whipped her head around staring at Rann. "What are you saying? What do you know?"

"After you went to sleep last night, your father came to the campsite. He sat with me and we had a long talk. He explained some things to me, Cassamie. Things that you need to hear; things that made an impression on me. All those years ago he did what he had to do because he had no other choice."

"No other choice. I don't want to hear anything he has to say. Why would you believe him? Why'd you even listen to him?" Rann saw the anguish in her eyes before she turned away to stare out the side window.

"When you've calmed down, let me know because we're going to discuss what needs to be discussed. A young girl's life is at stake along with ours and countless others." Rann turned back and started the vehicle. He backed out of the parking space, made a U-turn at the end of the street and headed back to camp. He'd intended to buy a few supplies but decided to pick them up later.

Cassamie meant to remain quiet in her anger. Rann had no idea what it had been like growing up with feelings of abandonment. How could he possibly understand? Yet, her initial anger began to seep away when she thought of the child. After a few minutes, Cassamie cleared her throat and asked, "What do you mean Sarah's life is at stake?"

"We'll talk about it when we get back to camp. I'll fix a fresh pot of coffee and we can talk. OK?" He looked at her and she nodded in agreement. The remainder of the ride was spent in silence.

Chapter 27

For what seemed to be hours, the demons listened to their leader go over and over what each was to do and the celestial or human who each was to fight against. Each insignificant detail had been listed from the particular strengths and skills of their target to their weaknesses. They would concentrate on the weaknesses. After going over the criteria one more time, their leader stopped and looked around the group. All except Apophis were in attendance. Apophis had been sent ahead to their final destination, the battlefield. His responsibilities were not as detailed as the rest, so he had no need to be a part of the rote explanations and strategies.

Jezebeth knew she was to confront both Giselle and Terrene. Terrene would be difficult to maintain visibly. She could quickly slip in and out of form and call on the terrain to assist her. Yet, Giselle would be the greater challenge. She was as quicksilver and cunning in her movements. Her gifts were numerous and she had few weaknesses. Actually, the only weakness was her faith in the goodness of others. If she thought for a moment that good existed in her foe, she would falter in her actions. Jezebeth would use her own skill of trickery to confuse Giselle and cause delay so that Jezebeth could go in for the killing blow. She would end Giselle's essence once and for all. She'd craved for the chance to fight the two assigned to her but she had truly wanted the human woman, Cassamie. She was the offspring of Grinstead and the victory of taking her life would've been sweet revenge against the celestial that had spurned her attention eons ago; however, she would gain enough satisfaction in the end when all had been slaughtered.

Jezebeth knew only hatred for any female with beauty and high cognitive skills. She coveted those for herself because she had once been human and beautiful. She'd also been highly intelligent but, in her time, women were to be silent and follow the commands of those in charge of them; fathers, brothers or husbands. Women had little say in what was to happen in their lives. In the ancient world, most women had no civil or political rights. They couldn't own property because that was a sign of power. Oh, how she'd despised those restrictions at such a young age. Though she'd inherited the brain capacity of her father and had proven her intelligence again and again; she had been overlooked merely because she was female. Her brothers got all the attention and the lion's share of the wealth. If only she could've been as her younger sister; patient, trusting and accepting of all that occurred in her life. For a brief moment, she thought of her sister with tenderness but quickly dismissed it. Jezebeth spent enough time foolishly daydreaming and she must bring herself back to the events at hand. The past couldn't help her.

She noticed Balan watching her again. He'd been probing and trying to read her thoughts. He would fail because she'd activated her personal aura to protect her thoughts from others, even one as mighty as he. Although the use of her aura would deplete some of her energy force, she would keep him out. Though he thought to fool her with his apparent indifference to the upcoming battle, she knew him well. He tried to read all of their thoughts to gain an advantage. His attitude of nonchalance hadn't fooled her for an instant but she'd allowed him the luxury of thinking so. She smiled when she thought of how easily she'd duped him, the prince of Hell. Through the millennia, she became adept at the use of trickery. When one was so much more intelligent than her adversaries, it came easily enough. Her father hadn't realized her skill until it was too late. His death had been the first as a result of something she'd done. Actually, it'd been accidental but, later, she realized it was inevitable. Deeds such as his could not go unpunished.

When Jezebeth was a human child, she belonged to a large and influential family. Her father was a respected citizen of Athens and a member of the Senate. He was an intelligent but harsh man. Jezebeth had three older brothers and a younger sister. She was most fond of her sister, Amintah. Her golden hair and blue eyes set her apart from the rest of the siblings. They all had dark hair with brown eyes as did their father but Amintah looked similar to their mother and had her gentle nature. Jezebeth's mother, Titain, came from an important family. Her grandmother was said to be a descendent of Hestia, the goddess of the hearth. In Greek society, usually three hearths were kept in a home. The third one, placed toward the South, considered a dangerous direction, had a continual fire blazing to ward off evil spirits and used for sacrifices and prayer.

The Greeks believed fire connected Greece to Earth and its permanence in history. As long as the fire was maintained, Greece would have the stability to last forever. Fire made up the center of the earth and gave them balance and security. It was one of the original elements made by the Divine One above and its importance had priority. The flames of the fire believed to be a communion with the deity and each life on earth connected to the fire. Therefore, Jezebeth and her sister shared a vital role in taking care of the third hearth. Both enjoyed making the pots and vessels to hold the oils and fragrances for the flames. Though Amintah's pots were strong and sturdy, Jezebeth's were beautiful and unique. She even made the oil that was put in the vessels, flammable so as to produce the highest flames of any seen in Athens. Growing older, she became well known for her skill. Both girls, along with their mother, tended the fires during the day.

In ancient Greece, women were given the religious tasks and responsibilities and all took them seriously. The fire was guarded at all times by the females in the family and the female slaves. Their flames had never diminished and continually burned brightly throughout the night. Some of the larger elongated earthen pots helped to hold and maintain the heat of the embers throughout the day and night.

Jezebeth had been seven years old when she first realized how little in importance she was considered by her father. One day after he returned from the Senate and was standing at the gate to their home talking to Philemon, another high-ranking citizen, she'd tugged on her father's toga and interrupted his conversation, excited to tell him of the beautiful pot she'd made for the hearth. He stopped her childish chatter by telling her not to interrupt his conversation and she should be taught proper manners. She 'd been shocked with the anger in his voice and embarrassed by the sympathetic look Philemon gave her. She was also alarmed at the look of contempt from her father. She hurriedly turned and ran back into the house. Soon afterward, when her father came into the house, she received her first beating for her disrespect and insubordination. Her mother, Titain, wept as she silently watched her child receive the punishment. Later that night, while gently rubbing salve on the red whelps, her mother explained to Jezebeth, a female's proper place in Greek society. It was a hard lesson but one she never forgot. Her first feelings of hatred ignited in her heart.

Her disgust with the inferior treatment of women in the Athenian society took its toll on her. Girls were not given the same opportunities for education as boys. Young girls were wed at puberty and prepared for their place in society by being taught to weave and spin, make clothes, food preparation and the rearing of children. When Jezebeth turned thirteen, she was wed to a forty-year-old man, one of great cruelty and disregard for his wife. Her father provided a handsome dowry to her husband This dowry was her inheritance, though she would never have any control over the funds. Her husband was not what he seemed. He chose to beat her on a regular basis. When she went to her mother and told of her troubles, her mother promised to talk to her father about granting a divorce. When her father heard of his oldest daughter's problems, her father chose to support the husband. They were connected in business and the returned dowry would have greatly affected that joint venture.

Jezebeth suffered through three miscarriages and was weakened by the physical and emotional trauma of the losses. Her fragile state brought about a mental breakdown. It was at this time, Balan came to her and took her as his own. Together they plotted against her husband and father and, eventually, an accident had taken all of their lives. Finally, she was free from the restrictions of mortal life. She never returned to Athens or tried to make contact with her family.

Today, Balan moved near Jezebeth and touched her on the shoulder. He knew her thoughts were elsewhere but had been unable to read them. She was starting to shake and he needed to bring her back to the present. He touched her once more before she turned to him.

"Is there something that you need?" Jezebeth gave him her most bored expression.

"No, I was just making sure you were with us." He smiled at her and turned away.

Jezebeth looked around and saw the Dog had left his position and headed off to the east. All were picking up their belongings and following him. She reached for the few belongings she'd brought and followed behind the group. Balan had moved up to the front along with Chernobog. Jezebeth knew even now he would be plotting how to benefit from the battle ahead. He was always looking for opportunities. *Even the Dog*, she thought, *should be cautious when in Balan's company*. For now, she knew they were headed toward a place near Max Creek. It was a remote area and was not close to any towns or human habitation.

People did travel to the area but infrequently and usually in the fall of the year. The spring rains and unpredictable weather kept most people away. Heavy rainfall could become deadly in the low-lying areas near the creek bed and flooding was a constant danger. This limited and restricted tourists from the area in the spring and early summer. People waited for late summer or early fall when precipitation levels were usually lower. She wasn't sure exactly how the location had been chosen for the battlefield but both groups knew of their destination. They would travel today and the battle would begin tomorrow. She was anxious to get started in order to finish it. She became wearier with the passing of time.

She wasn't anxious about the outcome but she was tired of the long wait. She spent too much time during her human life waiting for others to dictate the schedule of her life. She craved the freedom to be in charge, to know when things would happen, not waiting on the sidelines for decisions to be made. Even in the world of demons, there was a definite line of privilege. Perhaps soon things would change, even if she had to be the one to initiate that change.

Chapter 28

Surprisingly, it didn't really take long to reach their meeting spot. Sarah looked around and actually recognized the area. They were at the campground of Glen O Jones Lake, close to Equality. She'd been here before on picnics but had never camped out. She'd always wanted to but her parents weren't really the type to camp out. They liked to travel but they always stayed in a nice hotel or condominium. When looking behind her, she saw most of their group was here.

Lamechial lowered her to the ground and told her to wait over at the picnic table. He placed a cold soda, sandwich and brownie on the tabletop. He also gave her hand sanitizer. Gladly she used it and reached for the sandwich. Suddenly, she was starving. She ate the sandwich in a few minutes and started on the brownie. The soda was wonderfully cold. She didn't really understand how it could be so cold because she didn't see any coolers but then she remembered she was in the midst of angels and other interesting beings. The food was here and she was grateful.

Sarah looked around at the crowd and noticed Giselle and Terrene walk off into the woods. Lamechial and the other celestials were waiting around in small groups. It wasn't long until he came over to her to discuss their plan of action.

"Sarah, I want to inform you Giselle and Terrene went to meet up with our allies. Grinstead should be with them. When they've completed their discussion, we'll be joining them. If you're tired, it would be a good time for you to stretch out on the table and take a nap."

Sarah hadn't realized she was even tired but, as soon as he mentioned the nap, she yawned and stretched. She reclined on the tabletop and it wasn't long before she fell into a deep sleep. Lamechial remained close to watch over her. When Sarah awoke, she looked around the campground. Though she'd been here many times before, something was different about it. The trees seemed larger and the leaves were so thick that it was hard to see through to the sky. The underbrush looked so dense she wondered how anyone could even walk through it. It was starting to get dark but it seemed even darker here. She looked back toward the other campsites and didn't see any campers. To her right, there was a campsite deeper in the woods, more remote and she could barely make out the outline of a tent. Why would anyone want to camp at that location? It was away from everything. She doubted the site even had electricity because she didn't see any light or power poles.

Lamechial came and told Sarah it was time to learn the skill she was destined to master. He would help her. The gifts and skills she had, along with two others, were vital to the outcome of the battle. Giselle and Grinstead would be assisting them with their skills. He led Sarah away from the campsite following a path near the statue of Tecumseh, a Shawnee chief, designating the path of The Trail of Tears. The Trail of Tears, he reflected, was named because of the tears shed by those who witnessed the forced relocation of the Native Americans. The idea for cultural transformation first proposed by George Washington and Henry Knox was continued by President Andrew Jackson, a well-known Indian fighter, with the passage of the Indian Removal Act of 1830. The action of Congress initiated the movement of Native Americans from southeastern parts of the United States. The removal included many members of the Cherokee, Creek, Seminole, Chickasaw and the Choctaw nations including a limited number of African Americans. These peoples suffered heavily because of lack of food and supplies, exposure to the elements, sickness and disease along with the physical demands of the long, tiring and tedious journey.

Lamechial knew the forced removal of the Indians, more appropriately the Native Americans, remains a black mark on American history because of the racial actions and the over 8000 deaths that resulted because of the forced removal from their homelands.

His thoughts helped remind him of the injustices that had transpired through the years and inspired him now to end another injustice. He led Sarah to a clearing away from the roads and trails. Here she would need to learn how to hone her skill and capture the power of light. He knew Sarah was unsure of what he meant but she knew he had her best interests at heart and she trusted him. He could only hope she, too, would soon come to believe in their quest.

"Sarah, you must learn to trust yourself and your abilities. You have been gifted with a special and rare power. Few, even among the celestials, have possessed this trait."

"How did I get this trait, this power?"

Lam looked directly into her eyes before answering her question. "You were passed the trait by a celestial."

"Giselle told me somebody in my family was or is an angel." Sarah couldn't contain the utter excitement she felt with this possibility. Giselle had mentioned it and now Lam was explaining it. She was dumbfounded, as she continued to stare at him.

"Yes, one of your ancestors is a descendent of a celestial. Not all celestials are classified as angels and angels are classified by the role of their existence. They are celestials or beings who were created by the Highest One to live in Heaven, to watch and report on the happenings on this realm. From time to time, they come down to Earth to watch humans and sometimes interact with them. Certain humans are able to communicate with them but usually it's only those who possess the biological composition of celestial antigens in their system, otherwise known as their biological blueprint. This means those humans have had celestials somewhere in their ancestry."

"So, you're saying I'm part angel or celestial?"

"Yes, someone in your lineage was involved with a celestial."

Sarah was astonished. She couldn't believe what she was hearing again but she knew Lam wouldn't lie to her. His explanation defined the rarity in her blood and modern science was not able to explain it. So, this was what Giselle had tried to explain earlier. Lam told her modern science didn't have the technology to understand celestial composition. That made sense to her now. So, she really didn't have a disease but had a special genetic composition and one that had been passed down to her through her genes. Those genes altered by a heavenly being. Awesome.

"OK, you said you're going to teach me how to use light to fight off the demons, is that right?"

"Yes."

"Are we going to use any weapons? Do I need to learn to shoot or learn martial arts?"

Lamechial smiled at Sarah. Of course, she would think of fighting with man-made weapons or physical combat. He took her hand and led her over to a large rock for them to sit.

"Sarah, at times celestials do use weapons but that's rare and only when humans are involved in the battle. Celestials are immune to death caused by bullets, knives, bombs and all the other things that humans use to harm or kill one another.

"We won't be fighting against humans, although we will have some humans fighting with us. You are one of them and a woman named Cassamie James and her companion, Rann Steward, will be with our group; yet, Cassamie, like you, is not entirely human and her companion has special skills he learned to perfect and is useful to our cause. We'll protect you and them but you will be vulnerable because of the crucial role you play in this battle. The same is true for them."

"Well, if celestials and demons don't need the usual weapons, what do they use?"

Lam looked away for a few seconds then turned to Sarah and said, "They use light against the darkness."

"You mean earth light or Heaven light?"

"Both actually but you'll learn to capture the light from the sun, stars, moon or reflected light and bend it to your will. That's what we're going to practice now."

Sarah stood up and looked at Lamechial. She was amazed by what he had told her then turned and asked, "What I would like to know is how am I going to capture light, let alone make it work for me?"

Giselle and Terrene hadn't walked far into the forest before they were met by the sentries and led to where Grinstead, Myriad and Eurus were waiting. Grinstead got up from his perch against a tree and walked over to hug Giselle and shake Terrene's hand. It had been ages since he had seen Terrene and he was a little hesitant about how she would react to an embrace. So he touched her by a connection of their hands. Eurus came over to meet the two but Myriad held back.

Myriad was reluctant to face Terrene. So much time had passed since she'd been led to believe Terrene was a traitor. They hadn't been close for a long time but this was even more difficult than she had thought. When Myriad had first been informed about Terrene's alleged treachery, it had tormented her for years. It was unacceptable but with the damaging "evidence," she had been forced to believe it. Now, seeing her, she felt a wash of guilt for believing the worst. Myriad took a deep breath and walked up to her triad celestial.

Terrene read the torment on Myriad's face and reached out to her. As Myriad stepped closer, they embraced and the air charged with electricity. The broken bond was cemented once more and the air around them danced with energy, while the trees swayed in the breeze. The rustling of the leaves echoed the sound of profound cheering. Even the ground beneath them quivered with joy as the two became reunited. Finally, the earth was in sync. Mother Nature once more was aligned with the terrain of the earth and this union forged a strong connection. Pure power reverberated throughout the air and ground; giving the assembled celestials more leverage in facing what was to come. All were aware of the dynamics and symbolism of this union. For a brief moment, even the clouds moved aside to allow the rays from the moon to embrace the group. At this instant, Cassamie and Rann walked into the circle of light.

The humans could feel the electrified air and an energy force moving up from the ground.

"Tread carefully, for we are on sacred ground," Rann said, as he reached for Cassamie's hand

"Yes, I can feel the force beneath me and around us," she answered, while looking ahead to the group before them.

She spied her father first and tensed for a moment but Rann's gentle rubbing of her hand calmed her. Somehow Rann's presence emboldened her and she found herself able to move forward to join the celestial gathering of supreme beings even with her father among them. If what Rann had told her was true, her father had never deserted her but stayed away to protect her. It would take some time to accept this new information because she had harbored such negative feelings toward him for most of her life, at least for as long as she had been old enough to sense his absence. She would try to have an open-mind and hear what he had to say but, for now, she would watch and listen to gain an understanding.

Cassamie's gaze noticed the young girl in the midst of all the celestials, standing patiently, waiting for Rann and herself to join them. What connection did this child have to the group? For a moment, Cassamie wondered about the importance of this child's presence here then it hit her. This was the missing child. This was Sarah Bennington.

Chapter 29

The secluded meadow was still, not a breeze or rustle in the early morning dawn. All was stone quiet. Could it be nature at rest or something more? This land, rarely visited by man or beast, was uninviting and too far from any road or pathway. A few dedicated hikers or athletes knew it. They occasionally passed through the old, deserted conservation track; a track not utilized for over sixty years. Years passed to allow nature time to reclaim the region, which discouraged human activity.

Eons of time before, the site had hosted a battle, one of such magnitude and violence the land was left scarred and desolate for centuries. Good had prevailed but the corruption and vileness of those on the dark side had left a stench, a desecration of the area. Though the passing of time had helped to cleanse the blemishes of greed, jealousy, envy and hatred, the land became marked through the centuries as an area to be avoided. Evil resided here for a while until the purity of goodness, what was right and bound by love, had faced off against such elements of malice and damnation. Many evildoers were destroyed or sent back to the bowels of Hell but some of those representing what was good and just had also perished. They had been sacrificed for the good of all that would follow. They would be avenged and redeemed during another battle, one that would help settle the dispute over the dominion of man on earth. The time was fast approaching.

A sound could be heard coming from the west, headed east. If one would bend an ear to the ground, a heavy vibration could be felt preceding the sound of heavy footsteps and the racket of weapons being hauled over land Also, if one had an acute sense of smell, the putrid odor of burning brimstone and cinders could be detected, causing one to gasp for breath and hurriedly cover the nose and mouth. Evil was coming to the creek bed and valley beyond; coming with a single-minded purpose, one to kill and destroy all within its path.

The Dog was the first to enter the creek bed and look around, as if searching for something. He raised his massive head and sniffed the air then sent out his aura to assess the area for any celestials in the vicinity. When his surveillance informed him none were in the area, he quickly moved on toward the valley, only a half-mile away. Shortly behind him were Balan and Chernobog, both engrossed in conversation. Several creatures followed before Jezebeth entered the creek bed.

Her perceptors, her inner senses, reached out to gauge the region. Like the Dog, she knew no celestials were about. Yet, for just a fleeting second, she'd picked up on something, a faint essence, whispered across the air then was gone. It was so faint she knew it couldn't be a celestial but what could it have been? Perhaps, the long journey across the forest had weakened her for a moment and she had been mistaken. Trying to pick it up again proved futile. She was weary and must be over sensitive to the elements. She wished, briefly, they could use their supernatural forms of travel but knew this would only deplete a large percentage of their energy. That energy must be reserved for the actual battle. Weakened from keeping up her shield to prevent Balan from reading her thoughts, she'd already depleted some of her energy. When she entered the valley, she would rest and rejuvenate her powers and skills. If any celestials were within a mile of her, she would know.

Strangely, her thoughts kept going back to the time when she lived in Greece, during her human life. A feeling of sadness penetrated her thoughts. Sadness? What was wrong with her? Why was she dwelling on human emotions? She increased her speed to reach the destination more quickly for then she could rest and recoup her old self. She certainly had no reason to be thinking of times that had almost completely been erased from her thoughts for centuries. Why were they emerging now, after all this time? It must have something to do with this place. She knew it was important. Otherwise, they wouldn't have been in such a rush to get here. This spot had some imperative connection for the Dog but she didn't know what. This destination was chosen for a reason. He had insisted this site be the place for the confrontation. Even while her thoughts formed within her mind, she noted some change in the air, something causing her to remember and feel human emotion again. She had thought all of that purged from her centuries before.

A soft wind brushed across her face and settled at the nape of her neck. To Jezebeth's amazement, she heard a voice whispering in her ear.

"Yes, you're remembering. You're remembering how it felt to be human, the vulnerability of it and the warmth of human companionship. Remember your mother's love and your sister's; even remember the love you had for your father. He loved you, too. Haven't you ever wondered what made him change on that day? Could something have entered his thoughts, controlled him and led him down that dark path? Ask yourself who would want that and who would want to gain you as an ally?"

When these thoughts embedded in her mind, she felt the breeze leave and travel away from her. Jezebeth stumbled as she started to move again. She sat down on a nearby fallen tree to regain control. She felt chilled and defiled by the suggestion her human life had been manipulated and, perhaps, even her father had been controlled. She had never thought of that, never even had an inkling of that possibility; yet, somewhere within her, she knew it to be true and a feeling of desperation began building within her. She and all those she had loved so long ago had been targeted for a reason, a dark and violent reason. Whatever force had just awakened her to the possibility was certainly not one that belonged to the Dog. She knew it held no link to darkness. There was no intent of evil, only a message of warning. The gentle breeze that carried the message was beyond her skills of detection. Surely, this was a new form of celestial, a spirit in the purest, most innocent form, a newly made spirit, unencumbered by the strands of detection. Only that would explain why she'd been unable to sense its presence.

Strong forces were at work here, unlike anything she'd encountered before. The Omnipotent One was fully engaged in the upcoming battle. Jezebeth pondered the importance of this and what lay ahead. For the first time in her immortal life, she started to have doubts.

Balan knew something was definitely wrong but he couldn't pinpoint it. He felt a breech in the unity of those gathered in the valley, although he couldn't detect its origin. He knew there was no celestial nearby or the Dog would have known. Surely, Jezebeth, with her added skills, would be able to detect an enemy presence. At the thought of Jezebeth, he turned around to search for her and spotted her sitting on a log. She looked different somehow but he was unable to put his finger on it. She'd been totally unreadable during the last few hours. He also knew it was her intent to block him out. She despised the feeling of anyone taking control of her actions; amusing because she'd been manipulated from the beginning, while still human. A sneer crossed his face when he remembered how gullible she'd been then. Not the same being who reclined on a log, now waiting patiently for the next move.

Jezebeth had proven to be a good choice for him so long ago. She'd been useful to him throughout the centuries. She became quite resourceful with bringing misery to the lives of countless humans, even causing events leading to their demise. He chuckled as he remembered some of the suffering fools who had come under her spell. Yes, she would be just as effective in dealing with the celestials who they would soon encounter here and defeat. She had matured and grown adept at so many things. Almost regretting the breech that had formed between them, he looked away from her. He would deal with her in due time. Now, he had more pressing matters to attend.

As Balan continued to think about the upcoming battle, Chernobog had stealthily made his way toward the leader. Balan sneered as he observed Chernobog's maneuvering. If he thought he would gain favor in the eyes of the dark one, he was sorely mistaken. The Dog had only one use for him and it would soon be fulfilled, during the upcoming battle. Afterward, he would be discarded as was fitting for his lowly status. Chernobog was a fool to think he could coax his way into favor of the Evil One. He had no place in the lowest realm as anything but a servant to follow commands. Every demon had its place and he, Balan, far outdistanced them all, for he was a prince to their lowly stations. Soon, they would know their destiny. Suppressing a laugh of triumph as he looked out at the rest of the demons and creatures, he felt far superior to them. He could hardly wait for the battle to begin and that time was at hand

The Dog paused in the valley to await his legions and feeling their apprehension as they approached. This added to the thrill of the moment. He had brought a strong force with him but he knew they played as separate entities, not united. That didn't bother him, for each had been chosen for his or her individual strengths. These attributes would be necessary in fighting. He smiled as he remembered the thoughts of some of them as they traveled. No matter, for they'd fight when it came time to do so; however, just in case things didn't go as planned, he had a back-up plan. He wouldn't be staying around for the onset of the battle but they didn't need to know this. For now, he was confident in the outcome and the group would see that confidence in his actions; yet he couldn't help but remember the last time he'd been close by for another battle. The battle more intense than any other through the centuries and it was the one that determined so many factors afterward. He'd lost legions and had suffered defeat but he'd learned from the enemy's strategy and would put that knowledge to good use during this upcoming battle. Besides, many important celestials had perished and that brought a smile to his lips.

The Dog stopped in his tracks. He detected something; something so faint he almost missed it entirely. The hair on the nap of his neck stood up as he pivoted to face the detection.

Then there was nothing, only a light stirring of the air but there had been something. It was something so brief in form he'd been taken completely by surprise and even his aura hadn't warned him. He couldn't really deduce if it was a celestial but it was something. It was a new form, a subtle and almost completely undetectable form, even for him. He started to shake inside, to tremble so violently the Dog could no longer hold form. The beast was unleashed and burst upon the spot. A torrential rain of fire fell around those unfortunates standing nearby. The demons jumped back to avoid close contact with the Evil One but it was too late. In the beast's frustration and anger of being caught off guard and unprepared, an intense flame burst from his mouth spreading across the meadow with astonishing speed. The nearby demons were instantly incinerated. In an instant, they were annihilated leaving only an oily substance where they had once stood.

The incident caught the attention of all those in the valley. Chernobog was shaken in his tracks, for he only stood a few steps from the unlucky miscreants who met their demise. He was visibly upset and Balan found some satisfaction in his discomfort, yet, even he was affected by the incident. He took a step back to appraise the situation. What was their leader planning? Why the destruction of those chosen to be part of the battle? Was it an intended move or had he lost control?

Even as these thoughts formed, a strong wind burst across the meadow almost dislodging him from his stance on a small knoll. He witnessed countless bodiless demons destroyed. An instant later, a smoky blackout formed and no one could see through the density of the burning. There erupted complete chaos in the movements and actions of the demons. No one commanded them or took control. Screams were heard throughout the darkness of death.

Chapter 30

A peaceful interlude surrounded the group gathered in the woods at Glen O Jones Lake. The day was clear and mild, with a refreshing breeze feathering among them. It had been a long time since such a group of celestials, spirits and gifted humans had gathered. Their mission was of the utmost importance for mankind and all willingly accepted their responsibility.

Cassamie and Rann were seated on the ground near Malitar. Her father was in deep conversation with Giselle, Myriad and Terrene. As Cassamie looked passed them, she saw Sarah beside the cherub known as Lamechial. "Cherub" was not the vision she'd always formed in her mind when thinking of that particular type of celestial. The characterization of a cherub was a child-like, cute and cuddly winged angel, symbolizing love and innocence. Many children's books displayed them throughout the story lines to interest children. In fact, cherubs were used exclusively in nurseries, at weddings and Valentine's Day celebrations.

Ironic there was nothing "angelic" or "lovable" about this cherub. He seemed fierce and strong; yet, he displayed a definite gentleness toward Sarah. Most definitely, the child seemed comfortable with him, as she leaned against him. She looked exhausted. Surely, the child was overwhelmed from all she had been told and from all the training and instruction she had received. Cassamie knew the child needed rest. She could see the wary look in her eyes along with the dark circles beneath them. She needed a comfortable bed to regain her strength and prepare for what was to come. It was good they would be traveling to a house in the vicinity. In fact, it was the house where Sarah had been kept until recently. The child seemed willing and content to return and, evidently, she'd felt safe there.

Rann looked at Cassamie and gently touched her face. He smiled and whispered, "Did you think we would be in the midst of all of this when your Malitar first contacted you?"

"I had no idea it would be anything like this. Every other time he requested my help, it was your usual, 'run-of-the-mill angel-helper duties'." Cassamie grinned and reached for his hand. His close proximity reassured her.

"Typical, when I get into the mix, it has to go haywire." Rann moved a little closer to her and they both looked upward.

Hovering above their group were several, translucent spirits floating effortlessly through the air. Cassamie, continually amazed at the multiple beings in their midst, tried to discern what roles each would play. Although she knew this to be futile, because she had no idea about their abilities, yet, somehow, she trusted each would fulfill their obligations and roles. Some of these beings looked human, while others most definitely looked otherworldly still, she felt no apprehension or fear toward any of them, just curiosity. She moved a little closer to Rann and found comfort in his nearness. Cassamie smiled to herself while realizing the similarity in her comfort with Rann to that of the child with the giant Cherubim. Comfort came from trust and understanding. She corralled her thoughts and looked toward the woman, evidently the leader and the one in charge.

At the exact moment Cassamie concluded she was the leader, Giselle stood and waited patiently until all gave their undivided attention. She encompassed everyone in her gaze before speaking.

"My friends, we leave shortly to reach our sanctuary for our last night to rest and prepare. Early in the morning, we'll set out across the forest heading to the battlefield. We are the chosen force to meet and defeat the Evil One and his league of powerful demons. He has chosen the darkest from his ranks. Those creatures have no love or compassion in their core but only dark and deadly thoughts and schemes. I shudder to remember another time, centuries ago, when such a group formed not too far from here. The battle was long and fierce." Pausing, Giselle weighed the merits of providing the details at this time. She decided that story was for another time. Better to concentrate on the upcoming battle.

"Before and during the assault, we'll continually scan our opponents and take extra precautions to make sure none harbor goodness within. Although this is highly unlikely because they have been under the tutelage of the Evil One, nevertheless, we may find some with regrets or a trace of goodness within. If so, we must spare them and give them a chance and a choice.

"Now we head to a secure location to spend the night before the battle. Use your rest prudently in prayer and meditation. You need to gather all your strength, both within yourself and your exterior. Look around you and see the determination and goodness in each gathered here. Nothing has been neglected in selecting and preparing for this monumental battle. If you are here, it is a testament to your importance in the role you play as we set forward to vanquish the Evil One before us and reaffirm our covenant with the One Most High. Rest well tonight."

In unison the group moved as one through the forest to reach the house that would shelter them for the night and provide a safe haven for their plans, preparations and the much-needed rest for what would come tomorrow. Cassamie and Rann joined the middle of the group near the child. Once or twice, Sarah would turn around and give a shy wave but she never left the warrior angel's side and after a mile or so, he bent down and put her upon his shoulders. Cassamie warmed to the display of affection between them. Of course, the cherub was not her captor and had been no threat to her. Cassamie's own father had been the one to abduct her but she noticed no animosity from the child exhibited toward him. In fact, earlier Sarah had hugged Cassamie's father and held his hand for a few minutes before returning to the Cherub. Perhaps one day, Cassamie would feel some affection for her father but not now. With these thoughts, she turned around and found him close behind her. This startled her temporarily and she reached for Rann's hand. Even with the inevitability of the dangers they faced tomorrow, her heart hardened against a reunion. She prayed she would have control of her mind and heart for the battle ahead with no emotional distractions. She would pray for wisdom and bravery in her actions.

Chapter 31

When Cassamie and Rann walked into the large, inviting family room, the person Cassamie saw standing by the fireplace shocked her and left her almost speechless, while emitting a small gasp of surprise.

"Grams, what are you doing here?"

"Oh, child, it's a long story but I think it's time you heard it." Cassamie's grandmother looked around the group then smiled and said, "I believe my granddaughter and I need some privacy. If you don't mind, we'll go into the solarium. I would ask that someone bring us some hot, chamomile tea to help relax us before we begin a long, overdue conversation."

Then Grams turned to Cassamie, gave her a long, firm hug, took her hand and led her from the room.

Cassamie, still mildly in shock, dutifully went with her grandmother. She noticed Grams was familiar with the house and knew exactly which doorway to take to exit the large room. Cassamie followed her toward the side of the house where a long, rectangular room spread for several feet banked by beautiful, floor to ceiling windows. Outside the windows,

Cassamie saw a lush, plant filled setting. The rolling hills disappeared downward descending probably to a nearby stream or branch of the river. Tall, ancient, oak trees stood as sentinels, ever vigilant on watch.

As Cassamie surveyed the room, the light grays and greens of the décor added to the serenity of the setting. Grams walked to a long, low couch at the west end of the room and sat. She patted the cushion next to her for Cassamie to join her. Grams scooted across the couch and hugged Cassamie. Then she straightened, took a deep breath and began.

"I have a great deal to tell you, my sweet one and perhaps we should've had this talk a long time ago but I was hesitant to tell the story. Any thoughts of your mother have always been difficult for me and I see now I was selfish in denying you those details about her. I should have told you who she was and what happened in her life. I'm sorry for that but please forgive an old woman for the need for peace and shelter from the turbulent events of the past."

Cassamie reached out and squeezed her grandmother's hand before speaking.

"Grams, you owe me no apology. I sensed at a young age it was painful for you to talk about my mother, so I never asked you about her. I always thought I was to blame for her death and I didn't want to cause you further pain. I only wanted you to love me and you did. I never felt deprived of attention or affection. You and grandfather gave me a wonderful life. You were good to me and I always felt loved. Of course, I had a constant curiosity about my parents. The unknown was a challenge for me but it didn't deprive me of a happy life, perhaps it even helped to make me stronger. While growing up, I maintained that need to know about them. I gathered what I could find but it was never enough."

"I'm so sorry, my love but you will know now. You need this information before you go to the meadow beyond Max Creek."

"Max Creek? What does that have to do with anything? And whose house is this anyway?"

"It's our house, Cassamie. It has belonged to my family for generations. My maiden name is Timothy. My family lineage dates to the eleventh century, or at least that's how far back the documentation led. The Timothy name has been around since the time of Jesus. The surname Timothy is unusual today. You hear the name often as a first name but not usually as the family name. If you recall your Bible facts, you know that Jesus had a disciple named Timothy—the name meaning "Honored by God". We've long been sentinels of these woods, the forest now known as the Shawnee National Forest. Your ancestors were here long before the Shawnee chief, Tecumseh, ever stepped foot on this land. He was wise to comprehend the sacred ground but his acknowledgment was because of the suffering and pain encountered by the Native Americans involved in The Trail of Tears.

"You are a descendent of the noble family who was charged to maintain this home and surrounding land for a time that would require our strongest and most vital link to it. That time has come and you are that link; the Timothy, who must face the vilest of all beings created along with his evil companions. First, I must tell you about your mother.

"Shelby Annette Kensington was highly gifted with skills of perception and communication. During childhood, she understood things far beyond her years. She felt more intensely than others and had a depth of empathy for others' feelings. She knew what they endured and she carried the burden of their troubles in her heart. I think, because of this, her health suffered but I cannot be certain. It haunted her and drove her to recklessness at times. Your grandfather and I tried to shelter her. We tried to help and protect her from what she felt and perceived but we were never able to help her enough, unable to fully protect her from her own abilities.

"When she reached junior high age, her gifts were almost more than she could stand You know how mercurial young adolescents' moods can be and Shelby was often tormented by the problems that arose from all those young emotions. After a while, she realized the need to protect herself from the pain of others and she began to distance herself. By the time she was in high school, she only allowed a few friends into her life. She became somewhat of a loner by the age of eighteen. When she graduated from high school and attended college at Harvard, she completely severed her childhood friendships. It was as if she wiped the slate clean of her former friendships. Although she made friends in college, she learned to be detached and screen all the baggage that goes along with friendships. Most of the friendships she allowed were shallow, nothing developing into long-term loyalty and trust.

"She came home for the holidays and we'd go for regular visits with her. She looked healthy and well adjusted. She never complained about any troubles. We were confident she was enjoying her college life. She seemed involved in her studies. Your mother majored in Anthropology with a minor in Art History. She could talk for hours about the characteristics of certain races of people and what had contributed to their race and thus helping form their culture. When she came home during her breaks, she would flock to the New York museums and art galleries. She seemed to have a mission and was searching for something.

"One particular Christmas break, she seemed possessed with a line of research she had started, involving the Biblical interpretation of the strife that occurred between the heavenly angels and God. She spent hours at the local university libraries digging for any data she could find. You must remember this was long before the Internet, requiring only a touch of a few keys to retrieve information. She would come home carrying satchels filled with old books and manuscripts. At one point, I remember her asking if she could go to Rome and try to access the documents at the Vatican. Your grandfather thought she was getting too involved in her studies. He basically told her that and to the best of my memory, it was the only argument I ever remember the two having.

"I know your grandfather was upset and the next day your mother went back to Harvard, a full week earlier than she had planned. She got over being mad but she never again brought her work home with her, or at least she didn't do it in our presence. Although we knew she was still deeply involved in whatever she had been researching; she never again mentioned her desire to go to Rome. After a while, she seemed to be her old self. She came home often but she stopped discussing her studies and projects. One late night, she received a phone call on our home line. She appeared agitated and the next morning she headed back to Harvard. She told us she had to meet with someone regarding an avenue of research. That was the last time your mother came home.

"We went to see her in Boston but she was preoccupied and involved in her work. She told us she was getting ready to travel to Montana with a research partner and would be away from a phone at times but she would contact us when she could. She hugged us both, told us she loved us and would talk to us soon. We never saw her alive again. Seven months later we were called to a small-town morgue, actually not far from here. For some unknown reason, Shelby had traveled from Montana to this area. The authorities notified us and we had to identify her body. That was when we learned we had a grandchild, you, my precious one."

"Montana? What was my mother researching? From what you've said, she seemed totally absorbed with it. Also, she must have been pregnant with me when you saw her the last time but she wouldn't have been far along. Were you aware of her condition?"

"Yes, you're right, she had to be pregnant with you but I'm a little ignorant of her gestation period. No, I didn't realize she was carrying you and, under the unusual circumstances, I had no idea how many weeks she carried you. Perhaps we can find out when this is all over. I know you have so many questions and so do I. We'll find our answers soon enough."

"Grams, what does all this have to do with this house, this place in southern Illinois? Have I been here before?"

"I mentioned earlier, this property has belonged to my family for generations. Our ancestors were here to keep watch over this region. They were protectors or guardians with responsibilities to provide a sanctuary for those who would need it. To answer the second part of your question, yes, you've been here before but you were young at the time. We had attended a family reunion at Cave-in-Rock, a small river town not too far from here. That was the time you got separated from the rest of the children and your grandfather found you in the cave. Do you remember that?"

"Yes, I do, Grams, clearly. I've never forgotten it but I don't remember anything about this house."

"That's not surprising because you were asleep when we came here after the reunion and we loaded you up in the car early the next morning and headed to the airport. You didn't fully come awake until we pulled into the airport parking lot. We had to dress you in the car before returning the rental. You must have been exhausted from your excursion with your cousins. You slept for over fifteen hours."

"Well, that would certainly explain it but why'd we never come back here? It's beautiful and so peaceful. I would have enjoyed this region."

"Yes, you would have but it needed to stay secretive. I came many times throughout the years because I was the responsible Timothy until now. You will now have that role. I'm passing on your legacy, your responsibility. I have faith that you'll be a good steward of this region; however, I must explain some important details to you so you have a complete understanding of your inheritance.

"Grams, I've met my father. He's nearby. How much do you know about him?"

"Are you asking if I know he's an angel? Yes, I know."

Cassamie gently shook her head. "Today has been one of surprises. That's what you meant by not knowing about the length of the gestation period. Go ahead and tell me what you need to tell me." She reached over and picked up the cup of steaming tea that had been brought in earlier. It was delicious and she could already feel herself relaxing. She noticed her grandmother did the same before continuing. Cassamie was completely baffled that her grandmother was somehow involved in all of this but just how deeply, she had no idea. She was about to find out.

Her grandmother cleared her throat and began. "Cassamie, I'm not sure how extensive your knowledge of ancient history is but I've a pretty good idea it's rather extensive because of your inquisitive, journalistic mind. You know you were given the surname of James, one of the names of my ancestors. My ancestral records date as far back as the time of the Crusades and the attempt to recapture Jerusalem from the

Muslims. If you know anything about the Knights Templar, you know they commanded a large fortune that was sought by those jealous of their privileges, including many of the papacy and those outside the papacy. What most did not know was inside the Templars was an elite group that guarded Christian artifacts. This secretive group was known as the Timothies, hence, my family name. Eventually, most of the artifacts were delivered to the safe keeping of the Vatican vaults but some were kept shrouded in secrecy. Many wars were fought in attempts to obtain the documents and artifacts but, because of the groups' connections and resources, the Timothies have maintained possession of those artifacts."

"Grams, what are you involved in? What are we involved in?"

"I'll tell you everything but for now it can only be an abbreviated version, for at the present, our time is limited." Her grandmother cleared her throat, took a deep breath then continued. "We are guardians of artifacts known as the Triads of Good and Evil. These relics are actual coordinates of latitudes and longitudes, of ancient dates and sites of battles, clashes between the Light and the Dark. It's an ancient compass that has led those marked as participants to proceed to the locations of conflict designed millennia ago. There are additional relics and another of even more importance and in time, I will reveal it to you, however, there isn't enough time now.

"You know that a triad is a group of three. Throughout human history, the number three has always held great importance and symbolism. Even children's fairy tales utilize the principal of three. In the Christian faith, you understand the importance of the Trinity. In the darkest realm, they have their own interpretation for the number three, by doubling it, grouping it and using in triplicate. They've pitted themselves against the light since the Fall of many from Heaven.

"The Timothies have protected these triads with their lives for centuries. My father and his father before him and so on have continued to uphold their responsibility and duty. Throughout most of our tenure, little has happened except to hold the secret and the artifacts safely, however, I'm afraid your time will be an active and potentially dangerous one. You'll have help from the highest level and all the resources you require but there'll be danger and temptation. You must follow your heart and that great brain of yours; yet, even then, the challenges will be difficult. I have the utmost confidence in your skills and abilities. Are you willing to take on the responsibility that has been handed to you?"

"Grams, do I really have a choice? From what you've told me and the events that have recently occurred, I'm already involved. Anyway, I was brought here for a reason and I'm prepared to uphold my responsibilities. I'm overwhelmed with what you've told me but from what I've experienced throughout my life, especially most recently; I can't say I'm surprised by any of it. Even as a child, I knew there was something unique about our family. I always knew of your special skills of forewarnings and predictions."

"Yes, I knew of your awareness about many of the events of the past but I never saw the need to discuss them with you. I wanted you to learn on your own so I wouldn't be able to sway you in the decision that would, one day, be yours to make. That day is today and you've freely accepted your responsibilities, without my leading you to do so. That is a relief to me."

"Go on, Grams; tell me more about our family, our role as guardians."

"During the conflict between the Muslim Turks and the Crusaders, a branch of the Knights Templar took refuge in the underground caverns and passages beneath the temple of Jerusalem. Most of the wealth of the Templars was accumulated through their gifts from the Church, the many spoils of battle, such as precious stones and gold, the golden artifacts of the temple and earnings accrued from various kingdoms over decades. These amassed into a huge fortune, one even kings and factions of the Church coveted and plotted to possess. Hidden within these valuables were the elite Timothy's most guarded relics. The normal eye wouldn't recognize what they were. Only the trained eye would know them and be able to translate the coded messages. The compass was useless to the uninformed. This is what helped to safe guard the secret.

"One of our ancestors, Sigmund Orleans Timothy, was responsible for protecting the precious relics and maintaining their secrecy. At the time of his mission, he was thirty-seven years old, a married man and father of eight. His eldest son, James, your namesake, was a member of his battalion, with the duty of tending to the horses. He possessed a gift of communicating with horses, as you possess a gift for communicating with people and angels. Today, he would be called a horse whisperer for it was as if he could read the animal's thoughts and needs.

"A knight's horse was invaluable to him. He couldn't survive without a healthy, well-trained mount. For weeks at a time, the knight's only companion was his horse. The trust and dependence between the two were a bond as no other. James's services were priceless to the Timothies and his life was well guarded by the group.

"James suffered from an affliction of periodic seizures. When he was seven years old, he had a fall from a tree and landed on his head. He lay for weeks in bed struggling between life and death. The injury caused swelling of his brain. For five weeks he went in and out of consciousness but, miraculously, he survived. He appeared to fully recover, except for periodic bouts of mild seizures. Another difference was observed much later when he developed an unusual ability to communicate with horses. He could calm any stallion and was able to ride any horse while others were repeatedly thrown. The Templars, of course, treasured this gift and he was invited to join their journey to Jerusalem. At the time of the second Crusade, James was only twelve years old, a mere boy.

"Because of his skills, the Timothies protected him well, yet he was captured by Saladin, the Turkish leader and taken deep within the enemy camp. Saladin, a true lover of horses, had heard of the young man's success with the wildest of steeds and wanted to learn the secrets of his skills. He showed kindness to the young man and offered him friendship. Unfortunately, during his time of captivity, James suffered one of his seizures and flounced around on the ground. Shocked by what he saw, Saladin decided that James was possessed by demons and had him carried away and confined under guard.

"Days later, when James had control of himself, he realized the grave danger of his imprisonment. Being a bright young man, he quarried out a large stone from the wall and faked another seizure. He lay still as if dead. When the guard came to check on him, James knocked him out with the stone and escaped. He quickly found the stables, chose a golden stallion with a white star on his forehead and mounted the horse without bridle or saddle. Unknown to him, this particular horse was Saladin's favorite mount. The horse plunged forward and bolted across the compound, clearing the gates by a powerful jump. Horse and rider flew across the land to the Templars' stronghold."

"How old was James at the time, Grams?"

"He was only sixteen but held the maturity of a grown man. Remember in those times, young people were expected to act like an adult at an early age. Some even married and began families. Life was hard and demanding even on those so young. The life span during this time was much shorter. Even at sixteen, he was approaching middle age."

"Yes, that's right. What happened next?"

"He was able to provide the Templars with strategic information regarding Saladin's fortress and the Templars were able to defeat the Turks during this battle. James's contribution was invaluable. You may have guessed. Your surname was given because of this James. A name is a vital tool and holds much influence over an individual. The name James is a powerful one. Some of its meanings are: honest, benevolent, brilliant and a leader. You are all those things, Cassamie and so much more.

"Let me continue. From that time on, our family was fully immersed in the quest to free Jerusalem from the control of the Turks. Many Timothies gave their lives for the cause and were instrumental in taking the relics out of Jerusalem to safety. Those events led to this time and place.

"Soon another battle is going to take place at Max Creek and you, my child, will be in the thick of things. I pray you'll be well protected. I won't be traveling to the battleground but will remain here with a few reinforcements for security. You must eat heartily and get your rest because you leave in the morning. The trip is through the forest and valleys and you will cover about twenty-five miles on foot." Seeing the questioning look on

Cassamie's face, she added, "Even supernatural beings must reserve their energy. So, they will walk instead of using their powers."

"That makes sense. I'm in shape, Grams and I'll be OK. I plan on getting to bed early and it'll feel wonderful to sleep in a bed. It seems so long ago when I last had a proper bed. It's as if I've been traveling forever but it has actually only been a few days. Of course, I've had some help and someone has been working with me. Have you met Rann, Grams?"

Before her grandmother could answer, there was a quiet knock on the doorjamb. Cassamie and her grandmother both turned to see Giselle standing in the doorway.

Chapter 32

Around the valley, destruction could be seen throughout the field. Singed grass and burnt ground cover smoldered in the light breeze. The outer standing trees were unharmed but the stench was everywhere. The valley was surprisingly quiet. The birds and animals had left the area before the burning began. The remains of many demons were evidence of the destruction, which quickly became absorbed in the earth. Soon, nothing would remain to mark the spot. Sounds of moaning could be heard coming from those that had survived but they would soon heal.

"What just happened? How many destroyed? Where did Mephistopheles disappear? Has he deserted us before the battle even begins? Why bring a fiery destruction to some of his chosen team?" These thoughts bounced through the minds of those remaining.

Jezebeth survived the sacrificial cleansing without any damage. As she looked around, she saw many had not survived. She wondered why the sacrifice of demons was necessary to the

Dog. Where had he gone? The brief period of total blackout did not upset her. She had witnessed them before, especially with a large group of demons in attendance. The Dog used this method to confuse and disorient them. She just wondered why now? It didn't seem practical to destroy some of the beings who would be needed for battle but then she understood his trick. He was gaining energy from the demise of those of lesser importance. He hoped to strengthen the remaining ones with the distribution of new energy. *An effective plan but not one I would sanction. Listen to me. Am I regaining a conscience?*

The darkness lifted. Chernobog felt a resurgence of power vibrating throughout his body. He encountered a strong jolt that rooted him to the spot where he stood. He couldn't move. Though he used his tremendous strength and threw himself forward, he was thrown back into his standing position, unable to move. Time and time again, he tried to free himself from this hold but he failed each time.

Balan could see Chernobog's struggles but he was powerless to help him. He could move but only a few inches at a time. For every step he took forward, he would be transported back to a spot close to where he started his forward movement. *What is going on and where is our leader?* As he looked around the valley, he couldn't find him anywhere. *Why did he allow this to happen? It has to be part of his plan but why?*

Jezebeth remained on the fallen log, waiting and watching. She knew better than to fight against the forces working here. She wasn't entirely certain these forces belonged to the Dog. Perhaps this power was not from the lowest realm. Perhaps she was witness to the powers from above, the highest realm. She tried to remember back to her days as a human and the beliefs that her family shared. Her family had been religious and practiced the worship of the Goddess of the Hearth. She remembered their worship of a higher being that created the goddess but the goddess was her family's main deity and Jezebeth's training was based on that belief.

Now she wished she knew more about the One that held all the knowledge of their worlds. Always her information about him had been tainted by the beliefs of others—her parents then the cohorts of the Dog. Through the years, she watched the

Christian religion sprout, grow and spread throughout the nations. She briefly studied the Bible during one century but she had put it away when Balan ridiculed her. She knew more about the one known as Jesus than she did the Maker of All Things. She really knew little about the Omnipotent One. In pondering, she realized she would probably experience the full wrath of the One above, for she was sure this power was superior to her leaders. These thoughts played out in her mind and she, once again, felt the ever so subtle presence of another. She still couldn't discern what it was but it definitely was something. A spirit unlike any she'd encountered before. This one was almost entirely immune from her detection. She sent out her aura but it returned without any knowledge of the spirit. The only possibility was this spirit was newly formed and had never had its essence in the presence of the demons or the Dog. She wondered what kind of spirit was so undetectable, even by their mighty leader. He couldn't have known of its presence or he would have been prepared. He would have forewarned them.

As Jezebeth contemplated these thoughts, Chernobog and Balan continued to struggle against the forces working against them. Both were beginning to tire and each could feel their energy and auras draining. Never before had they been so overpowered that total movement was suspended. They desperately tried to summon their leader without success. The sun was starting to set and the battle would begin soon. *How could we fight with our movement so restricted? Would we be left as sitting ducks?*

Chernobog turned to Balan and called, "Where is our leader? What do you know of his plans?

At any other time, Balan would have gained great satisfaction from the fear in Chernobog's voice but he knew if he spoke, the same fear would be detectable in his own voice. He looked over his shoulder and saw Jezebeth resting on a fallen log. She looked somewhat peaceful, as if unaffected. Though he tried to attract her attention, she wouldn't look at him. Could she possibly know something he and Chernobog didn't know? That was impossible. She was his follower. She couldn't know more than he himself knew. After all, he was a Prince from Hell. The Dog would not overlook his superiority to choose her. Something was going on with her but he wouldn't worry about it now. He needed to concentrate his strength in freeing himself from this ridiculous hold.

Where were they? This was a valley but he saw or heard no creek or water source nearby. It couldn't be the battleground. Not here in the open. There was no element of surprise and nothing to hide behind before striking out. Balan looked around the perimeter of the valley. He could see a trail leading into the trees. He would send his aura out to follow the path and see where it led. Calling it forward he commanded it to seek out where the trail led. His aura, though weakened, floated across the field toward the pathway.

Chernobog expected no answer from Balan. He could sense even the mighty Balan was helpless and just as ignorant of the circumstances as he. He watched Balan try to get Jezebeth's attention but it was a futile attempt for she had distanced herself from them days ago. She was not concerned with their plight and would offer no assistance. The only one who would provide any help to him was Apophis and he had no idea of his whereabouts. Apophis was sent ahead days ago and no one to his knowledge had heard back from him. Chernobog began to feel a deep hysteria building inside. He hadn't felt this helpless since created from the bowels of Hell, called forth from the deepest, darkest region of the eternal fires. His essence forged with fire, magma, sulfuric minerals, brimstone and ashes. The Evil One called him up, molded him and commanded his service. From that night forward he had been confident of his strength and abilities. Now he held no such confidence for his maker had left him defenseless. What of the other demon reinforcements?

Balan abandoned making any progress across the field and decided to sit and wait for the return of his aura or the Dog to appear again from whence he'd gone. Balan knew he would return. For some reason, their leader had decided to leave them. Perhaps, he was testing them, once again. Balan was not afraid. He had confidence that the Dog would return for they would need him. No sense in worrying. The battle would require his services along with Chernobog and Jezebeth's. The few insignificant ones who perished were of no consequence to him. He decided to relax and await his master's return. Surely, he would return soon enough for the battle commenced on the morrow. Perhaps he should rest, not worry and regain energy. He sat down in the middle of the field and folded into himself.

Balan dreamed, a novelty to him because he hadn't dreamed for as long as he could remember. Unlike Chernobog, he had been human, long before Chernobog had been forged from Hell. Balan became a Prince of Hell as a reward for the deeds he performed by his human hands. Even as a young child, Balan lacked the ability to love and be loved. His parents were little more than uncivilized barbarians living on cold and barren lands of what is now known as part of the continent of Asia, near Siberia. His people, his tribe, were nomads traveling on hunt for the giant animals that roamed the earth so long ago. The giant mastodons, the prehistoric link to modern day elephants, were their chosen food source. These huge mammals traveled along with many dinosaur species and provided a huge source of food. Bringing one down required skill and astute cognitive acumen. His own father, a master of the feat, trained Balan in the process. Of course, at this time, he was not known as Balan. The Dog bestowed that name upon him, before he was known as 'Latar'.

At a young age, something was missing in his human make-up. He had no sense of right and wrong, no particular feelings of love for his parents or family. He only felt the need to learn as much as he could so he would be superior to others. Even his own father was no exception to his lust for what belonged to others. He listened to his father because he wanted to learn from him. When he learned all his father had to teach him and far exceeded his father's capabilities, he killed him. Taking all his earthly belongings, he left the familiarity of his tribe and ventured eastward.

He traveled through the biting cold, always headed eastward until one day he came to what later became known as the Bering Strait, the land bridge between continents. He crossed over the bridge and traveled into the continent today known as North America. He had been mortally wounded by a charging

Mastodon and left to die. The Dog came to him and offered him immortality. But there was a price, a high price. Latar had to agree to a total surrender to the demands of the Dog but he would live, though through a different channel of life. With little thought given, he agreed and became Balan, a prince of Hell, a servant of the one most evil. Balan, remembering these events became bored and fell asleep.

The spirit floated across the valley effortlessly. Phyllison, a newly formed spirit, was an angel of secrecy and almost undetectable by those of evil thoughts and deeds. She recently died from complications brought on by long suffering because of a disease. While human, she devoted her life to her faith in Jesus Christ and his Word. She suffered in pain and affliction for over twenty years but continued steadfastly in her faith. God guided her from her pain and brought her into eternity. Because of her blind faith and devotion in her Earthly life, He had chosen her to participate in this battle of Good against Evil.

Phyllison penetrated the enemy's camp in search of an inkling of goodness in these creatures and to turn some of the blackness against itself. She would seek out any goodness that might dwell within those working for the dark side. She detected something in the beautiful beast known as Jezebeth. Though evil for centuries, Jezebeth surprisingly maintained some human emotion—love. This love would be crucial in helping the celestials that would soon arrive.

When Phyllison first noticed Jezebeth, she was reminded of her older sister, Bonnie, who fought temptation throughout her life but had succumbed on many occasions. Phyllison knew the goodness in her sister's heart but for her it had not always been enough. If she could have only convinced Bonnie to buffer her heart by learning more about Christ and his teachings, then she would have strengthened her faith and resisted temptations. Phyllison had a loving and forgiving spirit. She had never been judgmental but supportive of what was right and good. Sadly, she felt she had failed her sister somehow and would try to make amends by leading this lost creature away from the darkness. To convince the demon to turn from the evil ways of the Devil and his minions of damnation, she called upon Jezebeth's memories of long ago.

Chapter 33

Cassamie slept soundly without interruption and was anxious to start the day. It was barely daybreak but she heard commotion throughout the house. When she walked to the window, opened the shade, she saw Giselle talking to one of the larger creatures that was now dressed in what appeared to be some kind of protective gear. Evidently, even these beings took precautions. She walked to the door and headed toward Giselle.

"Oh, there you are. I hope you rested comfortably. Your father has gone to see about Sarah then we should be leaving shortly. Have you seen Rann yet this morning?"

Cassamie looked around the compound and saw no trace of him, before answering Giselle. "No, I haven't seen him yet."

"He must have gone with Grinstead to help Sarah. Come and meet some of the group who haven't been introduced." Giselle extended a hand toward the huge creature. "This is Minnjatar, an important scout. He's been out in the field for days and has just reported on the whereabouts of our adversaries. They have already neared the battleground."

"The battleground?"

"Yes, Cassamie. There will soon be a battle, one that will put an end to this quest of the black force. We'll soon head in that direction and you, Sarah and even Rann will be a vital part of our defense, though you will not participate in the actual fighting, if it comes to that. When we get close to our destination, it will be revealed to the three of you what your role will be. Sarah has been told little but she has had instruction on how to use her gifts. These will be crucial at the end."

Cassamie was startled by what she was hearing but she had been expecting some involvement in their quest. She deduced earlier that she was brought here for a purpose and was prepared to do whatever was necessary. When Malitar first contacted her in Montana, she knew she would have a job to do. She just never expected it to be of this magnitude. She now realized what the events of her life had been leading up to; this was the top of the iceberg. She just wondered what specific role she would play and how Rann would be used. She didn't ponder too much about Sarah because she had been a pawn in this all along. Her role was critical to what brought them here. She knew if she waited patiently all would be revealed soon enough.

Taking a deep breath, she turned directly to face Giselle and said, "OK, when do we start?"

"We start now." Giselle reached for Cassamie and squeezed her hand "Remember, you too have celestial within you. This is what will be used to help ensure our victory. You've been led to this point from the beginning of your life. It is your destiny. She smiled warmly and said, "Come, follow me." She released Cassamie's hand and walked away.

Cassamie had no choice but to follow. What she was walking into, she had no idea, except to acknowledge it would be life changing.

As they turned toward the back of the compound, Cassamie spotted Rann, Sarah, her father and Lamechial, or at least she thought it was Lam. He was much larger than when she had first witnessed his transformation. It was hard to believe a small, cherub-like creature could actually change into this huge, fierce, powerful being but then again, she reminded herself celestials were not restricted with human frailties and limitations. Today, she'd be dealing with divine beings created by the Almighty God. Through him, all things were possible. She wouldn't need to remind herself again. Things were much different now and her life was starting to finally make sense.

Rann turned and noticed her walking toward them. He went to meet her and gently touched her face as she neared him. He wanted to take her in his arms but they had an audience and now was not the time. As he studied her face, he saw a strength and determination that hadn't been there earlier. She looked as if she'd resolved something in her mind and was at peace with it. Her skin glowed with the rays from the sun and her beauty seemed to intensify. How had he missed that look before? She was the same, yet she was different. Her nighttime sleep seemed to restore her but there was something more he couldn't quite pinpoint.

She looked up at him, smiled, gently touched his hand, slowly placed it to her lips, skimmed a soft kiss across his knuckles and gave him a dazzling smile.

The interchange between them did not go unnoticed. Grinstead stared before turning away. He hoped the feelings growing between the two would have a chance to flourish but he knew of the danger they would soon face. The Dog would do his best to harm Cassamie, as a move to get at him. Grinstead would keep close to her and protect her at all costs. Now that he had finally reached out to her, he would do everything in his power to keep her safe. He wanted to know her and make up for all the years that kept him from her. He had a lot to catch up on. He felt a hand on his shoulder and turned to see Giselle standing beside him.

"We'll keep her safe, my friend. You haven't just found her to lose her again. She is strong and the gift is fierce within her. I can feel it. I'm surprised you haven't."

"I know she's strong. I can sense the power within her. She is different today and I think even Rann can feel that difference. The powers have gathered today. I must trust the forces are enough to defeat this beast and his hideous minions. Yes, I know her gift is strong and her inner glow is noticeable today."

"Yes, and now is the time to move forward to meet and vanquish the enemy. Are you ready?"

"I've been ready for centuries. Today the will of redemption prevails. The forces of evil will be defeated and the innocent avenged."

"Let us hold to those thoughts. It's time to begin our journey, in more ways than one. Come dear friend, we'll lead them to victory." Giselle smiled, as she reached for Grinstead's hand,

The meadow glistened in the sun. Mild breezes flowed through the trees, whistling gently from leaf to branch to trunk and sliding down to the ground. New growth nestled beneath the trees, flanking the boundaries of the meadow. At the opening to the meadow, a blue mist swirled toward the center and settled to earth. The earth seemed to sigh with relief and satisfaction as the mist penetrated below the layers of the ground covering. The ground was replenished with the soothing touch of mist cleansing it from contamination centuries old. Now, the land was ready to support the ordained army of celestials in their battle against evil.

Off to the east, a huge army gathered on the outer perimeters of the meadow. The faces varied depending on their role in the soon-to-be-battle. Darkness would come but, for now, a glistening could be seen in the mineral deposits in the nearby overhanging of rocks surrounding the sides of the meadow and valley. The moment Sarah stepped from behind Lamechial, she knew her role and the precise location where she would stand. She moved away from the large group and positioned herself near the rocks on the western side. Something led her forward and she accepted the inclination, climbed about five feet up onto the rocky ledge. Lamechial followed her and presented his lion's face toward the north. His fierceness was more distinct now than ever before. He stood with his arms to his sides and his feet planted apart. The translucent cloud surrounding him enveloped both he and Sarah in its light. His massive wings, flowing behind him and encompassing a section of nearly nine feet, would prevent others from getting near their backs. His enemies would have to come from the sides or to face him head on but the enemy would meet one of his faces from any direction. Strangely enough, when Sarah looked at him, she felt no fear, only pride in his strength and appreciation for his companionship. She imitated his stance and turned to face the north end of the meadow.

The sunlight began to fade into shadows of the coming night and the other celestials entered the meadow. The larger beings walked into the center of the field distancing themselves from one another in strategic, metered paces. Each took position and commanded the area. Hofniel stood adjacent to Terrene as they turned to look toward the ridge of rock formations, flanking the meadow. On the outer lying borders, the shimmering spirits lingered in the heavy mists of dew filtering down. Various colors radiated in a pulsating rhythm. An unusual melody could be heard floating softly across the land. Its crescendo building as the sunlight faded into the night.

Standing on the highest rock ledge stood the child and Lamechial. Minnjatar left the group and joined them on the ledge. To the right and a distance away from Sarah, on a slightly lower rock formation, Cassamie positioned herself and kneeled. On each side of her stood Grinstead and Giselle. To the left of Sarah, also perched on a rock, stood Rann with Myriad, while Eurus floated nearby. Observing from the center of the meadow and imagining a line of connection, the locations of Sarah, Cassamie and Rann formed a perfect triangle, three equal sides in symbolic form of the Trinity. Each was equal distance from another with the elevation slightly fluctuating. It was not a random placement but a well-planned strategy for the upcoming battle. The gifts of the humans would reinforce and anchor the celestials' maneuvers and battle plans. The bodiless celestial spirits divided themselves in front of the rock ledge. They would add assistance to the humans in spreading the light.

Malitar stood off to the right on the outer border of the meadow. His attendance was not to interfere or fight but to watch and observe all that would transpire. He was a guardian of the events of this battle and one to record all and provide witness to the battle. Though difficult for him to remain on the outskirts, he knew his responsibilities and would follow through on them. Knowing the location of this meadow was crucial to the outcome of the battle along with the gifts and skills of the humans; he would bide his time. If they stayed focused and directed their power at the precise moment, the force should be sufficient to bring about victory.

Cassamie remained kneeling on her rock formation. Grinstead and Giselle were near and she felt safe in their presence; however, small needles of nervousness began prickling at the back of her mind. Amazement in what she had been instructed to do and the reasoning behind it echoed through her thoughts. A vortex was what Sarah, Rann and she would manipulate. Her father had explained the operation of a funnel shaped energy, thus, a vortex, created by the motion of spiraling energy, swirling centers of subtle energy coming from the surface of the earth.

The meadow here at Max Creek was a spiritual power center. From this information, Cassamie grasped that the energy is not exactly electricity or magnetism, although it does leave a slight, measurable residual magnetism in its strongest concentration. This explained the physics of the phenomenon and that alone, caused some apprehension. Rann, Sarah and she were vital in collecting and controlling this energy. Evidently, energy in vortices interacts with a person's inner soul. The energy of the vortex resonates with and strengthens the inner being, the essence of those who come within a quarter- to a half-mile of it. This resonance occurs because the vortex energy is drawn to the subtle energy, the aura of the person.

If the person's inner being, what she thought of as "the soul", was strong enough, because of the person's gifts and faith, then he or she could manipulate and control that energy force. It was similar to capturing the strength of a tornado and filtering that energy into a controlled force. In addition, vortices may be portals between dimensions through which passage is possible. In physics, a vortex is the name given to matter that is whirling around a specific center. Usually, this energy is unrestricted with no direction. A tornado moves about with no set pathway or purpose established except to continue until the energy is gathered and consumed. If this energy is tapped and given direction, a massive, powerful force would be at hand. It was all mindboggling.

She knew celestial particles were inside her as well as inside the child, Sarah. Rann knew of no such anomaly in his lineage but he did possess special gifts of intuition and perception. He believed these were a result of the stroke that somehow "re-wired" his neurological capacity and perceptions, opening up more of his brain and boosting his comprehension of the stimuli around him. Whatever the reasons for all of them being here, they were connected and needed to gather and manipulate the power found in this meadow. They, along with the selected celestials were united in a common goal, a goal to defeat Satan and all his chosen allies in this battle. Quite a goal.

The enemy was expected to wait until after sunset before beginning their onslaught. They would want darkness, the time when they felt most powerful, gaining strength from the fear of others. Cassamie remembered what she had been told only hours before. The time right before nightfall was the celestials' most successful time to harvest the purest power and energy possible. The hours around dawn and dusk are enriched with crepuscular rays, also known as "God's Rays". Beams of sunlight seem to shine through gaps in clouds. The columns of sunlit air separated by darker clouds or shadowed regions reveal the most obvious contrast between light and dark.

Crepuscular rays are near parallel but they appear to come together because of a linear perspective. Oftentimes they occur when objects, such as mountain peaks, block the rays or when clouds shadow some of the sun's rays, acting as a cloud cover. Numerous airborne compounds scatter the sunlight making them visible because of reflection and the scattering. When seen for the first time, these rays are observed in awe and inspire many to send thoughts heavenward. The rays have been named as various, religious nomenclatures such as: Jacob's ladder, Gateways or Stairways to Heaven, Fingers of God and Jesus Beams, plus many others.

With this knowledge, the celestials anticipated gathering the rays to fortify their strength against those of evil intent. Celestials' strength was not measured in physical stamina or by the mastering of weaponry. No machine could kill an angel or demon. The immortals waged their battles through the use of their minds and will. Even the emotions and thoughts of a celestial or demon could be altered or influenced. Satan himself was a mastermind of manipulating and controlling human thoughts and emotions and maneuvering the actions of demons and some fallen angels.

Of course, Satan could destroy any of his demons because most came from the bowels of Hell, or where God had sent them to purge Heaven and earth of their pestilence. All Evil was attributed to Satan because of his jealousy and covetousness of the One Most High. The turmoil in Heaven, when a third of the angels were thrown out, is a testament to Satan's shrewdness. In addition, he zones in on any defect or weakness in humans. She only hoped that the three of them would be able to withstand his invasive temptations of doubt and weakness. She would depend on her knowledge, skills and faith to succeed in her role of manipulating the rays of light and defeating Satan's purpose.

Cassamie looked around the meadow before seeking out Rann. He stood slightly to her right, about twenty yards away, not that far but far enough. Would they be able to carry out their responsibilities in the throes of combat, facing the vilest of creatures? She knew the celestials were nearby, yet they, too, would have their own foes to face. Taking a deep breath and steadying herself, she resolved to face the onslaught with courage. She was not alone, had never really been alone. Briefly she thought of her grandmother. She would be safe within the compound but she would be worried. Though her grandmother had gifts of perception and foreseeing, those gifts had not always been effective when dealing with her. Shaking her head briefly, she was still a little amazed with all she had been told. What a heritage her family had left her.

Cassamie's thoughts were interrupted by an explosive scream coming from the north end of the meadow. Everyone jumped to attention and readied for battle. Within seconds a large cloud of dust drifted across the meadow, as loud rumbling sounds resonated across the field. She peered through the quickly settling dust and the sight was appalling. Even though she expected to see unusual beings, the characteristics of the group were unbelievable, beyond anything she could have imagined. She could smell a putrid odor penetrating the surrounding area, similar to rotting flesh and pestilence imbedded in the beings that moved ever closer to them.

Her attention was drawn to the figure in the middle of the group. The size of the center creature was massive and grotesque. He appeared to be the leader but he didn't look anything close to the Devil, or what she thought the Devil would look to be. Her intuition told her it wasn't him but one of his demons.

Various other beings ran along beside him carrying unusual objects. One had a bucket of smoldering embers, while another carried what looked to be a type of crossbow. The rest of the beings were in a variety of battle gear with all of them wearing some kind of helmet. As she compared all those in the front of the group, their helmets were equipped with dark visors covering what must be their eyes. She wondered how they would see when nightfall came but then they weren't human and had other ways to sense their environment but why the visors? Then she knew. They were avoiding the light they knew they would face. Knowing the essence of the heavenly angels, they couldn't tolerate any form of light whether from earthly light or Heavenly light. Of course, the celestials embraced the light and their enemies thrived in darkness. It was that simple, had always been that simple.

Chapter 34

Cassamie's grandmother, Vera Mahan Timothy-Kensington, hadn't been idle while waiting at the compound. She'd been busy fortifying the perimeter of the house. She had told her granddaughter a great deal of information about her family but she hadn't revealed all. Not yet. She continued to shelter Cassamie from worry because her granddaughter would need to focus all her strength for what was coming, for what she would soon face. Vera would do all within her own power to protect this home and those left behind to guard it. It had stood as a retreat for countless others in the past and she was determined it would continue to do so long into the future.

Vera was what was known as a Delaphon, or a "Human Watcher and Protector". Even now, she held and gently rubbed the amulet secured around her neck; a talisman that had been passed down for centuries through the James family. Only the most sanctioned member could wear the stone for its powers were immense and only controllable by a true Delaphon, an ordained member of the secret order of the Timothies—human guardians of the true and just and human watchers of those most evil. Only a Delaphon could control and protect the stone. If another, somehow, took possession of the amulet, it would transform into a simple, unremarkable rock with no power. The true power came from the source wearing the amulet. Vera was the guardian responsible for the tool of goodness. When her life ended, the amulet would pass to Cassamie. Though Vera possessed no angelic powers or angelic wisdom, she held her unshakeable faith and obedience to the One above, along with an enhanced perception and ability to foresee many events.

At this exact time, she knew how important it was to safeguard this home against the foulest of all beings created. He would come. He would come to retaliate against her because of her role in preventing him from taking what he desired and hunted. Vera recalled that through the years, using his form as a harmless dog or a child, he had tried to get at Cassamie. One day after school, he had followed her home and another time, taking the form of a small boy, he had goaded Cassamie into climbing on a dangerous outcropping of rock. For he knew, any damage he did to her would be a direct hit against his sworn enemy, Grinstead. Up until now, Vera had thwarted his attempts to harm or capture her granddaughter. The measures she'd taken for the protection had weakened her somewhat but she had also honed her skills and gifts. Mephistopheles would come to collect his due or, at least, what he thought he had coming. Vera would keep him out, as countless others before her had done. She would go now to finish what she had started and what she must do to prepare. She knew time was running out.

Soon, she would collect her Bible, the one tool that could deter and eventually help destroy Satan and his followers. Though many had neglected to embrace the word of God in recent years, she knew his truth and Christ's love would find a way of resurging again to deliver many from the evil hold of Satan and his minions. Now she walked through the hidden passageway, following the signs in the stone only she would recognize, until she came to a small depression in the stony wall, covered by heavy moisture, moss and lichens. She quickly brushed away the heaviest deposits and felt for the small indentation. As she pushed inward, a hidden spring opened a compartment housing a smaller one that was engineered to keep air and moisture out. The inner compartment was made of several layers, alternating stainless steel, titanium and aluminum. When she punched in a secret code, another compartment opened holding three objects; a blue tinted vial, leather wrapped book and another package secured tightly by several layers of material then a heavy piece of some kind of animal hide.

Unwrapping this package, there appeared, at first glance, to be a jagged-shaped stick. Vera reverently lifted the "stick" holding it close to her chest as she whispered a few words of prayer and praise. This holy relic had been preserved through the centuries. Initially it had been coated with and protected by precious olive oil, tar and the rubbing of salts. Through the centuries other types of preservatives were developed. In modern times, more mechanical devices were used. Man's ingenuity had saved the precious artifact of faith.

Relics have existed throughout time by all religions but increased in intensity during the Middle Ages, as a result of the Crusades. Pilgrimages were made to visit shrines of holy people and the possession of relics became a large business. The pilgrim, a person making the journey to the Holy Land, believed the purchasing of a relic was a way to bring a shrine back with him or her. The word relic comes from the Latin *reliquiae* meaning "remains" or "something left behind." A relic is part of the body of a saint or a venerated person or it is another type of ancient religious artifact, preserved as a tangible memorial. Since the beginning of Christianity, followers have seen relics as a way to connect to the saints and ultimately form a closer bond to God. For Christians, this relic was "something left behind" by the most blessed of all and the one that had selflessly given all.

She was reminded again of the highest responsibility in protecting the "stick". She had guarded it since she was twenty-three years old, when her father had passed the cloak of authority to her. She had lived her life in the shadow of its importance and maintained a lifetime of love and devotion to its preservation. Being cognizant that the early church allowed the saints and their relics to remain in unidentified places of rest; by the latter part of the Middle Ages, the collecting and dealing with relics had escalated tremendously, spreading from church to royalty, nobility on to the merchant class. Obtaining and keeping a religious relic was a goal worth fighting for and one of great peril.

Though many religious relics existed in most countries, some of a higher authority than others, this relic was perhaps the most precious of all. The Timothies had been in possession of a part of the True Cross, a highly revered and sought-after relic. Through their most trusted and dependable members, the relic had survived the centuries in their safekeeping. The relic she now held in her hands had touched one so holy and pure the nearness of it brought her peace and a deep understanding of what must be done. Evil had run in this forest far too long, spreading pain, despair and heartache. It was time to rid the region of its vile influence and destruction.

She gathered the other leather package along with the small vial. She carefully closed the inner compartment, set the code, closed the outer compartment and smeared the moss back into place. She hid her belongings in a large pocket of her long, charcoal gray cape she'd put on before entering the tunnel. The unseasonably cool temperatures today would warrant her wearing the outer covering.

Cautiously, she made her way back to the basement of the house, climbed the steps and walked quietly outside the compound, heading toward the stream bordering the property. She knew she wouldn't have long to wait because the hairs at the base of her neck had already begun to rise.

In a flash, he was beside her. His nearness was almost more than she could bear but with sheer determination, she turned to face him. He had chosen a human form but far from the beauty he once held. Vera knew his former heavenly appearance was forever gone and forbidden to him but he could transform into other "human-like" forms, however, it would require a great deal of his energy for a short duration. A deep sneer marred the otherwise blemish-free face. Even in his physical deception, his evil nature prevailed. A smoldering aroma emanated from him. His eyes were serpentine with yellow rings around the elongated irises. There was nothing earthly or human about him.

As he stared at her, his sneer turned into a smile and she could see the cunningness in his maneuvers to soothe her weariness as he spoke, "Well, Vera, we meet again and this time you seem to be alone. What? No wayward angels to keep you company?"

"There are plenty of celestials near but I felt no need to ask them to join me here, after all, I've come well prepared. I've everything I'll need." She returned his smile and looked directly into his eyes. As she raised the amulet toward him, she said, "You know you have no power over me. I have nothing to fear from you. Your words cannot impact my thoughts and actions. You are powerless to influence me. Your presence won't hinder me. Shouldn't you be joining your group in the meadow or have you already accepted your defeat?"

Laughing lightly, he said, "Perhaps you have more to fear than you realize. I did just return from Max Creek where your precious granddaughter has foolishly aligned herself with an inferior group of celestials. Do you really think they can stop my legions? My most superior allies are on the brink of annihilating the foolish humans and damaging most, if not all celestials. You should have kept your granddaughter here. I'm surprised you were willing to sacrifice her but then you are merely human. It shouldn't surprise me."

Vera knew he was trying to weaken her resolve by attacking where she was most vulnerable—the safety of the one she loved most still, his wily maneuvers wouldn't work. Not here, not now, not with her. She took a deep breath, moved closer to him before she continued.

"Oh, I think she'll do quite well against those who serve you. You must remember she fights for the Light of the World, the true and just God, the ones you so callously and selfishly abandoned. Tell me, Satan, was it worth all that you gave up? You can never win. Oh, you've harmed countless others who were weak or ignorant of the correct path to follow but you will never defeat the Omnipotent One. He has allowed you to survive. You and your evil ways will soon come to an end because he gives you just enough rope to finally hang yourself."

Vera stepped back as she reached into her cape and removed the stick. She knew she'd baited him and his darkness would emerge. Just as she brought the stick out into the open, he made a lunge toward her but quickly checked himself when he focused on what she held. Even in all his hatred, greed and jealousy, he knew instinctively what she held in her hand He could no longer look at her and shielded his eyes, with his hand and arm.

"Yes, you cower before this holy relic because you and your evil influence on mankind were the reason for its existence. You didn't know my family possessed and guarded the precious relic, a reminder of the pain and suffering you caused the purest of all to endure. The Timothies were entrusted with it and kept it safe for centuries. Being the father of all sin, you know of its strength. You cannot tolerate the purity and sanctity of the remains of the wood used to hold and torture our precious Savior. We have preserved it, kept it safe and will give our lives to keep it until the end of time. Fear it with all that you are because if I touch you with the tip of it, you will disintegrate into the cinders that you feed. Go back to the Hell from which you came. She lunged toward him raising the stick to strike him, when he vanished.

Chapter 35

Simultaneously, Cassamie, Rann and Sarah all locked eyes. Rann smiled and gave a thumbs-up. This single gesture reconnected the three with confidence in their mission and she and Sarah each confirmed his signal with one of their own. A new sense of purpose enhanced their bond and their role in this most vital confrontation. They were ready to face whatever came. The last rays of daylight penetrated the meadow and Cassamie could actually see the celestials radiating in the afterglow. Their faces lit with a sparking purity while the beams seemed to travel through them and back again. She admired such beauty. The word majestic came to mind, as she observed the phenomenon. Never had she witnessed such beams of light, the crepuscular rays—the fingers of God. The rays filtered down in bright beacons refracting to find all celestials: anointing them with piercing brightness that chartered reflections. The intensity of the reflections, bouncing off the rocks, caused her to block the rays from her eyes by raising her arm above her forehead then putting on the eye shield. Moving on, the light energy bounced nearby and she encountered a supreme peace, a tranquility she had never known. Surely, this was the arm of God.

The demons had arrived. Chernobog was acting as leader with the support of Balan and Jezebeth. Elathan held back toward the end of the ranks. He wanted a vantage point for observation of the upcoming events and to make sure the lesser of the demons would not falter and run. He sensed something. Something had changed in the valley beyond this meadow. Finally, after what seemed to be hours, the creatures were able to move again. The strange force that held them captive had lifted and they were able to go forward. With the absence of the Dog, the four senior demons formed a plan of attack. They would move forward, without their leader. Puzzled as to what had happened to him, they realized he might be testing them. Darkness would soon be upon them and the time had come to act. The battle would begin with or without him. They knew the objective of this battle and would fulfill their obligations. To bolster the legions' confidence, they were encouraged to scream and shatter the stillness of the meadow. The piercing screams would herald their arrival to their enemies and weaken the opposing forces.

The celestials waiting in the meadow, prepared themselves and their human counterparts. They knew the awaited battle would soon begin. With the setting of the sun, the moonlight was immediately reflected on the metals and minerals within the rocks in the ledges surrounding the meadow of Max Creek. A faint, golden light penetrated the meadow and headed toward the advancing demons. The glow settled downward and seemed to hover a few inches above the ground. Fortunately, it wasn't yet detectable by the evil ones. Only minutes before, the celestials' power had been reinforced by the last rays of dusk. Even the humans felt the surge of energy and the enhancement of power. They had been trained well and, along with their inherent gifts, they were ready. To protect the humans' eyes, from the light energy that would soon engulf the meadow, they had been given eye shields. They'd already put them on. The true challenge would come when they had to keep a clear mind, remembering how to engage their powers and all of this during the intense maneuvers of battle. Training and instruction can only go so far because the faith, fortitude and determination of individuals decided most outcomes.

Grinstead reached toward Cassamie and pulled her into him for a crushing hug. He looked at her and said, "All that I was, all that I am, all that I will be binds my love for you and strengthens me to protect you. Daughter, you're ready and your inner strength will guide you when the task is at hand. Hold fast to your faith and trust in your abilities." He released her and Cassamie stepped back peering up into his face.

"Father, I will not fail you."

Giselle reached for Cassamie whispering, "We all fight together. The One most High is on our side. We battle for him and the good of all mankind. Let us honor him in all we do. She then uttered the words, "*Aw leigh oi noddeigh, unda kan sai tole imbeed*.

Cassamie had no understanding of these words but realized they must be the celestial language that gave praise and adoration. She reverently whispered, "Amen." Both Grinstead and Giselle smiled then jumped from the ledge. They were joined by Terrene and Myriad. The four stepped out into the meadow and walked toward evil.

Lamechial bolstered Sarah's determination by reminding her she was the youngest of them and virtually sinless from the evils of the creatures approaching. She would instinctively know when to act. He had prepared her well and she knew what to do. He would remain beside her at all times. Minnjatar would be joining the leading angels in the middle and return when necessary. Lam told her to be true to herself and not doubt herself, when it became too intense to think clearly. She was to use her training but to use her instincts more. She was smart and would know what to do when the moment came for action.

Rann watched the angels walking to the center of the meadow, headed toward the evil that approached. Myriad had left his side and joined the group in the middle. He looked over his shoulder and saw Eurus still floating nearby. She was in true spirit form and he wondered how effective she would be in battle. He had never worked with a spirit and was unfamiliar with their ways or abilities.

Perhaps reading his mind, she moved within inches of his face and spoke to him.

"Rann, you know nothing of battles between angels and demons but you will soon learn. I'll tell you this to ease your worries. The crucial battles are fought and won by sheer will and thoughts. You are aware of the psychological effects on mankind. Well, the same can be said of celestials and the evil ones. After all, aren't most temptations to man carried out through their mind and, thus, their thoughts?"

Rann soon found a newfound respect for his spirit companion and acknowledged her statements by nodding his head in the affirmative.

"Faith is based on blind trust in what cannot be seen or fully understood. That is the beauty of the true Christian religion. It has been thus since the Garden of Eden when Satan first tempted Eve and, therefore, Adam. You must remember we fight for our Maker, the Creator of all things. Prepare to stand in awe of all He can do."

At that exact moment, a horrific din vibrated throughout the valley. The evil ones attacked using the full impact of their wickedness. Rann had never heard a noise such as this. It paralyzed him where he stood. He frantically clutched his ears with the open palms of his hands, squeezing as tightly as he could to prevent the noise from penetrating his brain. He doubled over in pain as the sound battered his senses and every thought. He was helpless to defend himself against the onslaught. His head pounded with the piercing rhythm of the shrieking, high-pitched noise. He immediately felt nauseous. Regardless of his best effort not to retch, he found himself bending over at the waist and emptying his stomach. A cold sweat broke out across his forehead, as he crumbled to the ground.

Only a few yards away, Cassamie witnessed his anguish but she couldn't help him. She had her own battle with which to deal. The noise was loud but it did not infiltrate her body, as it did Rann's. She felt a mesmerizing force trying to command her thoughts and, therefore, her actions. It slid across her mind, seductive in its attempts to take control of her. A repetition of sounds floated near her ears and beckoned for her to step off the rock ledge and walk out into the meadow. She felt no pain, only a constant barrage of urgency in the voice, making promises to her of riches and wonders she would have when she joined their group. The voice reiterated over and over, "Come into the meadow. Join us here. Come to us. Leave the rocks. Come. Come now. We are all waiting for you."

Somehow, she knew it wasn't a real voice, only an illusion of one, a strong force with an ulterior motive, one she knew she must resist, at all costs. Then the sly voice said, "Come quickly, your father needs you. Can't you see him faltering? Come now. Come off the rocks before it's too late for him."

Cassamie jerked her head to the left where she had last seen her father walking and sure enough, she saw him stumble. She held back a scream, as she started to step off the rocky ledge.

Chapter 36

Vera awoke with a start. She didn't even remember falling asleep. She sat bolt upright on the couch, in a cold sweat. She felt both hot and cold at the same time. A disturbing dream had awakened her. She rarely ever took a nap, especially at stressful times, such as this. Carefully, she stood on shaky legs. She must get to Max Creek. Cassamie needed her now.

She ran into the kitchen and grabbed a water bottle, some crackers and quickly crammed both into a rucksack hanging on the pantry door. She would need to gather her weapons from the cavern again and head out in the Land Rover. It was imperative to reach Cassamie, as quickly as possible. She was unsure of the terrain of the meadow or the road leading to it. It had been years since she had visited the spot and it had been remote even then. She doubted much had changed since the site had been chosen as the battleground. Both sides wouldn't want any interference from humans, so it had to be a secluded area.

She looked out into the yard and noticed a few celestials near the creek. They appeared to be looking for something. She imagined they had gotten a scent of her earlier visitor and were investigating the scene. No matter. He wouldn't revisit them today or anytime soon; of that she was confident. Vera cautiously made her way outside and toward the front of the house to the shed where she kept the Land Rover. It started up immediately and she followed the circle drive to the lane leading out through the gates onto the road. When she entered the roadway, she floored it and sped down the road, throwing gravel and dust behind her. Now was not the time for a leisurely drive.

Sarah was insulated from much of the terrible noise by Lam's strong arms and sheltering wings wrapped around her. Part of one wing shielded her from the noise and the other covered them from the back, providing a haven of safety. Rubbing her shoulders, he gently whispered it would pass. She must resist the urge to listen to anything she might hear. He was right beside her; would not leave her side and she would be able to resist the urgings of the evil voices and sounds. He told her it was the demons' desperate attempt to get her and the others to leave the ledges. They would all hold steadfast and resist their attempts to deny the harvesting of the powers of light, the power that would soon come from the moonlight and bounce off the rock ledges, to initiate a vortex of light.

Rann had finally gotten control of his emotions and blocked the noise from his mind. He had drawn on his own deductions this was about what Eurus had warned him. No sooner had he made the connection, than Eurus floated down beside him, her spirit overlapped the spot where he regained his footing. Within the radius of her presence, he felt a steady easement from his pain. As he straightened to his full height, he realized the noise was gone from his mind. He was no longer sick. He looked at her, wiped his arm across his mouth then nodded to her.

"I believe I underestimated your strength, Eurus. I won't do it again. Thank you for your help. I feel much better and am now ready to meet my challengers."

"Yes, you are and you did well. Even I felt the sickness of their onslaught. That is how evil works. It hits in ways you don't expect. They are cunning in all things and look for the weaknesses of all. Most people's vulnerabilities are housed in their thoughts and ideas. Inner strength is the most important of all. So, heed this warning and remember the power of your mind. Stand strong against them. They cannot take more than you are willing to give." She seemed to embrace him, for he felt an immediate peace and sense of wellbeing. "I will now go to help my league of angels. You know what you must do and the time is at hand Hold to your trust and faith." Then she was gone to fight the evil, awaiting them.

For a tenuous moment, Cassamie almost stepped off the rock ledge but then her inner voice warned her that was exactly what Satan and his cohorts wanted. She must remain here on the ledge. Her destiny was to be here at the exact moment when the vortex would form. She stood straighter with a new resolve and looked over at Rann. He was waiting and watched her with a look so penetrating and filled with raw emotion. She, too, felt that emotion. She knew there was love in this valley and Rann would help her do what was necessary. She smiled at him and mouthed the words, "Be strong and true."

The meadow was blanketed in shining rays of moonlight with each beam penetrating with a powerful force so visible and bright even the celestials joined the humans in briefly shielding their eyes. The evil ones cringed where they stood and instantly brought down their eye gear and visors. Still, the rays were so strong the lesser of the demons dissolved where they stood and a layer of smoke settled to the ground and disappeared. The bodiless demons evaporated in a puff of greenish gray smoke. The moonlight alone rid the valley of one-third of the demons. A loud gasp could be heard among those remaining, before the creature in the middle called for a full charge. They bombarded the angels that met them and the physical battle began.

So much energy exerted through the meadow it temporarily became shrouded in clouds of dusts, hiding many. Strong adversaries pushed against one another; the impact could be heard for miles but would go unnoticed, for none were nearby. Though some beings had carried tangible weapons, these were dropped along the paths of fighting. Now the physical battle would be dependent on extreme will and psychological might. The horrendous cacophony of noise bombarded all but was quickly overtaken by a melody of such beauty the fighting momentarily stopped, as pairs of eyes looked for its source. None could see the invisible spirit of Phyllison as she sang overhead, with a voice of such clarity and purity, tears came to the eyes of many, including the humans and one demon in particular. Jezebeth was moved to tears and opened herself to the draw of the music.

Then it happened. The moonbeams reached the minerals in the rock ledges where Cassamie, Sarah and Rann stood. A miraculous force came up through the rocks and entered them. Their bodies became satellites for the energy force and awash with an intense blue light. Each remained rooted to their spot, raised their arms toward the heavens and tornadoes of light came crashing down to the meadow. The beams of cycling energy hovered nearby. All three, intuitively, in unison, took control of the vortices. Moving with a rhythm, seemingly filling the air, they manipulated their twirling infernos of light toward one another until all three joined together into one, massive, pulsating cyclone of penetrating, blinding energy. All the bodiless spirits used their forms as a catalyst to help spread the penetration of this powerful light energy throughout the meadow, helping to vanquish the opposing spirits.

The meadow was ablaze with light. Night had become day and the demons could no longer tolerate the light force before them. Many turned away from the celestials, trying to avoid the illumination surrounding them. The dark visors could not deflect the strength of this light. A few adamantly stood their ground, including Chernobog and Balan. They were not as sensitive to the vibrant rays because they had been in the presence of light before yet they were hesitant to move any closer. After the cleansing of the meadow by the light of the vortices, the few remaining demons gathered in the middle to try to recoup some of their energy and to come up with a new strategy. Each demon was a veteran of many battles against the light but none had seen such luminescent power, as this. Even Chernobog felt uneasiness with the sheer intensity of the beams, reflecting off the metals and the ultimate control of power by three humans. He felt an all-consuming hatred for them and quickly found his next target. He would go after the child, Sarah and her protector.

Unbelievably, during the intense beams of light, Jezebeth moved to the ranks of the celestials. Something reformed her while waiting in the valley totally immobile. She remembered sensing something earlier, something so subtle yet so pure. Was it a newly formed spirit? She didn't know but she did recall feeling a sense of overpowering peace and serenity. Shockingly, she began thinking about her past life as a young woman living in Greece with her family. It was as if scales lifted from her eyes and remembering she loved her family, even her father. Those times were so different and all men did not encourage children, especially female children, to voice their opinions. In her anger, somehow, she'd been manipulated and overcome by evil. She knew the creature responsible for her human deterioration but she also had to accept responsibility for her role in the wrong, which had been done. She would never be able to forget it but she felt an overwhelming embrace and acceptance of herself and a forgiveness of all the wickedness she caused. For the first time in centuries, she felt at peace, felt a part of something good, something worthy.

She dropped to the ground and kissed the earth where she stood. As she started to rise, she was thrown back down by a terrible, splitting headache. Something was within her brain tormenting her, taunting her and trying to control her actions. The force was strong and penetrating. Frantically she tried to process what was happening within her then she realized what it was, who it was that tortured her every thought. When she had stolen some of Elathan's power, it had given him a gateway inside her, providing access to her thoughts. He used his trickery to allow her to believe she'd been undetected, while she stole from his aura. How foolish she had been to believe herself superior to the Celtic demon. Now, she would pay the supreme price for he would control and eventually destroy her. Her thoughts and actions were his to manipulate and command

She writhed upon the ground trying to fight that which she could not defeat until the spirit, Phyllison, reached to enfold her in her protection from the dual trickery of the demon. The thin, golden light that had settled earlier to the ground embraced Jezebeth in its cleansing ray. The blazing light flowed all around her, caused no fear or pain, only peace; but its purity destroyed the tendrils of Elathan and he himself jumped in excruciating pain, as the light also surrounded him. He quickly withered away to fading puffs of smoke and descended downward. The demon had been destroyed and Jezebeth was free.

A complete transformation took place and her supernatural beauty was replaced by an innocence she had not known for centuries. Her soul was once again restored to that of a spiritual being purged of the wickedness that had overtaken it. Finally, she was free from the control of all demons as well as the wicked maker of all that is evil. She joined the celestials in their battle and sang praise to the light that had opened her eyes and pointed her in the pathway to what was right and good. She resolved that when the battle concluded, she would learn all that she could about the light of the world.

Giselle, Grinstead, Myriad and Terrene witnessed the transformation and knew that the newly anointed spirit, Phyllison, had found goodness within the demon and helped to sway her from the evil effects of darkness. This accomplishment would help to bring about victory. In unison, they turned to face the two leading demons standing only a few yards away.

Balan, in total disbelief of what had just happened to Elathan and the betrayal of Jezebeth, turned to lash his wrath upon one celestial he intended to destroy as retribution, Grinstead. Balan immediately attempted to goad him into a reaction.

"So, they welcomed you back into the fold. What a disappointment this must be to rejoin the same, pathetic group of spirits. Didn't you learn how fickle they were when they abandoned you after you were thrown out, cast away to this pathetic realm? Where were they then when you needed them? Did they come to help you? Did they defend you against the accusations? Of course not."

While listening to Balan taunt the angel, Chernobog detected the approaching presence of Apophis, an important ally in this battle. Knowing what Apophis's past role had been, he quickly regained some of his bravado. Indeed, when Balan finished, Chernobog added his own retaliation.

"When first thrown from the highest realm and landing on the mountain, you were not alone though it was not one of your celestials with you. Even with all your damage, you were aware of something nearby. It was something watching, observing and taking great pleasure in your suffering and weakened condition.

"When you meandered for days on the mountain, aimlessly searching, completely distracted and defenseless; there was one who watched and followed. You were completely unaware of him, functioned numbly, not perceiving, or caring about your danger. While alone in that cave for a great amount of time, did any of these celestials come to help you? No, not one single ally of yours came. In fact, there was only one creature with you on the mountain and in that cave. One being witnessed your exile from the beginning of your entering this realm and traversing hopelessly from one place to another. He waited and while you were most vulnerable, he watched, learned and acted. Do you know who was with you in your time of need?"

Grinstead listened to the bantering, appearing unaffected by the taunting words. Then he felt a quivering of the ground beneath him, all beside him witnessed a tunneling forming around his feet. A small mound of earth opened up and a serpentine head emerged from the ground. It was Apophis, the companion of Chernobog, with blazing eyes reflecting hatred and cruelty. Momentarily, Grinstead stumbled then froze in place, unable to move. His thoughts bombarded with the evil intent of the serpent beneath him, tempting him to succumb to his evil intentions and to turn against the allies beside him.

Apophis had waited patiently for the past few days for this moment. Plans made centuries before in a dank and dark cave, near the top of a mountain were now unfolding. The place where Grinstead sheltered in his lowest moments of despair and suffered the enormity of the punishment dealt to him. This was where Apophis had made his initial move.

As soon as Chernobog saw his old ally, he walked toward Apophis but Balan immediately checked his progress by raising his arm to detain him. Balan knew the moment belonged to Apophis but he sorely underestimated one of Grinstead's allies. Apophis poised himself in a striking position, leaning far back to propel himself toward Grinstead, with his deadly fangs in position. Just as he sprang, Myriad reached out, grabbed him around the base of the head, snapping the head sharply to the left and pulling with a great force until the head separated from the body. A terrific stench penetrated the area, as a green substance oozed from the snake's body. Then both pieces disintegrated into brown powder, before completely disappearing below the surface of the earth. In fear, Chernobog and Balan moved back from the celestials and retreated to the edge of the meadow.

With a look of shock, Grinstead turned to Myriad, "What happened? Why was I mesmerized by the serpent and hesitant to act?"

Myriad brushed her hands off and wiped them with a clean cloth she removed from her pocket. She answered, "He needed to be terminated. Bad business." She cleared her throat and touched Grinstead on the shoulder. "The old demon tried to influence you when you were weakened from your wounds and despondent from the events of the Day of Destruction. I'm not definite but I'm fairly confident he injected some of his venom in you all those centuries ago in hopes of using it sometime in the future. That is probably why you seemed a little disoriented during his appearance. Jezebeth can attest to the demon, Elathan, using the same technique on her, though his was mainly an attempt to hijack her brain. Yours was actually because of Apophis activating his venom that lay dormant in you for so many centuries. Even then Satan was threatened by you and tried to gain some kind of control over you. The residue of evil is hard to destroy but, as we know, it can be done; however, Apophis couldn't have had much influence on you but I decided not to bring it to a test and chose to deal with him. His tactic of deceit and secretive missions are over. The world is better off without him. His essence has returned to the hell from which he came. Now, let's deal with the rest."

Giselle and Terrene laughed while Grinstead nodded his understanding. The three knew how important it was to surprise the demons where they were most confident in their strengths and to hit them where they were most vulnerable and to hit hard. Myriad assessed the situation correctly and acted upon it. All joined hands and turned to face the demons that remained. They were united and ready to flex their strength in battle. The female celestials walked toward the demons but Grinstead held back.

He was receiving a strong warning from his preceptors. Quickly pivoting, he scanned to find his daughter. At this exact moment he observed her step down from the protective ledge. The rocks were sacred ground and could not be encroached upon by demons or creatures of evil but when she left the ledge she would be unprotected and vulnerable. In an instant, he disappeared from the group of celestials.

With the destruction of his one and only ally, Chernobog recovered and sent forth a warlike yell reverberating through the meadow. Gaining some control, he accepted his responsibility to take care of the huge cherub and relished the thought of destroying him. As he charged across the meadow toward the rock ledge where Lam stood enfolding Sarah within his wings, his vilest thoughts were to destroy both by a quick attack of tearing them to pieces. His excitement increased and he recklessly charged forward, without considering the abilities of who he would face and, thus, making a fatal mistake.

Lamechial immediately felt the demon's animosity and intent, while sensing his quickly approaching form. In an instant, the cherub intensified his size and facing the demon with the countenance of the Lion, he gently placed Sarah in the arms of Hofniel. It all happened so suddenly the child hadn't realized the danger before Lamechial launched himself from the ledge and cleared the distance to the demon in one strong leap, while bellowing his own scream.

The roar emanating from his mouth stunned the demon as he faltered in his tracks. Chernobog began to sweat and shake with fear. Too late, he realized he had foolishly underestimated the strength of his opponent but he would not back down now. He stopped and took position to meet the oncoming force. His last thought was the celestial was unstoppable. Lamechial sprang upon the demon lifting him completely off the ground and separating his head from the neck. The onslaught took place in the blink of an eye and allowing Chernobog no time to even emit a scream. His dominion finished as the rest of his body engulfed in flames and burned to cinders. The heat blazed so intensely the foul odor of evil consumed entirely in a matter of seconds. The demon was gone. Any remains returned to the underworld.

Lam turned to survey the rest of the battlefield and noticed the woman demon standing near Giselle. They were embracing. Strange but then he thought, maybe not so strange. He raised his massive head and sniffed the air. Yes, there was a new essence in the air all around. A newly formed spirit with the Omnipotent One's guidance brought about the conversion. Giselle, indeed, had assistance in finding "goodness" even among such evil. She was supreme at her job but, of course, God made her this way. The conversion would be a direct strike against the one most foul. He had lost his main force and still he had not shown himself. Where was he and what was he about?

There was only one remaining demon left, Balan, a high-ranking cohort of Satan. It was time to deal with him. Terrene decided it was her job to end the existence of one of the most heinous of the demon world. She took a step toward him before being detained by the firm hand of Giselle. Terrene turned toward Giselle, with a look of pure confusion.

Giselle smiled warmly at Terrene and said, "Dear one, I know you could easily smite him but there is another who needs to send him back in ashes."

Terrene looked to where Giselle pointed. Jezebeth? Did she believe the former female demon could defeat him? Giselle never made a mistake in judgment on the capabilities of others, be they human, celestial or demon. She would defer to Giselle's wisdom and wait for the outcome.

Giselle walked over to where Jezebeth still reclined on the ground with the golden light radiating around her. Giselle knelt down beside her and whispered in her ear, "You know that you can destroy him once and for all. You can send him from this earth never to return again, never to tempt or harm others, never to manipulate young, impressionable girls again. You have it within you to defeat him."

Jezebeth looked bewildered but trusting enough to ask, "How do I defeat one such as he?"

"You'll know. Don't doubt yourself. You are strongest with your newly formed faith. Act now."

Jezebeth rose and headed toward Balan. When he saw her approaching, a malicious smile formed across his face. He stepped up to her and with words dripping with sarcasm sneered, "So, you've decided to ask me to take you back again?"

Jezebeth paused and gathered her strength. She almost gave a hateful retort but felt the presence of the purifying spirit and knew exactly how to defeat the seasoned demon. She turned to face him directly and said, "No, Balan, I don't want to join you. I'm finished with your evil ways."

Balan burst out with a bellowing laugh and taunted her by saying; "You will never be able to free yourself from my influence. You belong to me." Then he reached for her but she quickly stepped back from him.

"You're wrong. I'm finished with you and all your evil ways but I need to tell you something."

"What could I possibly want to hear from you? You traitor."

Jezebeth, finding new strength, said, "I forgive you for interfering in my past human life. I forgive you for taking me from a family who loved me. I forgive you for your manipulation that brought about my father's death and countless others. I forgive you for denying me a normal, human life. I forgive you for influencing me when I was most vulnerable and bringing about the damnation of my human life."

With each word that Jezebeth spoke, Balan felt a deep prick within himself and his face stricken with a look of intense pain and suffering. It was an internal pain that struck with each listed grievance against him. In desperation, he looked at her with complete terror in his eyes. He knew nothing of "forgiveness" and only knew he couldn't tolerate the act. The act of forgiveness was incomprehensible to him. How dare she put him in this position.

Jezebeth moved closer to him and the golden light also advanced toward him. When she gently touched Balan, it was more than he could bear. He jumped back in terror and began gasping loudly. The light. He couldn't take the light. Slowly the light surrounded him and penetrated his evil body. The centuries old demon had no place for the goodness within the rays. His body began to tremble, a horrific scream came forth then an all-consuming flame burst from within and the demon was soon nothing more than ashes upon the ground. The light of all that is good and pure had destroyed an evil of such magnitude. Even his tenure of evil ways could not save him against the spiritual light. All those eons of time for him were erased and sent to a place where he could never return to this realm. Balan was no more and his ashes quickly descended down below to the home of constant turmoil, the Hell below.

Chapter 37

Vera bounced along the road, or what had once been a road. Now, it was an overgrown, rutted path overtaken by grass, vines, weeds and small saplings. She drove for as long as she could then pulled off to the side. She would travel the remaining distance on foot. The road ended at a line of trees and shrubs. It was probably the old trail used years ago or by dedicated runners and hikers.

She reached in the back and removed her rucksack and the bottle of water. She quickly took a drink and headed in the direction of Max Creek. She moved at a jog/run, in a hurry to reach the meadow where she knew the battle was taking place. Frantically, she pushed against the vines that tried to detain her movement. Her dream had revealed Satan would return with the intent to attack Cassamie. She had been his target all along. The child, Sarah, had merely been a diversion to get to her granddaughter and in this way, he would be getting at two of his arch enemies: Grinstead and herself. Praying fervently Grinstead would realize Satan's intent, she forged on.

Rann, Sarah and Cassamie worked their wonder and destroyed or disabled most of the demons. From a distance, they watched the action in the middle of the meadow. Cassamie saw her father, Giselle, Terrene and Myriad, otherwise known as Mother Nature, move toward the giant demon and his companion. Surprisingly, the female demon remained with the celestials. She changed right before their eyes. Miraculously, the light had transformed her—a demon of the dark world given a second chance. The female demon literally changed before their eyes and joined the celestials in destroying another powerful demon. What a sight to behold.

When Cassamie stepped off the ledge to walk toward Rann, she heard a loud, crashing noise coming from behind her in the trees. Whirling around she saw a sight she would never forget. The black dog was back only it looked much larger with a menacing fire in its eyes. He came snarling and baring his teeth. She had time to turn before he was upon her. She was knocked to the ground, squeezing the air out of her. She didn't have enough breath to scream, when she felt an intense pain with the tearing of flesh as the beast attacked her. The pain was unbearable and she struggled to remain conscious. Through the miasma of searing pain, she heard Rann's voice right before the black void swallowed her.

While Grinstead stood with Giselle, Terrene and Myriad, he felt a strong presence in the area. Instantly, he knew he had to get to Cassamie. Using his celestial speed, he was near her before Rann and Sarah had even witnessed the attack on Cassamie. The dog tried to attack Grinstead but the purest light surrounded Grinstead and the Evil One could not touch him; however, Grinstead was able to knock the Dog off his daughter. The force of his thrust threw the Dog over thirty feet crashing into a tree and momentarily stunning him. At the exact moment that Grinstead threw the Dog, Vera emerged from the tree line. She reached in her rucksack removing the blue vial and threw its contents onto the body of the demon dog. As the Dog righted himself and readied to attack again, he felt a searing pain along the back of his head and down his back. The holy water burned into the hide of Satan. Then Vera darted to the front and tapped him with the gnarled "stick", the most precious relic. The Dog howled in pain, burst into flames and burned down to brimstone. The celestials and humans witnessed the spiraling, smoking evil spirit disappear downward.

By now Rann and Vera had joined Grinstead beside Cassamie. Mercifully, she lay unconscious. Her wound was on the right side of her back. It was a nasty gash but didn't appear too deep. Fortunately, Grinstead had gotten there in time and prevented further damage. Vera leaned down to gently pour the remaining water from the vial into the wound. There were only a few drops left but she knew it would be enough to heal the wound and eradicate any infection or tissue damage from the attack. Vera reached down to touch the area around the wound. She softly used her fingertips to massage the reddened area. Vera added a few more drops and the reddened skin cooled and began the healing process. Before all their eyes, the wound began closing.

"There will be some scarring but it will be minimal; and eventually just a small reminder of the battle here today and the victory that was won. All in all, not a bad thing, don't you agree, Grinstead?" Vera asked the mighty angel.

Grinstead's face relaxed as he nodded in agreement, before putting his arms around Vera and saying, "Yes, we are victorious but I would never want to go through this again."

Vera looked at him carefully and knew he had suffered as would any parent. It had taken a toll on him. Perhaps, the celestials weren't too different from humans after all. Studying him, she perceived he looked more formidable now, though he showed the constraints of parental worry. She glanced over to Giselle and noticed she too observed Grinstead. Then Giselle transitioned her look to Vera, smiled and nodded the affirmation that Grinstead had restored his former honor as a high-ranking angel. This pleased Vera and she retuned Giselle's smile before speaking directly to Grinstead, while including all the celestials in her next comment.

"You know, Grinstead, Satan has forfeited his ability to ever bring any physical harm to Cassamie. He gambled and lost."

Looking at Vera, he replied, "Yes but he, being who and what he is, will not give up on causing chaos for her in any way he can. Though next time, I will be around to protect her if the need arises."

Giselle added, "You are right, Grinstead, however, he'll still have all of the Highest Authority to fight against and in the end, he will be destroyed once and for all."

The celestials knew Satan was not terminated. That right belonged to the Creator of all and He alone would decide the time and place; however, Satan had been marked and he could no longer appear in the form of the Dog. That form was lost to him forever.

After determining the danger was over and Cassamie would recover, Lamechial knelt down and scooped Sarah up in his strong arms. He had a wide smile across his face. The child had fulfilled her role and faced her responsibility with courage. She had helped save the day. Bending down, Lamechial whispered in Sarah's ear, "You have finished your role and now I am taking you to talk with Giselle and Grinstead."

Figures, she thought. *They have to talk to me and prepare me for what is to come. Now what? Surely, it's time to go. I mean, after all, we beat the demons.*

Grinstead and Giselle smiled warmly when Lamechial sat Sarah on the ledge beside Giselle. Grinstead remained standing with one leg propped up on the ledge looking even more impressive than before. Sarah thought he looked different somehow, as if he'd moved beyond this world and regained something.

Grinstead regarded the child and addressed her, "Well, Sarah, you did a wonderful job controlling the vortices. We are all proud of you. How does it feel to have successfully controlled the purest and strongest form of light waves?"

"It feels great and a little scary to think what we faced. It also feels good to know I will get to go home, right? What are we going to tell my parents?"

Grinstead chuckled and lifted her off the ledge, briefly hugging her before standing her on the ground in front of Giselle. "Of course, you're going home and you're going home tonight."

Giselle stood and reached out to gently push a strand of Sarah's hair away from her face before looking deeply into her eyes and speaking.

"Sarah, soon Lamechial will carry you home. He will wait just a bit until the night enters its deepest hours. Travel will move quickly because Lam, as you call him, will use the speed of a celestial. You will soon fall into a deep, restful sleep and not awaken until in the morning when your parents discover that you are home, in your own bed. When you are with your parents or any human, you won't have memory of the details of what has happened over the duration of your time with us. You will have amnesia about these events and all the beings and people you have met. You will be unable to speak to anyone about these facts and impressions you've formed. Do you understand what I am telling you?"

Sarah seemed to straighten before speaking. "Yeah, I get it. I kind of figured that would happen. Besides, nobody would believe me if I told them. But…I'm sort of sad I won't remember any of you."

Giselle spoke and felt a catch in her voice, "Sarah, I did not say you would forget us. When you are alone, at times, you will remember everything and know you are one of us. Also, the blood tests will no longer be able to detect any abnormality. The doctors will conclude it was an anomaly or a fault of testing, something unexplainable but not harmful. Your travels to different hospitals for testing will cease."

"That's super. No more tests and I think I get it," said Sarah. "You're going to do something to me that will stop me from talking to any other person about the things that have happened. Right?"

"Yes," Giselle answered, "that is exactly what will happen. Sarah, at times we will be nearby and will check on you. Now, are you ready to go home?"

Before waiting for an answer, Giselle rubbed her fingers tenderly across Sarah's forehead and softly chanted a few words. Grinstead caught Sarah as she drifted into unconsciousness. He gently placed her in the waiting arms of Lamechial and leaned over to place a light kiss on her cheek. In the blink of an eye,

Lamechial and Sarah were gone and Grinstead had moved back to his daughter.

Grinstead carried Cassamie to Vera's vehicle. Rann slid in beside her in the backseat and cradled her head on his lap. Cassamie was breathing normally in her shock-driven sleep but Vera assured Rann she would be fine.

When he saw that monster attack her, he thought his heart would stop. How had he come to this point in only a few days? Thinking back, he could not remember the precise moment when his feelings for Cassamie had turned to love. Smiling, he recalled his initial reactions to her, the "Clock Watcher"; however, one thing he knew, without a doubt, he would make it work. He was confident she felt the same way, for he had read her lips when they stood on the ledges, at the precipice of the battle.

Grinstead climbed into the front passenger seat of the vehicle and Vera started the engine. She backed up and headed away from the meadow, driving carefully so as not to jar Cassamie. She glanced at Grinstead, looked in the rearview mirror and informed them they'd go back to the compound to rest and recover. Stopping briefly, she turned and spoke to Rann, "You are welcome to stay for however long you can. I believe you need to understand the connections this land has to my family and the history of that link. Believe me when I tell you, I know Cassamie will be fine." She smiled, winked at him and drove to their destination.

The meadow near Max Creek was cleansed from evil. The demons were gone and could never again enter this site. The light of the vortices controlled by Cassamie, Rann and Sarah helped purify this land. The rock ledges, sanctified by the Holy Light, would always remain a safe haven for the righteous. The convergence of all forces involved brought victory on this day. Based on the supreme sacrifice given so long ago, the vessels of what were good and just had been victorious in battle. Nonetheless, the war was not over and there would be another day of deliverance from all that is evil in the world but, for today, all was well.

About the Author

Shirley J. Naas lives in a small, rural, one-stoplight town near the Shawnee National Forest in southern Illinois, the setting for her first novel. She shares her home with her husband, a quarter horse, a black Labrador pup, an older mutt, Keebler, named after a chocolate chip cookie, and two young barnyard kittens named by her grandchildren for their favorite Pokémon characters - "Persian" Paws and "Litten" Kitten.

A language arts teacher for many years, Shirley taught writing and literature to fifth through eighth-grade students. Countless field trips into the nearby forest influenced her writing. Incorporating her knowledge and experiences with middle school students gave inspiration for writing the fantasy, *Convergence*, along with personal experiences, folklore and local historical facts creating the characters and plot propelling the reader into the story. Her storytelling began many years ago when raising two daughters and hosting numerous slumber parties. Oftentimes guests requested bedtime stories spontaneously created in hopes of coaxing the rowdy group into a period of quietness leading to eventual slumber. Today, Shirley spends most of her time entertaining her grandchildren, enjoying family and friends, writing, reading and traveling in search of writing ideas and adventures.